Praise for Jade Chandler

"Chandler's first in her Brotherhood Bonds series, a spin-off of her Jericho Brotherhood books, is a scorching biker romance with gritty dialogue and an edgy storyline."

—*RT Book Reviews* on *Bail Out*

"Yes please! I need MORE of this wickedly erotic world Ms. Chandler has woven! Bottom Line: This is Ms. Chandler's debut novel, but you'd never know it by the excellent writing and editing. *Enough* is totally flawless...pick this one up STAT!!"

—*The Romance Reviews*, 5 stars

"This was a book that I found hard to put down. *Enough* is the debut title from Jade Chandler and I'd just like to say that I loved her writing style so much. Dare and Lila's story was red hot and had me hooked almost from the first page."

—*Night Owl Reviews*, 4.5 stars

"Once I started, I couldn't put it down."

—*Alpha Book Club* on *Release*

"*Release* is a nice smooth read that is so sweet."

—*Night Owl Reviews* on *Release*

"I had fun reading this book and I was thoroughly entertained."

—*Chick* on *Deny*

Also by Jade Chandler

Enough
Release
Deny
Shake Down

and Coming Soon in the Brotherhood Bonds series

Get Away

BAIL OUT

JADE CHANDLER

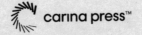

carina press™

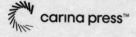

carina press™

ISBN-13: 978-1-335-62975-3

Bail Out

Recycling programs for this product may not exist in your area.

www.CarinaPress.com

Printed in U.S.A.

BAIL OUT

For original short stories and updates
on the Brotherhood Bonds series,
join my newsletter at www.jadechandler.com.

Chapter One

Elle

Daddy wanted a son but he got me. I'd worked my ass off to be the son he'd wanted, and for the most part I'd succeeded. I'd spent most of my childhood playing at Jackson Bonds while Daddy worked—the bail bonds and retrieval business was in my DNA—I was the fourth generation of Jackson to carry on the family tradition. I made sure I outperformed every person in the company, including my father.

I hurried into my office, threw my jacket over my black desk chair, and flipped on my laptop, brushing dust off my glass desk, a useless gesture. The screen came to life and I navigated to the Dallas PD website. I skimmed through last night's arrests online to see if anyone caught my eye. I was the best bonder in our company because I shopped for clients instead of waiting for them to come to me. A lesson Daddy had taught me when I was only a girl.

Despite trying over and over for sons, I remained his only child. In fact, we'd fought because after years of treating me like his business equal, now all he wanted to discuss was marriage and babies—my marriage and babies. I had a vague plan to produce the next generation of Jacksons, but my timeline and his didn't align. Daddy would never do this to his son.

I snorted at my own stupidity for letting myself go down the familiar trail of pity. Elle Jackson didn't do that—I refused to be that stupid. I had my shit together and no one doubted my skill or my experience. Shutting the door on my doubts, I triple locked and chained the door before shoving it deep in the recesses of my mind.

My phone buzzed showing Doris, my father's secretary, on the display. Doris had been a mother to me—the constant female presence in my life since Daddy whipped through women like some people traded in cars. Blunt, blustery and hard as nails, she'd taught me how to survive in our male-dominated profession.

Acid churned in my stomach eating another hole in the lining. I hated ulcers but had lived with them most of my life. Shoving all the shit down deep had consequences, ones I happily paid.

The phone trilled a third time and I swept up the handset. "Ellie, your father wants to see you, pronto," Doris greeted me.

"Hello, how are you, Doris?" I didn't want to see my father.

"Grouchy and old, now get your butt over here." She hung up.

Daddy had turned into someone I didn't know. Six months ago, he'd suffered a light heart attack, it'd scared ten years off my life. It had changed him, and not in a good way. He'd whisked his latest girlfriend, five years older than me no less, off to Vegas and made her Mrs. Jackson number four. Not stopping there, he had transformed from this badass bounty hunter I'd grown up with into this grandbaby-crazy man who only called me to talk about getting married. Of course, his harping triggered the Jackson stubborn gene, now I wasn't sure I ever wanted to pop out a kid.

I crossed the carpeted cubicle farm between my office and Daddy's. It wasn't far, but to me, every step felt like a hundred. No doubt he planned to revisit his plan for me to marry. Like I'd ever get married? Nope, not in a million years. Marriage was a joke and my father was its latest punch line.

"Hey, Elle." Janice, one of our bond assistants, stopped me. "Sign off on the three bond contracts we completed last night?" She held out a tablet for my signature.

"Morales, Juarez and Jones?" I'd read the update before I'd left my townhouse this morning.

"Yeah. We did good last night." She winked at me.

And she was right—those three bonds generated $20,000 in revenue, once the repeat customers made their court appearances.

"You headed to see him?" She nodded to the door behind me. The black door had Jack Jackson, President embossed in gold lettering.

"Unfortunately," I sighed.

She glanced around and then pulled me closer to her. "I heard him trying to convince Sal to ask you out yesterday."

Dammit. "Sal?" Disgust coated my mouth like the scum you woke up when you had a tequila hangover. Sal was thirty pounds past two hundred, oily, ten years older than me, and in command after Daddy and me. "How can I get him certified insane?"

Janice giggled. "I dunno, but maybe you have a case."

Closing my eyes, I searched deep for some calm. I had my daddy's eyes and his temper—the rest he said I got from my mama. She'd died giving birth to me, so all I had was his word on that.

"Luckily Sal would never give up his strippers for you." Janice walked past me back to her cube.

This lunacy was out of control; the whole office knew about his crazy scheme to marry me off. It could be funny except it threatened my position, made me a punch line to a joke instead of someone to respect. And I wasn't horseflesh to auction off to any bidder. My eyes stung and I blinked away the idea of tears. No matter how Daddy betrayed me, I refused to give in to the tears of frustration, rage, and hurt. No, I wasn't hurt. He couldn't hurt me because I'd turned my heart into a Teflon organ that no insult, no matter how horrible, would touch. How long before others began to see me as no more than a baby factory? It had been a long struggle to earn respect in this testosterone-filled business, now my own father sabotaged me.

Reminding myself I would ride out this phase of stupidity, I blanked my face. *Never show an opponent your hand.* One of Daddy's many rules of bounty hunting. Rules he'd repeated so often they were part of me. I just never thought my father would be the enemy.

I opened the door into Doris's domain. Neat, tidy and smelling of peppermint, just like always.

She eyed me over the rim of her small rectangular frames. "Took you long enough."

I squeezed my lips into a tight line and bit back the sarcastic retort. "Is he ready?"

"That's why I called." She turned back to her computer. "Get in there."

I walked into his office, a place that once was synonymous with safety.

"Sugar dumpling, how are you today?" Daddy stood, arms out for a hug.

"Good, Daddy, what did you want?" I inhaled the scent of fresh tobacco that hung on him. He'd been smoking his pipe in the office again.

"Come and sit down. You want some coffee or water?"

I shook my head and sat at his walnut table that matched his huge desk. The same desk and table he'd always had. I'd grown up playing in this office while he worked from morning to late into the night. The closet probably still held the toys he'd kept here for me when I was a child.

"Now, you know Doris is retiring in three months, and I've decided I can't do this without her. I'm going too."

I'd suspected this announcement. Since his heart attack, he spoke more about what we were missing in life. I didn't agree that I was missing anything. He'd spent 29 years grooming me to head this business, and I wanted the challenge. More, I had new ideas that would take our company to a whole new level. I'd leave my mark on the company, just like my ancestors had.

He leaned forward and grabbed my hands. "It's time the Jacksons gave up bail bonds for a quieter life."

I pulled back, frowning. What did he mean? I broke out in a sweat. He said we, didn't he? Well, he was in for a shock. I was just getting started. He'd hinted at retirement, but what did that have to do with me. This company was my past, present and future. It stood for us—the Jacksons.

How dare he try and steal this from me? I wanted to follow in my family footsteps, and I'd do anything to make that happen.

I tried to read his blank face.

Unable to discern a damn thing, dread built low in my stomach, climbing up my torso until it was hard to breathe.

"I'm not quitting." That should be clear.

He stared into my eyes and his lips tipped into a sympathetic grimace. "You won't want to work for strangers after I sell the company."

He blew me away with that bombshell. I fortified myself so I didn't show the devastation he'd wreaked with one statement.

"Sell the company?" My voice hitched from the way my throat had constricted. Anger warred with the confusion inside me. We'd talked about me taking over when he was done. Maybe he was truly impaired—like bat-shit crazy—if he'd rather sell our family business to strangers than pass it on to his own blood. Every move I'd made since I was a child had been toward running the business. I'd spent years by his side learning everything he had to teach, earned my major in sociology and criminal justice, and worked my ass off to be the best bail agent for the past seven years. The company was in my blood, part of me, like every Jackson before me. How dare he try and steal my heritage. He was in for a fight because I wasn't giving up just because he'd had a scare. He'd taught me to fight for what was important, and nothing was more important to me than this company.

"You don't need the hassle of this business. Lord knows it's not what it used to be." He frowned. "Was a time when a man's word was his bond, but now we get people skipping out more than ever. We ain't got unlimited time on this earth." He reached out for my hand but I jerked away from his touch. He let his hand fall to the table.

"I want the hassle." Trying again for calm, I hit irked instead of the freaked out I felt. It'd have to be good enough.

"And I want grandbabies." He smacked his hand on the table.

I stared at this man who until last year had never even mentioned me and a man in the same breath. The heart attack had scared him, I understood that, but this growing determination to plan out my life was alien. He'd never been that kind of father. I'd grown up with more independence than most, and I cherished the freedom he gave me. Where had that man gone?

So many thoughts whirred in my mind as the storm of rage built inside me. I tried to lock down the emotion, but he threatened my future. How dare he?

"I'm not popping out babies because you say so." I smacked my hand down on the table. We'd had this fight one too many times lately. His betrayal had become absolute when he threatened the company I loved. The one I should inherit just as he had and his father before him.

"And I'm not giving you another reason to keep me waiting." He lowered his chin in the same way I did when I'd dug in my heels.

We glared at each other, most likely with identical looks on our faces. I refused to say more. Arguing this point gave it legitimacy. Time ticked by as we each stared at the other. *Silence breaks the best man.* Another rule he'd taught me. His gaze never wavered, neither of us flinched or fidgeted. I shut down all thoughts that threatened my control. I'd win this argument.

Without breaking our stare off, he opened his mouth. "Get married and I'll give you the business." He narrowed his blue eyes at me.

"No. Pick another challenge. One I can do." I ground the words out from between clenched teeth. Breathing deep I searched for a reason he'd understand. "You got to live your life, why are you screwing with mine?"

Those eyes firmed into stone flecks. "I ain't got unlimited time on this earth and neither do you. You use this job as a shield—no men, no life—I won't let you pretend this company is a life."

I sucked in a sharp breath. His words sliced deep. I had a life.

"You and I are the same. You raised me to be you." I tried again to reach the man I used to know.

"I love, I live. You don't." He pointed a shaky finger at me and his face turned beet red. "I know that's my fault, letting you play at bounty hunting all these years—"

"What the fuck did you just say to me?" My voice boomed in the quiet room. Play at bounty hunting. How dare he belittle me. Rage colored my vision. "I'm the best in the city. And I'll prove it to you."

He huffed. "Fine! Bring in $500,000 in 30 days and I'll sign over the company to you." The look of satisfaction that flitted across his face pissed me off even more. He knew his demand wasn't even possible.

Pressure pushed against my eyes. Tears wanted to stream from me but the cold embrace of fury anchored me. Where had this stranger come from? He sure as hell wasn't my daddy. Fear mixed with the rage in me. Had I lost the company already? No. I controlled my future, not him.

"That's ridiculous. No one does that!" I shot back. "This company has been run by Jacksons since it began over 125 years ago."

"And a Jackson will sell it." He shouted, standing, arms pressed down into the walnut table.

I saw my future slipping away with each word. "You got a deal," I yelled. Regret rebounded through me in an instant. I had no real chance of meeting this challenge. No. I'd show him, do the impossible and he'd eat every last one of his traitorous words.

When Daddy's face settled into stark lines of determination I gulped down the doubts. I had no choice but to win even if no one raised that kind of money in a month.

His lip twitched and satisfaction showed on his face for a millisecond. Dammit, I'd played right into his hand. Anger beat in time with my racing heart. He thought he'd won, but even if I lost, he'd never, ever win.

"Whether I do this or not, one thing I can promise you." I stood with hands shaking. "You will never see a grandchild from me."

Acid ate at my throat and I struggled to breathe. I stormed from the room, not giving a single damn that he called after me. I had an impossible challenge to meet or I'd lose what I loved—my company. When had I started thinking of Jackson Bonds as mine? It didn't matter, unless a miracle blessed me, the company wouldn't be mine—ever.

Chapter Two

Elle

Parking my bright red Toyota Tacoma on the curb in front of my friend's apartment, I readied myself for step one in my master plan to win the only baby I wanted—Jackson Bonds. My high school bestie, Jessica, would help me nab a $100,000 bounty tonight, if I could go through with it.

I knocked and Jess threw the door open wide.

"Honey, I have found the perfect dress for you." She embraced me in a huge Texas hug before dragging me inside. I hate dresses because there was nowhere to stow my gun, and running, or worse, fighting in heels was impossible. Give me jeans and tees every damn day.

"You make up with your daddy yet?" She narrowed her eyes at me.

I rolled my eyes. "He's turned crazy. You can't fix crazy." I flopped down on her soft leather sofa.

He'd tried to talk to me three times since our blowup, but he'd stopped two days ago when I sent him an email. Simple and to the point, it had read: Take back this crazy challenge, sign the business over to me, or leave me the fuck alone.

Silence had been his response. Yup, we understood each other perfectly.

"Doris stopped by to see me today." I stood and followed Jess.

"Offering an olive branch?" She hiked up her right eyebrow, stopping on the stairs.

"Maybe." I snorted, still unable to believe Doris's advice. "Her solution to Daddy's crazy is for me to get married to some random fuckwad and then divorce him when I get the company."

Jess stared at me. "You doing that?"

"No," I shouted, not even meaning to shout. "If I need a dick to get the company then what's the point?"

She frowned at me. "I know some guys who'd do the whole marriage for a few thousand. You know the in-name-only kind of thing."

My eyes bulged. "Really? You think that's what I should do? No. Never. And no."

"More reliable than raising 500K in a month."

I folded my arms and stared at her. "Not. A. Fucking. Chance. In. Hell." Each word a staccato sentence of outrage.

"To my boudoir then. We got to fix you up."

I followed her up the stairs to her huge bedroom done in dusky pinks and deep rose colors. It was so girly I think my ovaries went into high gear. My own bedroom was low key with neutral colors I liked. I was Walmart and Jessica was Nordstrom's.

Laid out in the center of her bed was a bright red dress that caught the light. I'd never worn anything like it in my life. Maybe that was her dress.

She pranced over to the dress and threw it my way. "Go. Put it on." She waved me toward her bathroom. I followed orders and put on the dress, although I left my bra on, even if I could see it'd have to go for the dress to fit right. The dress was slit down the front almost to my belly button. I grumbled to my reflection as I wiggled out of the bra and left it on my pile of functional clothing then opened the door to my doom, otherwise known as Jessica.

"You're spectacular, those legs never quit." She clapped her hands together with obvious joy. "The right shoes, a touch of makeup and Joey won't be able to resist."

I hoped she was right. Joey DeRulo was the big bounty I hunted tonight. Jessica was a friend of the family and often partied with the five DeRulo brothers—all criminals. But then Jess earned her keep as one of the most elite call girls in Dallas. She'd modeled when I was in college and then three years ago had made the crazy leap to call girl to the rich, powerful, and sometimes illegal.

When she'd told me of her plan, I'd argued, cajoled and even begged her not to do it. This wasn't a career choice you could take back. She'd ignored my logical reasons for her own compelling reasoning—all she had to earn her way was beauty. She planned to make money while she had the beauty. Three years later, I couldn't detect even a hint of unhappiness with her choice, so I swallowed my doubts and supported her. Bonus for me, her new career gave me loads of intel for my bonds business.

"Now we get you polished up." She knelt on the floor with a yellow highlighter in her hand.

"What are you doing?" I squealed as she tickled me by marking the inside of my thigh.

"You're going to want a gun?"

"Yeah." I wasn't taking any chances.

"I marked the lowest it could go on your thigh. I bought some duct tape too." She winked at me as she stood. "But it'll hurt like a bitch when you remove the tape."

"Thanks for the thought, but I do have a thigh holster." Duct tape was getting nowhere close to the sensitive parts at the v of my legs.

However, I did worry about flashing a view of my gun when I sat in the scrap of satin. This was why I never wore dresses, let alone scraps of cloth that pretended to be a dress. "Remind me why I'm doing this?"

Jessica arched a perfectly manicured brow at me. "Daddy issues. You could just let the company go or get hitched." She grinned wide, knowing damn well neither one was an option for me.

"Fuck that." I fought for what I wanted.

"That's my girl." She patted my back. "Now go sit in that chair." She pointed to her girly vanity chair that spun in a full circle. I prepared myself for a Jessica Ann Beaumont primp session. The woman loved makeup and she knew how to apply it with a mastery I'd never developed. Okay, so I'd never attempted makeup mastery, but she'd never qualified at a gun range. We were opposite in all the ways that didn't matter, but in our core was a Texas grit any sane person should fear. Unfortunately, all my daddy saw was babies and boobs, but I'd show him what he so carelessly overlooked.

"Okay, war paint is on, now I'll touch up your hair and you strap on the gun."

"The plan—lay it out for me again." Jess and I had gone over the plan too many times but I believed in being prepared.

"I go into Lucky's first, and you follow forty-five minutes later—9:15 sharp. You say you're a *good head girl* to Santo, the bartender, he'll direct you to the party room—one of three. At the door you repeat the phrase." She stopped talking and gave me the hand motion to say it.

I didn't want to say it. The words demeaned me by their very existence. I blew out a burst of air and straightened my spine—grit—that was the word for the night. Tilting my head in that come hither way all girls knew, I lowered my already husky voice. "Good head girl."

Jessica gave me two thumbs up. "Damn you have a vixen's voice and a body made for sin. Joey won't be able to resist us—the one, two punch."

"So I get in and then…" I needed to hear the rest, especially the payoff.

"You come in and prance around, ya know, show off the goods and I'll intercept you. Kiss you, be prepared for tongue."

I opened my mouth to protest the necessity but shut it without speaking. If Jess said tongue then we'd French kiss—it wouldn't be the first time. Of course the first time we'd been 12 and practicing for our first real kiss with a boy. Disaster was the only word to describe that kiss. We'd grossed each other out on every damn level.

"I will introduce you to Joey, and here it may get dicey, we talked about this." She squinted her emerald eyes trying to see if I was really serious about this act. She'd questioned me time and again about how far was too far. My line was clear—I wasn't sleeping with anyone to get my collar. Short of that, I planned to do whatever it took to secure my fugitive.

"He may expose your breasts, play with them, suck

them or even want me to do those things." Her severe
tone made it sound like this was the end of the world.
True, I wasn't an adventurous lover and firmly hetero-
sexual, but this was work. Dirty work. The kind of work
that showed I had what it took to run Jackson Bonds.

"The whole room can diddle me if he leaves with
me and you." I added emphasis needing her to understand that I was more than okay with our plan—I was
committed.

"Fine!" She rolled her eyes. "The whole room diddles
you and then Joey suggests we go to his place upstairs,
but I'll remind him of the toys he loves at my place.
He'll come with us—"

"If he doesn't?" I bit the inside of my lip. This was
the weak spot in our plan.

"He will. He loves my sex swing and he doesn't have
one." She flipped her waist-length platinum hair behind
her. "Then we help him stagger out to the cars—he'll
be lit, count on it. Once we get to the lot, we move toward your SUV. You pretend to stun me. Stun the bad
guy and collect the cash!" She grinned at me with one
of her crazy-ass smiles. "Simple."

"Yeah. Simple." There were semi-truck sized holes
in the plan. But it was the best one I had, or anyone
had. Joey had been outmaneuvering bail enforcement
officers, AKA bounty hunters, which was my preferred
name, for over four months. Word on the street said he'd
be permanently gone in another week, so it was this
desperate plan or nothing. Nothing was unacceptable
now that my father was out to ruin my life.

I'd spent years planning my life and Jackson Bonds
played a central role in my future. But nowhere in my
grand life plan had I envisioned my father turning into

a sentimental idiot who would be the biggest obstacle to my dreams.

I almost toppled down the stairs in the heels, but I made it to the living room and my purse. Grabbing the thigh holster from my bag, I hiked up the dress to my hips as I positioned the uncomfortable holster on my upper thigh. When I straightened, the cold metal of the gun pressed into the sensitive flesh of my right thigh. Yeah, that sucked.

"Damn girl, you are smoking hot, even sexier than me." Jess whistled. "You'll have Joey in the palm of your hand." Her gaze trailed down me, stopping at my feet. "Walk back and forth, up and down the stairs until you have the balance right."

Rolling my eyes I complied, walking in circles downstairs before ending up back in her room. I glanced across the room to the floor-length mirror on her closet doors. No way was the woman staring back at me— Ella Jane Jackson wasn't a siren. At best, I'd describe myself as girl next door, but Jess had done some magic that made me not me. I shuddered and turned away, not wanting to think about how I looked or why I agreed to transform myself. I may never forgive my father, or myself, if I failed. But I wouldn't fail—it wasn't a possibility.

We left Jess's place and headed across town to Lucky's. In the parking lot, we bypassed valet and I parked myself. Jess squeezed my hand and met my eye. No words, just total confidence shone bright in her eyes. Her confidence built my own.

She hopped out of the car and headed inside. I studied the clock on my phone, hating each slow minute that passed until it was time for me to make my entrance.

My clock read 9:15—the magic hour.

My dress rode up revealing my gun as I tried to step-hop out of my truck. Damn tight dress. I rearranged myself behind the cover of my truck door. The gun chafed the sensitive flesh of my inner thigh and the too-high heels made the balls of my feet scream. Still, it was a small price to pay to capture DeRulo. Striding across the parking lot, I found a rhythm that felt sexy to me. Hopefully it looked like it felt, my luck I'd look like some awkward colt on these torture devices.

The bouncer eyed me with the kind of male appreciation that gave me confidence—definitely the type of look a sexy siren received. I let my thigh brush the bouncer's thigh when I slipped passed him into Lucky's Club, a nightclub where almost anything could be had for a price. Tonight I planned to be collecting. The smell of sweaty bodies and stale beer hit me in the entryway into the huge main room of the club. The room reminded me of a cave with dark walls and a smooth black floor. Neon lights ran along the black walls casting a strange glow across the dancers. The place screamed low-class, but then slime owned the club—the biggest drug pushers in Dallas, the DeRulo gang.

I squeezed through the maze of men and women who hadn't yet joined the throng on the dance floor. A hand pinched my ass and I wanted to kick the bastard in the balls, but I was undercover, so to speak. If Joey DeRulo scented who I really was, he'd run the other way. Tonight was his first night back in Dallas, and it'd be the last night he enjoyed the freedom. I planned to collect the 100K on his head, or I wasn't a Jackson.

I pushed through the people four deep who waited for a drink, landing in an empty place beside a badass biker with Jericho Brotherhood on his cut. Rusty-red hair and harsh jawline shouted stay away. He tipped his bottle of beer in my direction and one corner of his full lips tipped up into a smirk.

Normally, he'd be exactly my kind of trouble, but tonight I had a mission beyond the bits between my legs. And believe me those bits were already excited by his cut biceps, wide chest and don't fuck with me aura.

"You're sexy." His gaze traveled down my tight dress and then back up to my eyes. His cinnamon eyes held an unspoken promise of all things sexy, but tonight was a work night. Dammit.

I held his gaze a long moment before turning to the bartender who appeared in front of me in seconds. Having most of my overly generous top half on display appeared to work for bikers and bartenders. Hopefully it mesmerized Joey too.

I crooked a finger at the young hunk behind the bar, and he leaned forward until my lips were less than an inch from his ear.

"Good head girl." I spoke the code words just as I'd practiced.

The bartender sagged and stepped back. "Second door on the left at the top of the stairs."

I winked at the biker then made my way toward my prize. After weaving through the edge of the crowd, I hit the stairs and moved up them with purpose, a hundred grand in purpose.

At the second door, a hulking goon stood at the door. He leered down at me and again I reminded myself not to knee anyone in the balls. I repeated the password but from a safe distance this time because I didn't want to get too close to the creep. He opened the door which led into a huge room. Gathering my confidence, I stepped inside determined to see my mission to an end despite the nervous flutters in my stomach and the tight ball of apprehension making it difficult to breathe.

Low lighting and smoke made seeing difficult, but I spotted several groups gathered around sectionals and lounge chairs scattered across the room. The far wall showed the second-floor club room where women danced, that was a generous word, in front of the one-way glass. Few watched those girls because most focused on the center of the room where Joey held court.

Women displayed themselves in various levels of undress, artfully draped across the furniture like expensive trinkets for sale.

How would I compete with all of them? What would be so special about me?

Jess said my tits were the special sauce Joey craved. With no choice except to believe her, I sashayed through the room showing off my assets and casing the place. I counted ten guns and too many thugs to battle. Jess and I would have to play the game.

Jess stood up in front of me. Her dark eyes undressed me with frank appreciation. Suppressing a shudder of heebie-jeebies from her come hither look, I did my best to appear enthralled. Shit, maybe a stranger would be better.

"I like you." She purred. "Come closer, *chica*." Her finger trailed down my hair.

"Jess, bring your girl here," Joey called in a hot second.

Wow. I hadn't expected such a quick response. I could do this.

"Loosen up, Elle, you got this." Jess caressed my ass. "We get him hot and then head to my place."

I refused to give way to the nerves trying to overwhelm me. I could flatten an attacker in a half dozen ways and kill without hesitation, but I freaked out over a bit of slap and tickle. *Do the job, Jackson.*

Jess pushed me down next to Joey, the better to get an eyeful. To me my boobs had always been pesky things I banded in sports bras to be able to do my job without pain.

Joey's half-lidded gaze widened and his mouth went slack. "Aren't you a sexy one." The slurred words confirmed he was out-of-his-mind high, just like Jess predicted.

Jess slid her hands over my breasts and they popped free from the red dress. When she lowered her head to my nipple, I forced myself to relax and let my head fall back to better observe my prey. She bit my boob, I yelped, which reminded me I was supposed to be enjoying myself, not castigating myself.

Nope, girl, now wasn't the time to be proud, but time to get the job done.

I focused on Joey, who ate up Jess's every move. "Kiss her." His hot, foul breath wafted across my cheek.

Jess grinned wide before she lip-locked me. Fuck, she was a damn good kisser. This I liked—a world better than our awkward attempt at twelve. I leaned back from the kiss, still on script.

"Baby, think of what we could do to you at my place. You love my toys." Jess gave a sultry pout.

Joey's eyes popped open. "Let's go now."

Chapter Three

Rebel

Nursing my third Bud, I glanced up the stairs where the smoking-hot blonde in the red dress had disappeared. Now there were two things I wanted up there—the woman in red and Joey DeRulo. Damn if it wasn't a toss-up which I wanted more. It should be a no-brainer—Joey earned the Jericho Brotherhood a hundred large, no chick was worth that kind of cash. But if one came close, it'd be the hot number who'd whispered to the bartender and not given me a second glance.

I held a finger up for another beer. When the bartender set it in front of me, I peeled a ten off the stack and gave it to the guy. No change and no tab. It paid to tip well and I had a rep, the Brotherhood's rep, to uphold. Outsiders didn't understand what I'd give for my club and my brothers. My life was theirs, no question, that was the easy part. A life of loyalty, where your brother's back meant more than your own, was the price of belonging. I'd pay it three times over and know I'd gotten a bargain.

We'd cut the disease from the heart of the club, and it more than flourished. Hell, the Prez had more recruits than he knew what to do with. And my new business, Brotherhood Bonds, had already taken three recruits, along with the two brothers who helped run the business. My brothers backed me in the play for the bond business, and I'd prove their faith in me was a fucking great investment. No one ever believed in me like the men I called brothers. Acceptance came with the cut, but I'd always needed to go beyond the expected. Race the fastest, earn the most, live hard and work harder.

When I'd run Bound, our sex club, it'd been a constant headache. But justice was in my blood. My dad and his dad had been cops. While I'd never had cop in my DNA, hunting criminals fed something inside me. I bonded the scum too but that was business. Hunting satisfied me in a way nothing had since I joined the Brotherhood.

If I scored DeRulo and another couple big payouts, then I'd be ready to take on more brothers. Everyone in the club profited when our businesses did good.

The bonds business had only been running a year, but we were in the positive and growing every week. The DeRulo bounty pushed our growth into new territory. I glanced up the stairs and spied the same meathead guarding the door. No one in or out in an hour, not since the hot number in red went inside. Fuck, I wanted a taste of her, but I'd never see her again. No reason to spend another minute in this mob hangout once I'd tagged DeRulo.

A loud voice drew my attention back to the stairs. DeRulo wavered at the landing, barely escaping a fall that would have taken out the two blondes who tried to hold up the heavyweight. Built like a linebacker, two broads were not keeping him upright long. Somehow the threesome made it down the steps, but I had no more time to watch their precarious progress. I punched the button on my phone and told JoJo to bring the SUV around. With quick steps, I ducked outside to the shadowed alcove between the club and the garage. From here I could make a move to intercept them whether they went for the valet or garage, provided JoJo showed up in the next damn minute.

A sultry laugh floated on the night air. It came from the blonde I'd noticed at the bar earlier that night. The laugh and her knockout appearance distracted me from the mission. Damn, I wished we had time to tangle. JoJo still hadn't made it to me when the three weaved their way into the parking garage.

Fuck. I might have to incapacitate DeRulo and worry later about how to get him in the damn truck. I fell into step behind the trio with my eyes zeroing in on the ass outlined by the slinky, red dress. The other blonde was hot too, but something about the shorter, busty blonde made me salivate.

The three stopped in front of a red Toyota truck. I stepped forward to intercept DeRulo when my blonde dropped her friend and shocked DeRulo with a compact Taser.

Anger shot through me at the realization she was taking my bounty. I had no idea why, but without JoJo there wasn't much I could do about it. Where was the bastard?

Joey DeRulo grunted and the woman pushed him toward her truck. He fell inside and she bent low. Was that a thigh holster riding high on her beautiful leg?

Damn. He'd just been had.

The pretty little number had to be a bounty hunter. She swung DeRulo's legs into the truck and slammed the door. The friend's eyes opened and she said something to the woman by the truck. A bitter taste coated my throat—this was a setup and they had to be playing for an audience. I scanned the garage and saw the camera in a corner.

Reluctant admiration flitted through me even as the pissed off settled deep in my chest. I'd knock JoJo out for this stunt. While I'd expected competition, I hadn't even considered this.

Dammit, she'd been undercover cozying up to my mark while I'd sucked down beer at the bar. Who was she? I hadn't met her before because she wasn't the type I'd forget. The red truck backed out and zoomed out of the lot.

Wheels squealed on pavement when JoJo slid to a stop in the lot. Too little, too late. I stormed out to the curb where the black Hummer sat. I climbed inside and glared over at my brother. "Where the fuck were you?"

"There was a goddam fender bender just as I pulled out." He stretched his neck looking left and right. "What happened to DeRulo?"

"A chick happened. A goddam seductress nabbed De-Rulo right from under my nose." I blew out a breath and let my head sink against the headrest. Outmaneuvered by the woman I'd fantasized about all night. One thing was certain, I planned to learn everything about her.

I woke early the next morning before my alarm on my phone even sounded. Throwing back the black comforter I stood and stretched my neck. Today would suck, no doubt I'd be razzed about letting a chick beat me to my score, no matter that she was a helluva woman. Even if she wasn't my competition, I'd have checked up on her.

A quick shower and protein shake later, I was headed

out the door to my Harley for the weekly Council meeting at the clubhouse. The cool spring air woke me up more than my shower. Spring in Oklahoma was my favorite time of year. Maybe I'd spend the afternoon letting the miles of road strip away the shit from the past week.

Turning off the highway, I drove up the long driveway to the clubhouse. The cement block building hadn't changed, but now two houses dotted the horizon behind the clubhouse—Dare and Jericho's new places. Bear already had his place down the hill, the area was turning into a regular Brotherhood compound, not that I'd ever plant roots here. Too rural, too much like my past. Ardmore suited me perfectly, bigger and less personal. I loved my brothers but I had no desire to have any of them in my fucking back pocket.

I parked next to Rock's bike; he just didn't have style with his basic bike, but few had my sense of style. I strode through the front door and was stopped before I made it ten feet. Delta updated me on his latest chase up in Oklahoma City. We had a good system—JoJo tracked bounties and made bail up there, I worked Dallas, and Delta worked all three.

I moved on, only to be stopped by Dogg who wanted to shoot the shit. No time for that. I glanced around the full club room, spotting Mama and Pixie serving breakfast. The whole place resembled a garage more than a clubhouse with its concrete floor and walls. The tables were rejects bought from sales across the county. If I decorated this place, it'd match, be top-line, just like Bound or any of our other businesses. When Jericho had rid the place of the Old Man's hokey treasures, he'd left it stripped bare.

Giving Dogg's shoulder a squeeze, I moved on, managing to avoid more conversation. In the chamber, Jericho heaped a huge glob of biscuits and gravy into his mouth. Never a fan of that particular breakfast, I knew it was his favorite. I sat beside Jericho, nodding to the other guys.

Dare gave me a shit-eating grin. "I hear a woman bested you last weekend, stole your skip."

"Maybe you should think about going drag," Viper chimed in.

"I'd make a fucking gorgeous woman." I preened, not showing an ounce of weakness. These bastards would skin me alive if I let even a smidge of weakness show.

The table erupted in laughter.

Thorn strode in and shook his head at me. "Brother, you need me to teach you how to fight?"

"Why?"

"No woman's ever beat me." He crossed his arms. "Pathetic."

I sighed and bit my tongue, anything I said would only make it worse. Nothing we enjoyed more than razzing each other, hell, drinking even came second to giving each other shit.

"Okay, leave Rebel alone, maybe he likes being whipped by women—each to their own." Jericho cocked a brow at him. "We need to talk recruits."

Everyone settled. Club business came first.

"I need to put a brother in charge of recruiting, add him to this council. It's too damn much to keep up with, how they're doing, where they go, when they need to change up places." He shrugged and stared at each of us. "Shit, I'm glad we got so many wanting to join, but it's a fucking headache."

No one spoke.

"Who should we have do it?" Jericho smacked his hand on the table.

"Zero," Rock grunted. "But he still works for me. Or you two do." He glanced at Dare and Jericho. "I can't lose another experienced inker."

Dare stroked his chin. "We could work it out where J and I alternate Saturdays, and you could keep him say 30 hours."

"That's better than we have now. And Zero has a way with the newbies." Rock leaned back in his chair.

"That's settled. Rock, let Zero know about the job and have him talk to Dare." Jericho cleared his throat. "I've asked Mama to put together a calendar of events we're gonna do as a club." He passed out the list. "Pick one to own."

Rebel scanned the list. "I want the Poker Run." I loved riding and poker. "I've even got a charity in mind."

The other guys signed up and then Jericho moved to the reports on businesses. We continued through the list of revenues. I stacked up okay, but I wanted more—to be number one. This week that was Bound, although the sex club and the porn business had been beating each other out over the past few weeks. Not that the tattoo or protection business was losing cash. We all were competitive asses who liked to be on top.

"In the last year we've moved from 56 members to 70 with 24 recruits, and at least half that many wanting a slot now." Jericho grinned. "I like the way we're growing, feels damn good to be here."

Getting the club out of the hands of Jericho's dad had only been the beginning of the trouble, but we'd weeded out Renegade and the other bad seeds. We were stronger than ever.

My gaze settled on Rock, reminding me of my one failure. I planned to fix that shit, but it bugged the hell out of me. Avery's dad, who'd skipped out on his bond eight months ago, was still in hiding. The club had bought the property her dad had put up as collateral just to make everything right there, but as far as I was concerned, Gerald was top of my list.

Rock stopped me on the way out of the meeting.

"What can I do for you, brother?" I met Rock's serious gaze.

"Anything on Gerald?" He dropped his eyes to his boots. "I hate that bastard breathing free air."

Regret burned low in me that he even had to ask.

"Me too." I hated to let Rock down. "Nothing. I've got a net wrapped tight around Oklahoma, and feelers out all over the place."

Rock nodded. "We'll get the bastard."

The next morning I sat in my office at Jericho Bonds. Dunkin' Donuts coffee on my black desk and a pile of papers scattered in front of me. I reviewed the latest bond contracts, stacking potential bounties in another pile to go over next. I fucking hated paperwork but being the boss meant paperwork. My phone rang and I hurried to answer it. With luck, it was a bond or an urgent bounty needing my attention.

"What can I do for you, Rebel?" Gus's rough voice greeted me. Gus knew every damn thing about bounty hunters in the southwest, and every damn thing that happened in Dallas.

"I need to identify a player. She's probably five foot seven blonde with a nice rack and she's a bounty hunter."

"You meet Elle Jackson? Did she swipe Joey from you?" The old man cackled, ending in a coughing fit. I held the phone from my ear as he hacked into the receiver.

"Who does she work for?"

"Jackson Bonds, boy. Her old man runs that plum. Word is she's on a hunt for cash, though no one knows why. Hell she's been living at the jailhouse and scraping up more bounties than three men do in a week." Gus cleared his throat. "Despite the tasty package, you need to know she's a badass and could hand you your nuts on a fucking silver platter."

Did that make me feel better? Nope. Not in the least. I didn't care if she was the fucking queen of bounty hunters, I didn't lose to anyone. And if luck hadn't been against us in Dallas, I'd have taken her bounty in a second flat.

"Any other intel?"

"Not on her." Gus typed on his keyboard. "But Jack Jackson, her daddy, had a health scare some time back and word is he's gotten strange, looking to sell his business instead of pass it on. Lots of folks speculating that she's trying to raise the cash to buy the business." He paused and I wondered if he was done.

"Do you—"

"Ain't as if old Jack didn't inherit that business from his daddy. Ellie will make the fourth generation of Jackson to run that business—oldest bail bond business west of the Mississippi. A goddam shame if she's scrambling to purchase it."

I agreed but then I'd learned family disappointed you every damn time. My own family no longer spoke to me because I wore the Brotherhood cut. But they'd given up on me long before that when I'd only been a teenager. A sixteen-year-old son with a hankering for the wild life hadn't set well with my father, the County Sheriff. The more he'd tried to set me straight the more bent I became.

"Good to know. Keep me updated if you learn more," he told the old man. "I got a case of that bourbon you drink like water and—"

"The good stuff?" Gus barked into the phone.

"Only kind I deal in, old man. And I'll drop it by when I'm down that way next." I chuckled at the whoop on the other end of the phone.

"Boy, you have the best bribes." The old man laughed.

"And you have the best info in the business." I knew the value of keeping my contacts happy. Besides the old cuss was likable in a crusty kind of way.

While Gus had retired from the bail bonds business, he had contacts everywhere and, more important, he was often paid to suggest bounty hunters for the big contracts. I was all about securing the big contracts because of the cash and the chase. I wasn't sure which I craved more.

The day passed in the worst way possible, with me in the office doing paperwork. I needed to find an assistant, or at least needed something to distract me. As my clock hit four, I finished the paperwork then sent Gus an email about three skips I wanted to hunt down. He'd get me a shot at the contracts if anyone could. I rolled the phones over to our cell numbers and headed out. I locked the glass front door on the brick building Brotherhood Bonds called home when my phone chirped. I drug it from my pocket and answered. "Brotherhood Bonds."

"Yeah, uh, I need bond bad." A shaky voice spoke into my ear.

"You got the right place, man. How much? For what?" It always came down to those two things.

"My name is Jeb Randall and this is all a bad mistake. I'm locked up at the downtown jail in Dallas."

It was always a mistake and everyone was innocent. Those two things weren't my problem.

When I didn't respond he cleared his throat. "I got 500,000 bond. They say I killed my wife, but man, I didn't do it." Nervous tremors shook his voice.

"You got something worth $50,000?" I pushed the speaker button while I searched his name on Google. The story came up right away. A man, 45, arrested for killing his wife in a hit and run. He had two children and a good paying job. I had no idea if he was innocent or guilty, but he looked like a good bet.

"My house has that much equity, maybe more." He paused. "Will you bail me out?"

"Headed your way. I'm starting the paperwork, see you soon."

"Thank you, thanks so much." He rattled on as I disconnected.

I connected my phone to the Bluetooth in my helmet then dialed the sergeant on duty, telling him to start the paperwork. As we talked, I sped down the road toward Dallas. I'd be there in a little over an hour and with luck the paperwork would be done.

The air smelled fresh outside Ardmore but that would change when I approached Dallas/Fort Worth. I parked between two cars right in front of the Lew Street Justice Center. Striding inside, I greeted several of the cops I'd gotten to know over the past few years. They gossiped worse than bikers, especially after I poured a few drinks in them.

Benny, the desk sergeant, grimaced when he saw me head his way.

"What?" I didn't want to hear what he said next.

"Randall made bail thirty minutes ago." He gazed away, down at the papers he shuffled. "Elle Jackson bonded him."

That damn woman. She'd struck again. "But he called me." Anger tinged my words despite my efforts to tap that shit down.

"She was here talking to lots of the newbies, actually bonded four out, Randall included." Benny shrugged. "Sorry, man."

"You know what's up her ass?" This was the second time she'd caused me to lose cash.

"Heard from a birdie that her old man isn't giving her the company, she has to earn it somehow," Benny said. "Man, she's almost living here, bailing out all she can."

A growl escaped and Benny flinched.

"No worries, Benny, we're good." I shoved down my frustration. "I may just leave Dallas alone until she's done going crazy." Even as I said it, I knew it was bullshit. I didn't walk away from anything.

"You're not the only one pissed. She's stepping all over everyone and that's not her style, or the Jackson style. No one knows what, but shit is definitely not right between her and old Jack." He lifted his cap, scratching his mostly white head.

"You give me a call if you learn more about their beef?"

Benny nodded his head before I even finished the question. "You got it, Rebel. She's on a crash course, and I hate to see it. She's better than this."

Chapter Four

Elle

I carried two bottles of bourbon up the front steps of the house with peeling white paint. Knocking on the door, a smile crossed my face. Gus had been like an uncle to me growing up. He and my daddy had been best friends for years, and maybe he could help me in more ways than one.

The door creaked when Gus threw it back. "Girl, I've been wondering when you'd slink over here."

Almost as round as he was tall, Gus held a chubby hand wide, inviting me inside. I followed down the narrow entry hall and into his worn-out living room. Nothing had changed in years, everything exactly where Mamie, his deceased wife, had liked it.

I sat on the couch while Gus settled his girth in the brown suede recliner he practically lived in. His eyes lighted on the bourbon and his smile widened. "That's the good stuff. Hand that over here."

I chuckled and complied, settling back onto the brown and yellow floral-patterned couch. There'd be no talking to Gus until he'd had a couple of swigs of the bourbon. I scanned the room taking in the photos of his children and wife hanging above the television, the only upgrade he'd made in the ten years Mamie had been gone.

"Ahhh." He sighed and set the bottle on a tray next to him. "That hit the spot. Now tell me, girl, what kind of trouble are you in?"

I gulped and nervous flutters moved down my spine like dominoes falling. "Why do you say that?" My voice squeaked. Damn, so much for playing it cool.

He shook his head. "Everyone knows you're in some shit, no one knows what kind." His small brown eyes bore into me.

I didn't want to admit to anyone what my father was doing. It'd been so hard to even tell Jessica, but if I wanted Gus's help, I'd have to pay the price

So I told him about Daddy and how he'd changed, ending with the stupid deal I'd agreed to.

"You should get married, then divorce the deadbeat after Jack signs over the company." Gus leaned back in his chair hiking up the foot recliner.

"Why does everybody say that?"

"Jack ain't going to let you win any other way." He shook his head.

"I got DeRulo, and I've signed at least another 150K in bonds in the past two weeks, I'm halfway there." It surprised me how successful I'd been.

"And how you plan to get the other half?" He squinted his eyes at me.

He knew what I wanted but the old man was going to make me ask, maybe even beg. "I want you to convince Jerry to let me go after Stone Larson alone—that's a $200,000 score right there."

Gus sputtered, coughing up his last drink of bourbon. The bottle still held inches from his lips. "Girl—"

"I need the cash and I can do it," I pleaded. Pride had no place in my life right now.

"That man's a dangerous killer who has a whole gang supporting him. No way any one man or woman—" he nodded in my direction "—will take him down alone."

"Have Jerry give me 72 hours on my own, then send in the clowns." I leaned forward, meeting Gus's eyes.

He grimaced and set down the bottle. "Forty-eight hours, and then there will be three others on his case." He eyed me. "I need you to understand how dangerous this is and be careful." He drank more of the bourbon before turning my way again. "You won't get him alone, no one will, but I know this kid, Rebel, biker and bounty hunter. He'd make a helluva partner on this one."

"Why wouldn't I use one of the bounty hunters we have?" She frowned at him.

"Because your daddy will give the credit to whoever in the company helps you." Gus's face drooped. "He's not going to play fair."

"I'm his damn daughter. He has to abide by the terms." I didn't want to think about what it meant if Daddy was working against me.

"And you wrote those all out?"

"No, but…but that's ridiculous, we're family," I stuttered. Fear flashed through me and took root deep inside me. He wouldn't go that far, play dirty, just to keep me out of Jackson Bonds.

The next morning I stalked Daddy's office, waiting for him to get inside. Gus's words had haunted me and kept me from sleeping last night. Five minutes after nine I stormed through the reception area. Doris raised her eyebrows and went back to her coffee. I threw open the door and stomped inside.

Agitation eroded my confidence and I felt like, and probably looked like, a little girl on the verge of a tantrum. Why did parents have the magic power to reduce you to your worst childish behavior?

"Sugar dumpling, I've missed you. Sit down and tell me about you." He grinned wide and gestured to his table.

Those words pricked my heart, it was what he'd always said when I came to see him. Once upon a time the words had warmed me, even made me feel safe. Now they stirred the sickening stew of emotions curdling my stomach.

"So this deal we made—"

"It was a mistake, I know." His condescending tone matched the way he patted my hand. "You ready to be reasonable?"

"Yes, Daddy." I kept my tone even. "I think we need to define the conditions of our deal."

His eyebrows bunched together like two wooly caterpillars on the move. "Now what's this about?"

"The terms, I want to be clear on them. I'm already halfway to the goal so—"

"How do you figure?" He blustered.

"I raised the first hundred with DeRulo."

He nodded.

"Another 150 on bonds and—"

"Whoa there, you don't count bonds signed, only bonds delivered." He tapped his pipe in the ashtray.

"Why?" Heat melted the calm I'd been able to maintain.

"Way it is on the books and you know that—what do we count as revenue?" He lit his loaded pipe and the comforting scent of his tobacco filled the room.

Shit. Shit. Shit. We didn't count bonds as revenue

until the bonded appeared in court and the money was ours, free and clear.

"Exactly." He must've read the look on my face. "And I'm not cutting corners on this." He leaned back in his chair. "You got 15 days—"

"Seventeen days," I corrected him.

"Seventeen days to raise 400K, it's not going to happen." He puffed his pipe with his eyes lit with satisfaction.

Damn him.

"What choice do I have if I want to keep this company?" I gritted out the words.

"Get married, I said that."

I surveyed his face looking for humor or a sign he bluffed, but my father was dead serious.

"Have Doris type this shit up." I stood, shoving my rage deep down. "So I'm clear what I can do to earn the company I deserve—the one you got with no strings attached." I turned sharply and marched out of his office before I said something I regretted.

A couple of people started to move toward me as I walked to my office but I waved them away. I would scream if I opened my mouth. My phone pinged, and I opened an email from Gus. It was to the point. You have 48 hours starting now. The contract was attached. I grabbed my purse and stopped by the front to let our receptionist know I'd be out on a case the next two days.

He tried to ask me questions, but I knew better than to tell him. It'd take exactly ten seconds before my father knew and that wasn't going to happen. He'd flip a gasket if he knew I planned to bring in Stone alone. While not a suicide mission, it was going to be dangerous, especially since I couldn't use anyone at the company to back me up.

Chapter Five

Rebel

I got word from Gus that the contract on Stone Larson was in process. By Friday at this time, I could bring in the badass and earn 200K, making up for losing De-Rulo. I headed to my place, a small two-story house on the outskirts of Ardmore to pack a bag. I crossed the hardwood floor of my living room to the kitchen where I poured more kibble for Harley, my huge-ass tomcat. His water container was full and the pet door gave him free access in and out of the place. He and I were tentative roommates who got along best if we weren't on top of each other for long.

"I'll be gone three or four days. Someone will look in on you." I met the cat's yellow eyes. "Don't shred them this time."

He licked a paw as if he considered my request. The bastard could be mean as hell if he got in a mood. He'd scratched up the prospect who had drawn cat duty last time I was in Dallas. I ran up the stairs and threw some clothes in a bag. I grabbed my shaving kit off my black dresser. I should make the bed, but I left it, even as it bugged the neat gene I'd inherited from my mom.

I started out the door, but turned back and got my club jacket from the closet. The jacket would be necessary to hide my piece. I knew Stone a little. We'd played poker one night when I'd been at a roadhouse outside of Fort Worth. A member of the Angels of Death, he was beyond lethal and his club would back him all the way. Unlike the Brotherhood, the Angels made their cash in the worst ways possible—drug trafficking, along with a handful of other totally illegal sidelines. At least Stone wasn't an officer in the club, if he was then we wouldn't have created the bad blood between our clans, even for the 200 large.

I stopped to pet my huge black cat before heading out the front door. I locked it behind me and hurried down the steps to my bike. I stowed my gear in my saddle bags and headed south. I tagged JoJo to tell him I'd be out. Delta had left two days ago on some personal mission, so we were a man down until he got his family shit straight.

Dusk settled on the streets of Dallas with dark approaching fast. I turned off the interstate into Angels territory, wanting to scout out a few places tonight. I parked next to another chopper-style bike and headed inside Roscoe's, a dive bar. While a group of Angels dominated the floor with five or six tables pushed together, I saw Devils, Bastards and Dragons all present. I waved to Domino, one of the three Devil's Brigade members at the bar. Eyes followed me on the path from the front door to Domino at the far side of the bar.

"Hey, brother." He clasped me in a back-slapping hug. "Long time, no see."

I sat on the bar seat next to him, one he'd cleared for me. "Too long. Let me buy you guys some good whiskey." I gestured for the bartender and ordered our drinks.

We shot the shit awhile, remembering other nights we'd gotten drunk together.

"Tell me if the stories are true?" His light smile didn't hide the serious glint in his eyes.

"What stories?"

"The Brotherhood cleaned house, got rid of some in a very permanent way." He let his words trail off.

"Man, we're solid, better than in all the years I've been with them." I wasn't talking about our club business with anyone. "We're busting at the seams with prospects."

"That's what I hear. Bones sent us up this way to see if we can reap any new prospects." Domino shifted in his seat. "I hate recruiting. Any advice for an old friend?"

The Devils weren't as bad as the Angels but they weren't even close to legal. Normally based outside of Austin, Domino was far from home. I assessed him and an idea hit me. "Maybe we could trade info." I let my eyes linger on the group of Angels in the middle of the bar.

"Could do that." He stroked his beard. "I talked to Shorty earlier. He says they're getting ready for the party of the century, tomorrow night at their compound—welcome home bash of sorts."

Stone would be in town, and I wouldn't have the contract yet but surveillance wouldn't hurt.

"My understanding is he's still a loner, not much for staying on site." He grabbed a handful of peanuts and chomped on them.

I ordered another round of whiskey. "Good to know."

I leaned back in the chair before I threw back all the whiskey in my tumbler. Setting it down hard on the scuffed wood bar, I signaled for another round.

"If you made a run up to Bound there's maybe ten hopefuls hanging on. We don't have the capacity to add them."

"You picked out the best, then," he growled.

"For us, anyway, but we're not the same kind of clubs." I shrugged, looking straight ahead. "We got this recruit problem by going to the Daytona Bike Show a year ago. All of a sudden word spread and we're turning punks away—good damn guys we have no room for or no willingness to make room for."

"Daytona? No shit?" He eyed me then smiled wide. "You heading back there?"

I shook my head. "We got more recruits than we can handle, and that was from one visit. We cancelled our plans to head up to Sturgis." I'd been glad that had been canceled because I'd been on the list to go. I hated recruiting because glad handing wannabes wasn't my idea of fun. I'd rather punch their too-eager faces.

"What we think?" I snatched up a hand of pretzels and swallowed them before speaking. "There's a longing to belong—to be outlaws."

"These boys you turned away. Was it because they were too violent or too weak?" Domino cut through the bullshit.

"Some of both. You know our businesses, there's a type that fits and a type that don't. But some of those boys might like your style."

"You fucking Brotherhood boys always stay right on the line, not really stepping over to our side." Domino chuckled.

I narrowed my eyes at him. "You talking shit about mine?" My voice dropped low.

He leaned back, palms up. "No way. Each to their own, but makes me think a ride up to Bound might be worthwhile. And that's not even counting the girls working there."

I settled back and sipped my drink, calm now that I'd made my point. More than a few clubs thought because we didn't run guns or drugs, we were weak. As a club, we'd made it a priority to set those assholes straight because reputation mattered in our world.

We shot the shit another hour or two and I drank more whiskey than I intended but that suited me just fine. Back at the hotel I set an alarm for ten before I sacked out for the night.

My alarm beeped, creating a reverberating pounding in my head. Fucking hangover. I scraped the hair from my forehead and pushed myself up. Silencing the alarm, I shuffled into the motel bathroom. The water was hot but the shower spout too low. I dipped my head under the water stream and let it wake me up.

In my room, I dressed in a T-shirt, jeans and my Brotherhood jacket. It provided better cover for the piece I wore shoved into the back of my jeans. Since I might run into Stone, I needed a gun. No doubt he'd be packing.

JoJo had called last night while Domino and I drank ourselves stupid. According to JoJo's friend, Stone had a woman in Dallas, one few supposedly knew about. I had my doubts he'd show there, but it was the best lead I had.

I started my bike and drove the six blocks to the address. I drove by once and then parked around the corner. Sitting around on a bike for any amount of time was suspicious, to say the least, so I walked half a block down to the bus stop bench and sat down. Eyes focused straight ahead, I could still see the house in my peripheral vision, but no motorcycle sat in front of it. Probably a dead end.

Twenty minutes passed. I sat there ignoring each bus that stopped beside me. Since this area was lousy with drug dealers, I'd look like another dealer or mule. My mood soured faster than my ass went numb. A red truck drove by and my attention focused on the blonde driver behind the wheel. What the fuck was she doing here?

I pulled my phone out and punched Gus's number.

"Hey, son, what can I—"

"Why the fuck is Elle Jackson after Stone?" I didn't believe in coincidences.

"Calm down. She's got an exclusive on him until tomorrow night, so you steer clear."

"How?"

"Her old man's doing her wrong, and she finagled a chance to get the bounty first." His breathing was so fast each word sounded like a wheeze.

"You did this."

"I knew that girl when she was a baby." He didn't even sound guilty. And why would he? Elle was a family friend, and I was just a new kid on the scene. I got it, even if I didn't want to understand.

"She can handle this?" Why did I ask that? It was none of my concern.

"She says so." Doubt sounded in his words.

Fuck. "I'm out of here. Not watching her take more money from me."

"Son, you should—"

I hung up before he said anything else. I stood and

headed back to my bike. I kick-started the motor, putting my foot on the gear pedal, but I didn't go anywhere. If she missed him then I'd have no idea where to look for him. He wouldn't be back here. Anger clawed its fingers deep into my chest. Who was this girl? Why did everyone act like she was royalty? No one ever gave me special treatment. In fact life took pleasure in bitch-slapping me every chance possible.

I turned off the bike with a jerk of my hand and pocketed the key, stalking back to the bus stop. The princess was parked across the street from the girl-friend's house, well away from me. I stared forward and clamped my jaw tight. Even if Stone killed her, I wouldn't care. Nope. No interference from me. But after Stone kicked her ass, I'd follow the biker, so I'd be ready to pick him up when my contract went live.

I recalled the generous splay of tits she'd laid out on the bar at Lucky's. Fuck. I wiped the image from my mind along with her tight ass in the red dress. She'd done just fine taking down DeRulo, but there'd be no con-game with Stone. Hell, I planned to bring JoJo in when it was time to take Stone down. I didn't trust the odds of taking him down one-on-one. Maybe 60-40, but I liked a higher percentage on my side.

The garage door opened on the run-down bungalow and Stone rolled his bike backward out of the garage. Blondie dropped the pickup into gear and blocked the drive, along with my view. Then Stone ran across the front yard before the crazy woman tackled him at the hips. He faltered but didn't go down.

Damn, she had guts. I wouldn't want to go hand-to-hand with him. She brought her Taser up to the small of his back. He jerked and went down, but he wasn't close to out. I started to stand and made myself sit back down. This wasn't my business.

Stone flipped and kicked out. The blonde flew through the air and hit the dirt hard. Stone was on top of her before she got up. The sun glinted off a metal blade. Son of a bitch. Stone liked knives and he was going to kill the blonde idiot.

Not thinking past that, I stood, pulled my Glock and fired. He was too far away for an accurate hit but I fired again, hoping to scare the bastard away before he carved a smile across her throat. I ran full out, shooting again. Stone glanced up, saw me coming with the gun, and moved off Blondie. He ran for his bike, I heard it start as I crossed the street toward the woman who was still down. Fuck, had he already killed her?

Chapter Six

Elle

I tried to cough and breathe at the same time, and I choked again. The bastard had knocked the wind out of me when he'd landed on my chest. The gunshots had saved my life. I craned my head and spotted the red-head I'd seen at the bar a few weeks ago. What the hell?

I successfully sucked in a lungful of air and pushed myself up to sitting just in time to see Stone ride away. Dammit. Fury filled me. I'd lost my one chance to get him. He'd be smoke in the wind now. By tomorrow, four other hunters would be on his trail. My odds would be slim to none. How could I even hope to go after him again? He'd overpowered me in seconds.

"You okay?" The ginger leaned over me. "He cut you?"

Frustration and rage bubbled up in me. "You scared him away!"

The man leaned back staring down at me like I was certifiable. And maybe I was because I felt my company slipping away from me. Who would I be without Jackson Bonds?

"I kept him from killing you," he shot back. Flat lips and brows angled down in anger.

"I think I'd rather be dead." I stood and my head swam, staggering back a step I righted myself. "Who the hell are you?"

He handed me a card. "I'm Rebel."

The card read Brotherhood Bonds.

I gave him the stink eye. "You did scare him away so you can get him yourself." I fisted hands on my hips.

He stared at me a minute before turning away. "You *are* crazy." The words drifted toward me.

Well, now what? A thought hit me and I chased after the man walking away from me. He had a fine ass and broad, straight shoulders. He was just as cream worthy as the night in the bar.

Get your head on straight, Elle, you need him to catch Stone, not in your bed.

"Wait up," I shouted after him.

He didn't slow. I picked up my pace and ran until I was in front of him. I turned, facing him. "Stop."

His expression turned arctic but he stopped. Arms crossed across his chest, he looked good enough to eat. But that was beside the point, I needed his help. "You owe me."

His jaw slackened, incredulity passed across his face. "Say again."

"You lost me Stone, so you owe me," I asserted, standing arms across my own chest.

"How do you figure?" He spoke with a slow deliberateness as if he thought I was stupid.

"You just do." I stomped my foot. "So now we're partners, we'll bring him in together."

His brows crinkled then he threw his head back and laughed. "I got men to help me. Surely Jackson Bonds does too?"

Hell, he knew who I was, that wasn't good. Every bounty hunter in Dallas was gossiping about the feud between Daddy and me.

"You have one of the five contracts, right?" I started again.

He blew out a breath before he nodded his head once.

"Stone isn't going to go easy. You need help."

"Not your help." He glared at me, stepping around me, moving off again.

Shit. Desperation drowned me and I blurted out, "What will get you to help me?"

He walked on two steps before slowing and turning back to me. "The truth."

Why couldn't he have asked for a kidney or even my spleen? I had no desire to tell him the truth.

He gave me an expectant look then his face shut down.

I was losing him. "Fine! I'll tell you." I sucked in a breath and my ribs screamed in pain. "Meet me at the diner two blocks from here."

"I know it." He moved away.

I turned back to my truck trying to figure out what the hell I should say to him. How little could I get away with? Maybe I could make up a story? One that didn't devastate my pride or make me sound pathetic.

I backed out of the driveway I'd blocked, should have run the fucker over, but too late for that. I drove to the diner, parking in the side lot. I hadn't found a plausible story to tell what's-his-name. What had he said? Rebel. I wonder how he got that name.

Never show your fear. I stood straight and reminded myself I was a Jackson before I strode into the diner. Rebel sat in the far back corner and a cup of coffee already sat in front of him. I tried to ignore the pulsing buzz of attraction. My nerve endings were sending up serious smoke signals. I'm sure the signals read *Jump him. Jump him now.* Stupid body. I had a lot more at stake than a night of fun.

I sat across from him. "I'm Elle Jackson." I held out my hand.

"I know." He eyed my hand before clasping it in a crisp handshake. Not too firm and not gentle like he feared I'd break. Already, I liked him.

"Are you sure you want the truth? I could think of lots more pleasant things to do." Like getting my fingernails pulled out.

Fiery eyes dropped to mine and his lips tugged up in a half smile.

Shit, that wasn't what I meant, but it'd be a better trade than the truth.

He must've read something on my face because his fell into serious lines. "The truth."

I glanced down at my fingers and tried to get my thoughts in order. When I was ready, I looked up at him. "My father is crazy." Shit, that wasn't what I meant to say.

His lips twitched into that half smile again.

"He raised me to take over the business, then he had a heart attack, and now he is determined to sell the bonds business to save me from myself." My hands shook. "He gave me two ultimatums—raise $500,000 in bonds or he'd sell the company."

He stared at me as if he read every hidden thought in my mind. He spooked me, not only because I wanted to taste him more than take my next breath, but because he saw too much, made me feel too much.

"Why not use one of your own guys?" He lobbed the question at me, but I knew harder ones were coming my way.

He was too smart, too hard, and too damn perceptive to let me off easy.

"He's…" My voice shook and I stopped until I pulled myself together. "He's being a prick." I spewed the words that pissed me off even more than the ultimatum. "If I use one of the people at the company, he won't give me credit for the bust, even if it is my contract. That's another thing—we can split the bounty, but it has to be turned in on my contract."

"I didn't agree."

My world started to crumble, but I shored up my shaky core. *Fake it 'til you make it.*

"But you will." I spoke with ferocity as if I could will the world to bend to me. I wish.

His lip twitched but he didn't smile.

"How did you convince Gus to give you the 48-hour contract?" His eyes turned cold.

So that's what had him on edge. He hated that I'd gotten an advantage on him. Rebel might be more competitive than me. Wouldn't this be fun? Not.

"I went there with bourbon and begged." I hated admitting how I'd had to play on Gus's love for me. He'd been like my uncle growing up. "I'll beg you if I have to."

"Nope, just answer one more question. What was ultimatum two?"

Why that question? Fuck. My mouth opened and closed. Just say it, I castigated myself. But the words wouldn't come. I stared out the front window trying to get my shit together. The simmering anger built into a raging fire. I wasn't doing this. "That's none of your business."

"True enough." He placed cash on the table and moved to leave.

"Stay." I placed my hand on his wrist and electricity sparked between us.

My pride had already been decimated. Why did I care what this stranger thought of me?

"I can get married." I spoke through gritted teeth, but I made sure he understood that option wasn't happening. It'd be the same as letting my father win.

The bastard threw his head back and laughed, I contemplated choking the life out of him even as his sexy laugh sent quivers through my belly.

"Princess, there are hundreds of men in Dallas who'd line up for the honor. Pick one, get the business and divorce his ass." His dancing eyes landed on me. "What's the big deal?"

"The big deal?" I sputtered. I threw my hands up. "I don't want to be married. My daddy didn't get married to inherit the business nor my grandpa or his grandpa."

"You'll kill yourself trying to catch Stone, but not get married?" He leaned forward. "What the fuck does it matter how you get the company as long as it's yours?"

"You ever had everyone look down on you, think you aren't good enough?"

His face went black. "Yup."

Something ate at him. I filed the information away before I admitted the next ugly truth. "They look at me like that now. Why the hell would I add to it? Or give that windbag who calls himself my father the satisfaction of making me?" I shoved down the hurt and let the pissed off reign free inside me. It burned away all the other emotions.

Cocking his head to the side, he stared at me. No doubt reading the sad shreds of my soul. I felt like I'd been chopped up, wrung out and spit out a mangled mess at his feet.

"True enough." He held out a hand. "You got yourself a partner."

Relief, cool and sweet, poured through me. With him, my impossible mission was still within grasp. Or maybe I deluded myself.

Chapter Seven

Rebel

I threw my jacket on the bed of my motel room and sprawled in the one chair. Thumbing through my contacts I found Charlie and hit send. Charlie was a good time guy who always had the best lowdown on parties. I needed an invite to the Angels' party tonight and he was my best shot.

"Amigo, what's up?" His happy-go-lucky nature rang in his words.

"Dude, I need a night of drunken hell-raising." I always was down for that. "I'm in Dallas for a chick but she fucked that shit up, so now—"

"Compadre, I have the perfect party for us." He laughed into the phone. "Bikers, willing women and booze that flows like a river."

"Sign me up, bro." Score. That had to be the Angels' party. "When's the party start?"

"You know me, it never ends. I'm over here at the Cantina. Drop by and we'll go wild."

I glanced at my watch. Three o'clock. Shit. I'd be pushing my limits to party with Charlie and still be upright by the Angels' party.

"So I got a pinch of business for the club," I lied, not wanting to meet up too early with a man who beat my impressive tolerance for alcohol. "Can I text you in a bit and catch up with you?"

"Long as it's before seven, man. That party is by invite only. Come with me or stay home." He chuckled. "And I know you don't want to do that."

"You got it, man. I'll catch you by five for sure."

We shot the shit a few more minutes before I clicked off. I kicked off my boots before I climbed in the bed. A quick nap before I met Charlie. With that dude, I never knew where we might end up.

In bed, I scrolled through my contacts to Elle's number. We'd agreed to share information. I hit the text button and stared at the blank screen. Then I typed: Meeting up with a guy. May have more info on Stone by ten tonight. Will text you if I score details.

Not ten seconds went by before my phone pinged in response. Let's take him tonight.

The woman was eager but crazy. No way to grab Stone while he was surrounded by his club. It'd be a suicide mission. He'll be surrounded by Angels, but we can tag and follow. Take him once he's away.

Seconds passed to minutes with no response. I set an alarm for an hour from now before I plugged my phone in to recharge. I let my eyes close. Images of Elle dressed in her tight jeans, T-shirt and boots replayed in my mind. Hell if I didn't find her sexier dressed for work than I had at Lucky's when she'd all but pranced around naked. Not many women could take down a man in five-inch heels or tackle Stone to the ground, for that matter. Her in-your-face aggression turned me on most of all, and I planned to taste her in the most personal way before we parted ways. The need to taste her had been the only reason I'd agreed to help because no matter what magic she pulled out, she'd never raise the cash. It was beyond impossible, and I should know, I was the king of longshots. But that deal wasn't even a longshot, it was a pipe dream and my blonde beauty was headed for a painful crash with reality. Not mine. Why had I even thought that? I loved women and one would never be enough for me.

When my alarm rang, I rolled over to silence it before I headed to the bathroom. I splashed cold water on my face, staring at the stubble that had grown on my cheeks. I needed to run the razor over my face soon. Never one to be clean shaven like Dare, but beards were a pain in the ass.

I changed into a Brotherhood tee and slipped on my cut. No guns tonight because no matter how well I was armed, the Angels would be better armed. I'd settle for my fists and the two knives I carried in ankle holsters. I don't think Stone got a good look at me today, but if he did then I might run into a bit of trouble. Trouble liked me because I loved that bitch. Part of me hoped someone would call me out, nothing beat a fight.

I opened a small case and removed two trackers. They were decent quality but nowhere near as sophisticated as law enforcement trackers. Within a mile or two, they did the job and the app was easy to use. Tonight would be a success if I managed to get one of my beauties on Stone's bike and leave the party alive. I was almost certain of the second, but the first might be tricky.

Charlie still held court in the middle of the Cantina, so I headed his way. The dude was as chill as anyone I'd ever met, but there was serious shit underneath the chill because Charlie rode nomad for the Bandits. And nomad meant one of three things: enforcer, spy, or bat-shit crazy. Maybe all three. But he'd been in a bad spot a couple years back, outnumbered seven to one and I'd jumped in to help out. We'd been tight since then.

I'd never choose the nomad life because it defeated the purpose of joining a club—the brotherhood. I suppose there were lots of reasons for joining, hell not all my brothers had joined for the same reasons.

"Charlie, how's it hanging?" I strode toward him, a smile on my face.

His long hair swung behind him when he stood up and embraced me. "Dude, it's been too long." He stroked his scraggly beard and stared into my eyes. "You ain't got any shit going against the Angels?" He and I had spent many bottles of whiskey talking about my bounty business. I knew what he asked me.

"No shit, man, not today anyway." I met his stare. He had the coldest fucking eyes when he wanted to but I had nothing to hide.

"Give Rebel your chair." He glanced down at a guy sitting next to him. I spied his cut, another Bandit, a lot younger than either of us, maybe new to his patch. The kid all but jumped out of the seat and found a place down the table. "Whiskey, two bottles," Charlie shouted toward the bartender.

In under a minute, the bottles and fresh tumblers appeared in front of us. Charlie and I drank to old friends and then another to new friends since I didn't know half the people partying with the guy tonight.

"Tell me this shit about your club. Word is you're stockpiling recruits. You expanding?"

Everyone was interested in the Brotherhood's business these days. Jericho had shaken shit up and the waves still rippled through our biker brethren.

"No and never south." No reason to even poke at that bear. Texas had a club within spitting distance of anywhere. California was the only place more crowded with MCs. "You seen the Old Man?"

I needed to know if he'd been spouting shit about us. We had few beefs with clubs and none of those were with serious fuckers like the Bandits. I'd personally end the bastard if the Old Man tried to start trouble.

"He tried to stop by but he wasn't welcome. Hasn't been welcome in any club I know of." Charlie leaned back and puffed on his cigarette. The bar was no smoking, like every damn place these days, but no bar owner ever asked him to stop. If Charlie was in your bar, then hundreds maybe thousands of dollars hit the till each night.

I nodded and drained another glass. "We cleaned up and needed replacements, when we went looking they came to us like we were the fucking Pied Piper."

With a laugh he drained his glass. "Good to know." He leaned forward and the table quieted. "You guys hear how me and Rebel met?" Not waiting for any response he launched into the story of our first night out.

My phone pinged. Take me to the party. I can do undercover.

Can you fuck in public? I shot the reply off and deleted the text stream. No way was I taking my bounty hunter into the wolf's den. She may have survived De-Rulo's kind of party but not mine.

Another ping sounded. Do you wanna fuck me in public?

My cock wanted to take her up on the proposal. In a hot minute.

Charlie laughed and looked at me. "Man, never met anyone who just jumps in like you did that night."

If he only knew. "Shit, we Brotherhood boys started fighting on our mama's tit. Nothing we like more. Hell, you should meet Dare and Thorn."

"Thinking about heading up to your sex club. Heard good things about that place." He winked at me.

Most of what he'd heard had been from me. I'd run the club for four years and bitched more than once what a pain in the ass those damn women were.

My phone pinged three times. Charlie's eyebrow cocked.

"The girl trying to find her way back to my bike."

He laughed. "Must have a hot pussy to go with the mouth that got her in trouble."

I ignored my phone and bullshitted with the guys around me. I drained the whiskey and poured more trying not to look at my phone.

When my phone started ringing, I growled and walked out of the bar. Time to set Elle straight. She pushed my cover story with Charlie.

"What the fuck are you doing?" I snarled.

"This is my score. I need to be with you. Why are you ignoring me?" Her sexy voice did nothing to keep my cock down.

"Princess, you can't handle my parties. Naked babes are everywhere and we party with bodily fluids. You down to fuck?"

"You?" A breathy sigh revved me up.

"Yeah, me." Damn I wanted her. "And if you wander off, it makes you free game for anyone there."

She sucked in a breath. "I can live with that."

My cock was taking over the rest of me. This was a bad idea, but damn, for the first time in forever I wanted this woman on the back of my bike, in my lap, with my cock buried deep in her. I would no doubt regret this. "Charlie is my way in, so if I text you, it's because Charlie is on board. Do what I say and you'll be in."

"Yeah. Make that happen." Did she want me or her eyes on Stone?

"No matter what we can't take him when he's surrounded by his club," I warned her again.

"I know, but I need to be there. If I lose this contract, I'm done."

She was done either way but I wouldn't be the one to burst her bubble of denial.

"Look, I'm gonna send you a pic. If, and that's a big if, I work you in then you best bring some scissors when you come. You need to get the shirt from my saddlebags and make it look like it does on the bitch in the picture. You come in any other way and I'll send your ass packing."

She gulped and I waited for her to open the pic.

"Really?" she whispered.

"Totally, that's the most any girl will wear tonight."

"Okay, got it." Her voice was smaller now.

I felt like a fucking jerk, but she'd been the one to shove her way into my world. "You don't need to do this. I can't even cut you out."

"I need to be there." The kick-ass defiance rang in her tone now. "Make it happen."

I walked back into the bar. Charlie's shrewd eyes followed me and a troublemaking smile met me when I sat down and drained two glasses of whiskey.

"Where'd you go?" He elbowed me.

"Business."

"Chick business. The same one who screwed you over."

"Let's just say we disagreed and I walked." I poured more Johnnie Walker. "Now she wants me back, made all kinds of wicked promises." I swallowed the whiskey. "But man, we got plans so she's in the cold."

He narrowed eyes and studied me. "I've never seen you look twice at a chick you've fucked. This one got a golden pussy?"

"She's got something, and all my good sense says to run the other way."

Charlie laughed loud and all eyes rested on us. "Who says it has to be one or the other? I'd like to meet the girl who gives you the cold sweats."

Damn. Part of me wanted Charlie to dismiss Elle. Elle. The woman had dug under my skin and infected me with a bad case of lust.

"Brother, I'm good hanging with you. She had her chance."

"Give her another." He drew a drag from the cigarette that never left his mouth.

"I'll make her earn it." I pulled out my phone.

Send me a picture of your tits and all is forgiven. I hit send. Let's see how much she really wanted to be on the back of my bike.

Chapter Eight

Elle

Today had been craptastic. When I'd returned home I'd checked my email to find the rules of engagement, at least that's how I thought of them. My father had detailed the conditions of our agreement—a hasty, anger-filled moment that now defined my existence.

The conditions were simple, all the more brutal for their simplicity. There were four simple conditions on raising the $500,000: I had to raise the funds with bounties or completed bond contracts, so I couldn't bond my way out of this deal. All contracts for bounties had to be in my name. The money had to be collected by sworn contracts by 5:00 p.m. April 17—only twelve days left to raise another $300,000. All expenses, including any Jackson Bonds labor, must be deducted from the revenue raised. I'd considered flying out to try and grab another couple high bonds, but the costs would eat the profit fast.

In short, I was fucked.

I had opened the bottle of wine before I'd even read the terms he'd set for the marriage. I had no words to describe how small I felt at having my father dictate terms of marriage. What fucking century was this anyway?

My phone buzzed. And I was buzzed, the thought made me giggle. I was definitely tipsy. The message was from Rebel. What had I gotten myself into with him? I swiped his name and the message made my head swim.

Send me a picture of your tits and all is forgiven.

Disbelief and anger swarmed together building momentum in me, a lethal combination mixed with the wine. Who the hell did he think I was? I was not some biker babe with no sense of self-worth.

My fingers tapped against the screen as I typed out my response. *Fuck you, you misogynistic bastard.* My thumb hovered over send.

Then sense flooded back into me. He wasn't my rat bastard father, and this wasn't his idea of fun. Okay, maybe it was, but this was my undercover assignment—the one I'd begged him for. I deleted the words and stared at the screen.

My father had led me to this desperate situation by backing me in a corner. His terms for raising the money were impossible but his terms for my marriage were easy in comparison. Except I never wanted to marry, never planned to marry, and sure as shit didn't do it for business. Of course he knew all that, which is why the conditions hadn't been nearly as harsh. They sounded so very simple. I must show proof I was married before he retired on June 30 and remain married for 60 days after I received the company. The final condition wasn't so hard either—I had to live with my husband while married.

All my life women had traipsed in and out of my

house on the arm of my father. He collected them like others collected figurines. Always in love, he'd married three of the multitude, of course none of those marriages had lasted long. Janice had stuck it out five years, Beth had lasted two and Megan was at the six-month mark.

Of course he and my mother had been married ten years before I was born. A complication from her pregnancy had ended her life the same day mine began. I think he truly loved my mother, and his response to the grief was to find a replacement, but none of them had ever lived up to her memory. I'd shunned the idea of love before I'd reached 15. After the third marriage, I'd sworn to never marry. Marriage was supposed to be forever, but it wasn't, no one stuck around forever. Besides love was for suckers like Daddy. Love broke people, like it had him, and I never wanted to experience it. I'd lost enough.

I refocused on my phone. I'd spent precious minutes fuming when I needed to act. He'd said there was a time limit and I was running out of time in every facet of my life. Did I back down? Trust him to do the job right?

This was my life and I was in control. I'd take a hundred pictures of my breasts to keep that control. I stripped off my top and unfastened my bra leaving it behind on my couch. I headed to my bedroom and full-length mirror. How would a biker chick do this? Probably with fuck me eyes and a pretty pout.

I could make fuck me eyes. I could do anything. Thinking of what I'd already said to Rebel, this wasn't really a big deal. Hadn't I promised to have sex tonight? And good God I wanted him in the worst way. I remembered the way his eyes burned into me, claiming me even before I knew who he was.

After I snapped a few pictures, I picked one in under a second and sent it off to him. Not giving myself time to process that I'd not only taken, but sent my first nude picture. I hurried into my closet and found a skimpy strapless bra I'd worn with a sundress. I hoped it'd work for the T-shirt thing he wanted me to create. My phone pinged. Rebel had sent an address with a warning to be there in thirty minutes. Thankfully it was only ten minutes from my place. I called a cab then focused on makeup. Red lips, dark liner and mascara. That was all I had time for. I stuffed my driver's license and cash in the skin-tight shorts I'd packed myself into. Finding some high-heeled slides, I slipped them on my feet as the cab honked in my driveway. Hoping I'd done enough to be a biker's girl, I headed out.

The bar where Rebel was hanging out had been part of a reclamation project in midtown Dallas. The neighborhood had gone from blight to trendy bars, night clubs and a few shops. It was all part of the effort to bring more people back to the heart of the city. I'd moved into one of the early rehab projects and I loved my townhouse, it was cute and close to everything, especially work.

Work brought me back to the night in front of me. What had I signed up for? I considered calling Jess for advice but rejected the idea. I was a big girl and if I was going to earn the cash I needed, this wasn't the last time I'd be crossing into foreign territory.

Rebel territory.

My spine tingled with anticipation and my nipples poked out of the tight half shirt I wore. One of the reasons I hated skimpy bras, they had no nipple protection, but then tonight that might be the least of my worries.

Committed to my new undercover assignment, I tried to get into character. What would the others expect? I knew sexy, right? Right. The catty voice of self-doubt called bullshit on my answer. I'd spent lots of years suppressing sexy so others took me seriously. A blonde with double E's didn't inspire confidence, so I'd strapped my breasts down just like I had the sexy side of me, the side who wanted Rebel to do naughty things to me tonight. Heat burned in my cheeks and I banished my fledgling desires to the dark pit of my mind. I had exactly ten minutes to deconstruct his shirt and get my ass inside. I gave the driver some cash and booked it to his bike—flashy with fire and skulls painted on it. No other bike looked like his and somehow that fit the little I knew about him. No one would ever forget him.

Making quick work of the shirt, I cut up both side seams and stripped the shirt of sleeves. I cut around the neck then put it on to see how deep the vee would have to go. The picture he'd sent me showed off lots of boobage. By the time I'd murdered his shirt it was literally tied together. Brotherhood flashed across my chest. The back still showed the Jericho Brotherhood clear enough, which I figured was the point of this whole shirt thing. Or maybe he just wanted me to dash across town like a crazy woman.

Inhaling deeply, I straightened my spine and stuck out my chest, leading with the assets. I didn't text him, I was here because a part of me, an important part of my feminine core, wanted to see his reaction to me in his shirt.

Tonight I'd put myself into his care completely, while I trusted him to keep me safe, I didn't know if we were on equal ground in the attraction department. I hoped my entrance showed me just how much he wanted me.

Swinging open the door, I felt eyes on me. A large group of guys staked claim to the center of the bar, so I walked in that direction. Our eyes met a moment later and the stark lust in his gaze almost made me trip.

Damn. He definitely wanted me. I don't know if anyone had ever stared at me with his kind of heat, but I lit up, burning hotter by the second.

He scraped back his chair and strode to me. His gaze traveled up and down me in the seconds it took for us to meet.

"Fuck, baby." He claimed me in a kiss. His mouth devoured mine as if he was a starving man and I was the first meal he'd had in weeks. I wrapped arms around his neck and let him plunder me, surrendering to the pleasure cascading through me with an intensity I'd never even guessed existed. Lost to his touch, my body sagged into his, my knees quivered and toes tingled. Kisses really did make your toes curl.

He cupped my ass, pushing me up against him. I gasped and he deepened our kiss with his tongue dancing across my lips and back inside. I rubbed against him, my body seeking more of the delicious sensations rocking my world. He slipped back from me, not even an inch, but the space left my intoxicated senses demanding more heat, more delight.

I blinked and tried to find myself again but the yearning to be connected stole my reason. His hands slid down my arms until he grabbed my hand, turning and tugging me behind him. I followed still in a drugged haze from his touch.

A wolf whistle penetrated and I glanced around.

Every man in the place stared at us with hunger in his gaze. I glanced down catching sight of Rebel's fine ass moving forward. But then every part of him was more than fine.

He sat next to a Hispanic guy with long hair and a grin splitting his face then pulled me down onto his lap. His erection pressed into my ass. Flutters of heat moved through me. He definitely wanted me and oh boy did I want him. In fact if he kissed me like that again, he could do anything he wanted to me no matter who was in the room. I understood a whole other kind of physical attraction, one that surpassed my wildest imagination, skyrocketing past any experience I'd ever had. I was almost thirty and had my share of lovers, but nothing even compared to his hello kiss. My mouth went dry. What would it be like when we had sex? Suddenly, I had to know, and soon, hours felt like eternity and knowing became more important than anything, even spying on Stone.

"So you're the woman tying my boy in knots?" The Hispanic guy took me in from head to toe but his eyes met mine. Points for him, most guys talked to my boobs.

"Who, me?" I had no idea what he talked about. Rebel might want me, but I'd be a distant memory the next day or maybe the day after that. He didn't have a relationship vibe.

"Blondie, this is Charlie, pay no attention to the stories he tells." Rebel smiled.

My God, the man had dimples and my heart flipped in my chest.

"Elle, this is Charlie, everybody's friend, but nobody's friend more than mine." Rebel's words confused me, but I smiled at Charlie.

"Oh, honey, your smile is so sweet. You new to our life?" Charlie blew out smoke rings.

Smoking was illegal but no one seemed inclined to stop him. A quick glance confirmed half the guys were smoking. Not sure what to say, I just nodded. We hadn't created a cover story, but new, yeah I was new and no way would I convince anyone otherwise.

"Breaking her in to our life? Man, that's a tough job, but you have compensations." Charlie met Rebel's gaze and something passed between them.

"I deserve hazard pay." Rebel pulled me back into his chest.

I liked it there against his hard muscles. The scent of whiskey and leather surrounded him and I'd tasted the whiskey in our kiss. "You want a drink?" He murmured in my ear.

The tickle of his breath in my ear created an ache low in me. I wanted him to bite my ear, suck my neck, and kiss my body they way he'd taken my mouth.

"You keep giving me those fuck me eyes and I'm taking you before we go." He growled in my ear.

My chest swelled and I wanted him. Against the wall, right here, what did I care?

Get your shit together, Jackson. I tried to shake away the fog of sex that had descended on me when his lips touched mine.

"Your girl made it just in time, compadre. Let's hit it, boys." Charlie stood and the rest of the table followed his lead.

Rebel set me on my feet and stood behind me. "You look perfect in my shirt. Stay glued to me."

Charlie grinned at Rebel. "Boy, never seen you have

it so bad. Never thought I would." He smacked Rebel's arm and walked around us.

Rebel didn't follow, he waited until the other guys moved before he led me out, trailing maybe twelve other bikers. Some of the guys found bikes and headed out. Others waited on their motorcycles. Rebel walked over to his bike, parked right next to Charlie's, I think they called that kind a chopper. He threw a leg over and waited for me to get on behind him. So no helmets. Totally legal in Texas. Was that against the biker code? I had no clue but filed it away to ask him later.

"Don't get lost." Charlie threw the words over his shoulder before he revved his bike and pulled out of the lot. Rebel laughed then zoomed out behind him. We were moving fast, and it hit me, Rebel had been drinking for who knows how long. Shit. Was he safe to drive? Let alone drive this fast?

I swallowed my fear, deciding I'd just have to trust him. I'd all but begged to be part of his world tonight, so I'd take what came without questions and hopefully without fear. For once in my life, I wanted to be wild, to dig into the long-denied part of me and see what surfaced. Bubbles of excitement fluttered through me. I have no idea if it was the freedom of being on his bike with the wind in my hair, if it was this thing building between the two of us or if I just needed to let loose. I'd kept myself contained, in control, all my life, but tonight if I was brave enough, I might give up my control and live wild. What could it hurt for just one night?

When we slowed, I caught where we were, an old stockyard in one of the less desirable parts of Dallas. A part where taxis never ventured and cops tried to avoid. My first step into the wild.

Rebel parked next to Charlie. I slid off the bike first, once he stepped off his bike he drew me to him. My chest hit his. My softness against the hard planes of him. Breathless, I let my hands roam over his chest, wanting to feel his skin against my skin.

"We'll catch up." He spoke over my shoulder.

A laugh was the only answer.

His lips met mine and this time I did the kissing, pressing my mouth to his, my tongue exploring. He groaned before he took control pulling me under with a touch. His hands found my breasts and squeezed. I moaned even as his mouth moved from mine to nibble at my ear. "You are so fucking hot it's killing me. You don't stop tempting me I'm taking you here."

Wasn't that the plan?

"Baby, I'm trying to be the good guy here, wait until we make it to my room, but damn, you in my club shirt is stirring me up."

I let my hand run down the smooth surface of his stomach and grabbed his erection. "We don't have to wait. Not sure I can." And that was the damn truth.

"Fuck."

Pain shot through my ear. He'd bitten it hard and while it brought me out of the fog, it turned me on too.

"This way." He stepped back from me, then wrapped an arm around me. We walked up the line of bikes toward a dark corner at the far end.

Were we going to do this? I'd never had sex in public, I mean this wouldn't be like having sex in front of someone, which he'd warned me about and I wasn't sure if I could do that, but sex where we might be discovered, I was up for that. Or maybe I was so turned on I was up for anything.

Once we reached the dark corner, he pushed me against the back of a building. The air smelled of city and an earthy scent still clung to the stockyards. A street lamp glowed in the opposite corner of the lot and a sea of bikes were between my dark corner and that light.

I closed my eyes then did the thing I'd avoided because once I looked, I wouldn't be able to look away. I opened my eyes and met Rebel's cinnamon gaze. So damn sexy. "What do you need?" His hands rubbed in circles on my breasts. My body quivered. I needed him, everything he'd give me.

"I want it all. Every bit of you until you have nothing left to give." I hadn't meant to say the words rolling through my mind.

"My kind of girl. I demand everything. You'll give me more than you know you have." His dark words created a curl of need in me.

Our lips collided and my body pressed into his. His skillful hands unfastened my skimpy bra and then it was gone.

He broke the kiss. "You won't need this." He threw it behind him.

My God, he'd thrown away my bra. I never went without a bra. I opened my mouth but no words came. He'd slid that masterful mouth down to my breast, teasing my nipple, pulling gasps of pleasure from me. My body thrummed, on edge needing more but not wanting to give up the exquisite delight of his lips.

Heat built inside me and I arched into him. His hand snaked down my pants, slipping aside the thong I'd worn tonight. How'd he gotten there? The spring breeze hit the bare patch of skin low on my torso. My shorts were unbuttoned, I totally missed that. His mouth suck-led me while his fingers slid through my wetness.

His low groan created goose bumps along my skin. "Please, yes." I was so close. Overflowing with need, I pushed into his hand, faster and faster.

"Take it, baby, yeah." His words drove me on.

The force built bigger and bigger until I cracked open and the yearning transformed into satisfaction. "Rebel." I clung to him as my body shuddered and then calmed. Never. No one had made me come like this.

I stroked him through his jeans needing to touch him, relieve him like he had me, but he pulled my hand away, holding both my hands to my side. "Don't touch." He grinned at me. "I want to wait, savor the hunt."

A new flame of desire lit inside me at his words.

"Tell me now. What are your limits?"

"Limits?" I didn't know what he meant.

He closed his eyes before refocusing on me. "What do you want to do tonight? At the party? What do you not want to do, no matter what?"

"Besides Stone?" I stalled for time because I wasn't sure. I wanted a lot, but not too much. If it didn't make sense to me how could it make sense to him?

The smile was back. "Yes, besides him. We'll get back to Stone in a minute."

"I only want you." That was easy. After the brushup with Joey, I knew I never wanted to be one of three or more.

He nodded but stayed silent.

"I've never done wild, let myself go there."

His eyebrows raised. Was that anticipation in the glint of his eye?

Damn his silence. "Could I do what I want? Tell you

what I want and you do it when I want it? No stopping me, like now." I looked down at his boots afraid to see what was reflected in his eyes.

His thumb settled under my chin and pushed up. I searched his face for a reaction, maybe even disapproval. That's what I feared.

All I saw was satisfaction.

"I can do that. But you'll have to use your words." He searched my face. "Can you do that?"

"Oh yeah, I can so fucking do that." I grinned wide.

He smiled back. "You're like Christmas morning."

I cocked my head not understanding what he meant.

"Christmas always holds the best surprises. Looks like my Christmas is in April."

Heat crept into my cheeks. Why was I blushing? I didn't blush, ever. Yet tonight I'd done it twice. Rebel brought out parts of me I didn't even know were in me.

"So about Stone?" I had no idea what to do with that Christmas comment.

He chucked my chin. "His bike is about a third the way down the line. I got a tracker to stick under his fender."

He had tracking gear. My level of infatuation shot up, I loved a man who was prepared.

"When we get close, I'll say fall and you stumble. I'll place it as you get up." He kissed my nose. "Angels will always have us, everyone not part of their club, in their sights."

A chill chased down my spine. The Angels of Death were serious players, and I didn't want to screw up. "So our cover?"

"You're my woman, we're partying with Charlie and

ended up here. We go everywhere together, get me on that?"

"You said it before, twice," I huffed. "I can defend myself."

"My girl wouldn't and a girl here not in the sights of her man, well then, she's everyone's girl."

I gulped. This world didn't have normal rules. What the hell was I doing?

"I got you. You be wild, let it all out, know I won't ever be more than a touch away." He sealed his promise with another kiss.

Eventually we moved from our dark spot, ambling toward the noise of the party. He kissed the top of my head which was sweet. A hot sex god with wicked fingers shouldn't be sweet too.

"Fall." He nuzzled my ear.

One step, two and I fell. Somehow he broke the fall, not that I needed him to. He knelt. "You okay, Blondie?" His hand shot out and if I didn't know to look for it, I'd never have spied him sticking a tracker on the bike.

"Damn you got skills." I laughed, standing up.

"Oh I know, and you haven't even sampled my best skills." His arm tightened around my waist. "I can hardly wait to show you."

"That sounds promising." We turned a corner and the noise amplified. Music, the buzz of conversation and more met me head on. I'd never been to a biker bash, but this seemed supersized to me.

"Is this normal?" I kept my voice low.

He shrugged. "Normal isn't part of our vocabulary."

"Where are we going?" I couldn't tell one group from another.

"To Charlie." He held me tight and we walked in a slow stroll, in no hurry apparently.

We passed five naked women lying on a table, holding shot glasses in interesting places. Bikers lined up for shots and some of the men must have had talented tongues that lapped more than the liquor because the sounds of pleasure didn't sound fake.

A bonfire blazed in the distance and the music came from there. People danced, maybe doing more, it was hard to tell from this distance, and I didn't really want to get closer. I don't think my wild ran toward that kind of hedonism but it definitely intersected squarely with the sexy guy holding on to me.

"Compadre, thought we'd lost you to the pleasures of the night." Charlie's eyes landed on me.

"Ah, Charlie, glad to know I was missed." Rebel clasped the guy's shoulder.

Bikers liked to touch, well he'd touched me all night, but it surprised me how often they touched each other. I'd never guessed they were like that.

Charlie glanced to the guy on his left and he moved away. Rebel sat beside Charlie, no one said a word. The whole interaction lasted seconds—it was like there was some pecking order everyone but me knew about. Maybe in a club that'd make sense, kind of like a wolf pack, but here the order was distinct. I had no idea how that happened. I wondered if anyone had ever studied MC dynamics, they had a distinct way of life.

He settled me close to him on his lap, curled into his chest, my thoughts about biker anthropology vanished. Just my useless sociology degree surfacing. Dad had insisted I graduate from college, and I'd ended up with a double major—sociology and criminal justice.

"You want a beer?" He spoke directly into my ear, low and private. Every time he'd talked to me around the bikers, he'd done that, like our conversation wasn't meant for the others. He made me feel special and I soaked up the intimacy.

"Whiskey and beer for my girl." He spoke to someone. I must have missed the question.

A few minutes later, a half dozen totally naked girls paraded over. One stopped in front of Rebel bending low and showing off her boobs, mine were bigger and better. Where had that come from? When had I become jealous?

Rebel took the whiskey and beer. The girl faded away. So was she one of the girls for everyone? I shivered. No, I'd never want to be her. I liked Rebel's protective presence even more.

He set his bottle of whiskey down and twisted the top off the Bud Light before handing it to me. I drank down the ice-cold liquid, realizing I'd worked up a thirst somewhere in our adventures. He winked at me before unscrewing the bottle of Johnnie Walker. He and Charlie clinked bottles before he drank.

Charlie had acquired a redheaded drink girl. I glanced away. Lots of the guys had found women and in that moment, I realized two truths—some things you could never unsee and I needed more beer. Lots more beer. I finished my beer and Rebel handed me another. Where had that come from? I glanced at the dirt. An iced bucket of beer and four bottles of whiskey set on the ground. Shit, the naked girls and blow jobs had distracted me. I'd missed whoever delivered our goodies.

"Turn around here." Again the low tone, just for me. I wiggled around until my body faced him and my legs were on each side of the chair. The metal chair rocked while I settled in a comfortable position.

"That's better." He drank more Johnnie Walker, half the bottle had disappeared.

"How much of that can you drink?" I bet it was a lot.

"Charlie, what was the count last time you drank me under the fucking table?"

"You passed out at five."

I made the mistake of glancing over. The redhead had her head buried in Charlie's crotch, sucking him off. What did I do with that?

"Five, darling." He showed me his dimples with the smile. "Now kiss me."

That sounded like the best idea I'd heard since we'd left our dark spot. One minute we were kissing then he moved to my breasts. I moaned and nibbled his ear. "You're working me up."

He grunted but didn't move from my breasts, I think he must be a breast man. The idea amused me. "Tits or ass?" I whispered into his ear. He kissed me. "Both, baby, why settle for one. I want it all and you got it."

His answer set something free inside me. No one ever said that, all the guys I'd ever dated were all about my breasts, but Rebel wanted it all. I remembered his words, *I demand everything.* Tonight he'd said I could have anything I wanted.

Was I brave enough? Maybe.

His hand moved between my legs, rubbing the rough jeans material into me. I dug fingers into his shoulders, throwing my head back to give him better access to my body. He bit down on my nipple and I shouted out from the climax exploding inside me.

"More?" He breathed out the word.

Oh yes, I wanted more but not the kind of more he was thinking of. I slid my hands under the bottom of his shirt to touch the chest I'd salivated over all night. I rocked into him and his head fell back, eyes fluttering closed. Breathtaking.

My mind made up, I moved down to his belt unfastening it before I unbuttoned his pants. His hands stilled mine. Eyes open, the question was reflected in his eyes. Did I want this?

"What's this about?"

I rubbed his hard length.

Desire flitted across his face. "Use your words." His breathing heavy, eyes lidded, but he still wanted to be sure I wanted this.

Hell yes this was about me and the need I had to taste him. I'd never done this because I'd never had any desire to suck someone's dick before. No one had driven me crazy with teasing touches until all I could think about was touching him. But that had changed. This was my night to explore all my untapped desires. "I want to suck you. Here. Now."

Chapter Nine

Rebel

My head spun and not from the whiskey. *I want to suck you. Here. Now.*

The words echoed in my head. This night had turned into the best kind of adventure. I'd known I'd taste her, but I'd never expected this from the woman I'd met this afternoon. Too straitlaced, uptight and in control for this kind of play. I was wrong and I'd never been happier to be wrong. Everyone had fantasies and I was the lucky SOB who got to live out hers.

Elle's hand wrapped around my cock to free it from my jeans. She started to move away so I lifted her, making it easy to free her legs. She knelt in my lap, stopping to kiss me with her sweet mouth. Was it her fantasy or had all the others pushed her to try this?

Once she pumped my cock, my brain shut down. I'd been hard most of the damn day because of her, which meant this wouldn't last nearly as long as I'd like. Hell, just thinking about her lips on me was almost enough to send me over the edge like a fucking punk kid.

Sliding down me until she rested on the ground between my feet, I'd never seen a more beautiful image in my life. Our eyes locked and she gave me one of her sexy smiles then slipped her lips over my cock. I groaned and fisted hands in her golden hair while I forced my hips to remain still. This was her show.

"Lucky bastard." Charlie spoke low.

I glanced over to where he watched my girl, a dark hunger in his eyes. No matter what he wanted, Charlie wouldn't poach my territory, and honestly his life was beyond wild. He'd give her nightmares instead of fantasies and we both knew it.

"Don't I know it." My eyes closed, my body tensed, but I wasn't ready to give in yet.

Her tongue circled my tip making me groan and thrust up. Growing braver she circled the tip again before sucking me down. I wanted it to last but my body had been primed too long. I stared down and my chest tightened. Somehow she'd squirmed under my armor and my heart stuttered to life. I'd been in high school the last time I'd felt like this—moony with infatuation.

We moved together and my knees tightened, my hold tightened on her head.

She stiffened.

I clasped my hands behind my head, giving her control to end this the way she wanted. My balls tightened and the release hit me hard and fast, a freight train racing through me. One that ripped open my scarred heart, leaving it vulnerable to the blue-eyed girl who stared up at me with a huge smile on her face. Satisfaction lit her up and made her even more beautiful.

I tugged her to me. Before she'd settled onto my lap I kissed her, not wanting space between us. Emotion had never been my friend, and I walled most of that shit up. But something in our exchange reached down and pulled it free from where I hid it. I poured what I felt into our kiss, needing to rid myself of the weakness trying to plant roots in my heart. I had no room for those kind of weeds.

When I broke our lip lock, I was grounded again. How had one blow job almost unmanned me? Elle was the dangerous kind of girl—the kind you wanted to keep. But I didn't keep any woman, let alone one like her.

I stood her up so I could fasten my jeans and straighten her shirt, tucking those delicious tits back inside. The shirt, that's what had my head tripping. I never claimed a woman with my clothes, put one on the back of my bike, any of that girlfriend shit. I'd done two of those things today.

I leaned back in the chair with Elle on my lap. She faced Charlie, who'd lost his chick some time ago. I swallowed the whiskey, hoping to find the perspective I'd lost.

"Tell me how you met this bastard?" Charlie directed the question to Elle.

Her eyes flicked to me, I nodded to her. No reason to lie and most likely Charlie knew or would know who she was soon enough. The biker had this way of having information I'd never expect him to know.

"I do the same thing as Rebel?"

"You're a biker?" Charlie laughed at his own joke. No female was a biker in our world. Property, an old lady, our bitches—they had many roles but none were members of the brotherhood. It didn't work that way.

"Bounty hunter." Elle's cheeks held a rosy hue. She had a delicious blush that made me want to find ways to heat up those cheeks.

Charlie arched a brow at me. "Am I going to have trouble tonight?"

"Nah, just letting my girl live out her biker chick fantasies." I kissed Elle's cheek.

"How's that going?" He grinned at Elle. "Live up to the fantasy?"

Wow, now her cheeks were crimson. Charlie cackled and lit up another cigarette.

"The experience is so far beyond the fantasies. The fuel I have for new fantasies, now that I'm looking forward to." There was the confident woman I'd seen this afternoon. Badass and she didn't care who knew it. Damn, I needed to rein this shit in before I started acting like the lovesick fools at home.

I handed her another beer and the conversation turned to bounty hunting. Elle told him about her family tradition of hunting outlaws.

"*Chica*, your family been hunting mine for generations then." Charlie launched into one of his favorite topics. His long outlaw heritage, going all the way back to the Wild West. His stories, as outrageous as they were entertaining, had Elle laughing. I liked to see her happy, it suited her better than the pissed off attitude she'd worn earlier today. Hell, it felt like I'd known her forever, but it'd been just a day.

She kissed my neck and bent my ear to her mouth. "Bathroom." She whispered the word. Unlike most of us, she probably wasn't good taking a couple steps into the darkness and pissing. Most women wouldn't be, and I'd be a fool to suggest it.

"Be back in a bit." I nodded to Charlie before grabbing her hand and heading toward the bonfire where there'd be food, a bar, and bathrooms. "This party is like our lake parties," I told Elle.

"Really?" Disbelief clear in her voice.

"Yup. Wild times." I loved the lake and the hell we raised when we were there.

I saw the line of portable shitters and steered her toward one. When she stepped inside, I blocked the door because I wasn't taking any chances with her safety. Once she finished her business, we headed around the bonfire behind the food tables. Stone held court in the center of his brothers. This was his going away party because of the price on his head. He'd move to a club in Mexico or be inside a prison by week's end. My vote was prison.

Stone glanced my way and something flickered in the look between us. Probably my overactive imagination but I moved faster wanting to have Charlie at my back if shit went sideways. We'd made it a few yards away before we acquired three shadows. I assessed our options. The gate out was closer than Charlie.

"You notice the three following us?" I spoke low.

She nodded. "What's the play?"

"Head to my bike."

We crossed between two buildings leading to the parking lot when guys ahead of us blocked the path. Angels closed in from both sides. Fight it was. I had seconds to explain to Elle the consequence of a woman fighting a biker on his home ground, so I hoped she'd listen.

I flipped her around, putting her back to a wall and my phone in her hand. I had Charlie's number up. "I'm going to dispose of this trash. You cannot help without starting a war, so shit goes south, call Charlie and wait for him. Get me?" I'd spoken in a rush before the two groups converged on us.

"I can—"

"Nope, not here. No doubt you're lethal, Blondie, but not here."

Her eyes lit with understanding and she squeezed my phone tighter. "Should I call now?"

"Nah, only if I go down." I turned toward the five guys. Two looked like Angels but the other three were prospects, if that. Maybe I was the price to become a prospect. An Angel had to kill to become a member, no way they'd pull that shit tonight. This wasn't something to go to war for, just some side entertainment.

"Stone says you overstayed your welcome," a member said to me.

I assessed each of the five. The spokesman was the most dangerous, bigger than me and no doubt carrying weapons he longed to use, maybe a knife or brass knuckles, likely both. The second member was scrawny, he had a habit. But he'd be quick, no doubt. The other three, not a worry as long as I took them out quick.

"We were just leaving." I smiled holding my hands out.

"We have a going away present for you," the small one said before laughing a high-pitched wheezy laugh. Definitely high, that might work to my advantage or make him extra deadly.

I was under orders not to throw the first punch with any other club, which sucked balls, but orders were orders.

"Restrain him." The big one nodded to the three prospects.

Two came from the left and one from the right.

"Going to fuck your bitch when we're done with you." The soon-to-be-maimed idiot on the right sneered at me.

I didn't waste any more breath on words. The idiot on the right swung wide, but I ducked. Now I'd fuck them up. I swept my foot out and tripped the fucker who'd threatened Elle. He hit the dirt and the other two reached me. A right hook to the shorter one and he hit the dirt. A left jab made the last prospect stagger away. I stepped back, grinding my boot into the loudmouth's hand. Bones snapped and I kicked back hitting him square in the stomach then kicked the fucker's head. One down.

The high motherfucker ran at me with a knife in his hand. I sidestepped his run and kicked up, the knife went flying into the night. I circled and kicked him in the back, propelling him into the brick building. He collapsed to the ground. Two down.

Two bear-like arms squeezed me from behind. My ribs cracked. Fuck.

"Going to break you like a fucking toothpick." The big one leaned forward to speak and I whipped my head back, smacking him in the nose with my head.

He dropped me and I stumbled to the ground. One of the two prospects aimed a kick for my head but I grabbed his foot and twisted. Snap, his leg cracked and he hit the ground. Three out of the fight. I stood and faced the two remaining attackers. The prospect looked at the big guy who had blood gushing from his nose.

"Get him, you want that prospect patch, put him on the fucking ground." The big guy tried to circle around me as the other guy ran at my side.

Fisting my hand ready to strike, I tracked the real threat. I heard the kid rush at me and snapped my fist back, connecting with the kid's jaw. He crumpled. I kicked back, making sure he was out of this fight. One left.

The big guy was strong and cunning. I'd broken his nose, which meant all bets were off. I watched his hands, making sure no gun appeared there. "Come get some." I egged him on. I wasn't being led away, leaving Elle unprotected. Not a single fucking chance I was that stupid.

He lumbered forward and we sized each other up.

"Should I take a nap? This is your show. You done?" I goaded him.

His eyes turned cold, or maybe I should say colder. The eyes always led the attack. He moved in, headed for my gut. I could take that hit to get in close enough. His fist connected as I kicked his knee out, I heard the crunch of the joint dislocating. He was down, grunting. I kicked his head.

One thing that fucking traitor Romeo taught me— never leave them awake to call for help. I surveyed the scene, no one moved. Everyone out. I backed to Elle, holding my hand out to her. "Let's get out of here before someone decides to check on them."

We headed for the gate.

"Hold it, motherfucker." A low growl at my back.

I whipped around to see Charlie.

He laughed. "Man, you're a mean motherfucker. You get the best pussy, and five to fight."

"You called him?" I snorted.

"You went down on your knee." She grinned at me. "Besides if I couldn't kick ass someone else should get in on the fun."

Charlie walked up to us. "Compadre, this woman,

she's my kind of crazy. You can call me a friend, Elle Jackson."

I stared at Charlie. He took his friendships seriously. Elle had no idea what Charlie had committed to, but I did. Charlie would kill for his friends and I'm sure he did much worse for his brothers.

"Thanks, my friend." I clasped his shoulder. "But you know seven is our lucky number, nothing less is worth bothering you for."

"Fucking cocky shit, too." He shook his head and walked with us out to my bike. "I'll have a couple words with Diablo."

"No need. You know I like a good rumble." I didn't need any more trouble with the Angels because I was going to start plenty tomorrow when I took Stone down with Elle. The fucker had signed and sealed that outcome when he'd sent his thugs after me.

"And I like my friends respected." The dark tone allowed for no arguments.

"We good?"

"Golden." His smile returned. "I'd offer to split a bottle with you, but you got something better to split tonight."

He watched us get on my bike before he turned and headed back to the party. I had a feeling someone would be on the wrong side of his fist very soon.

I drove out of the gravel lot and about five blocks away before I pulled over.

"Why we stopping?" Elle asked.

"Need to find some kind of place to stay within a couple miles of his bike." I flipped my map program open on my phone and searched for a motel. There was one 1.2 miles from here, most likely seedy as hell, but it was better than the corner. "Found a place, but it won't be pretty."

She glanced over my shoulder. "Yeah, they rent by the hour. I've stayed there a few times while I was hunting."

Of course she had. The hot woman on the back of my bike was a bounty hunter just like me. I bet she'd stayed in as many rat-infested dives as I had.

In the parking lot of the Sleepy Time Motel, I checked the tracking app, Stone's motorcycle showed up clear and bright—the place was our home away from home for the rest of the night. Glancing down at my watch, I couldn't believe it was already one. We had maybe four hours before Stone left, if that. We wouldn't be getting much sleep tonight.

I checked in and paid the oily midget behind the counter a hundred bucks to keep the room until four tomorrow afternoon. I also made him give me a clean set of sheets—even I had standards. Once I had the key, I walked down to the room and let Elle inside. Closing the door, I was surprised the room appeared decently clean, nowhere near my personal standard, but much better than I'd hoped for. Elle stood in the center of the room as if she wasn't sure what she should be doing.

I tossed the sheets and my cut down on the one chair in the room.

"Come here, baby." I held my arms open and she fell into them.

Her kiss ignited a fire I'd only quench buried deep inside her. I backed her toward the bed until her legs bumped the mattress. I stripped off her shirt. "Need you naked."

Giving me a brilliant smile, she kicked off the heels before she shimmied out of her shorts. I couldn't take my eyes off the creamy skin of her hips and those stellar legs.

"Your turn." Her sexy voice hit me square in the chest. "You okay, did they hurt you?" Concern laced her words. No one worried about me, the way I preferred it, but Elle's concern touched that part of me I'd been trying to shove away.

I kicked off my boots and padded around her to remove the bed-bug infested bed spread. I threw it in a corner.

Her lips twitched. "Neat freak then?" Her eyes went from the discarded spread to the sheets I'd brought in with me.

What could I say? I liked shit in its place, in good damn shape. "Likely, helluva lot neater than most my brothers."

She laughed, a high clear sound that brought my cock to full attention.

"Now, I'm thinking about some very dirty kind of things." I shed my clothes, moving made my cracked ribs ache, and my stomach would be black and blue come tomorrow, the big dude had packed a wallop. Not that I'd admit any of that to Elle. I'd have to be half dead for the pain to even register against the need I had for the naked beauty in front of me.

Her gaze slowly tracked down me before moving back up.

"Like what you see? Because my view is incredible." I stalked toward her. She sat back on the bed as I approached. "Just where I want you." I dropped to my knees. "I need to taste your cream."

Eyes widening she stared at me. I wanted so much from her and we had so little time tonight, so I bent to my work. I needed to hear her call my name when she came.

She tasted sweeter than I imagined and she was wet and ready for me.

Satisfaction coursed through me, building with every moan escaping her sweet lips. Trailing my fingers through her wetness, I pushed two fingers inside her while I sucked her clit. She bucked under me. I glanced up to find her eyes on me and her hands just under her tits.

"Touch yourself," I commanded.

She plucked her nipples with a greedy need I approved of. Jacking my fingers deeper, she made the best noise ever. I focused on my mission, needing her to give me another of her sweet releases before I rewarded myself with something I'd wanted since I first saw her in Lucky's.

Not that she wouldn't be screaming my name then, but first I wanted her third orgasm to come from my lips. I grazed the sensitive nub with my teeth and she shot up.

"Please, like that." Her breathy words stoked the blaze inside me. A generous and expressive lover, I could give her pleasure for days, something I'd do another day. Tonight my hunger was too raw for slow. Remembering the way she'd knelt between my legs pushed me to take her higher, and let her fly free.

"God, that's good. I'm coming." She panted the words, rocking her hips into my mouth to take what she craved.

Her body tightened. "Rebel." There it was. My name as she crashed down, this orgasm so much more powerful than the two I'd given her already. Goddam she was a perfect match for me.

Chapter Ten

Elle

My world exploded and still he flicked my clit, sending shattering waves of bliss through me. My body bucked, out of control, the sharp edge of pleasure turned almost to pain. Yet he didn't stop.

Slowly the room came back into focus, the waves turned into shimmers of delight. Rebel's body covered mine as his mouth worshipped my breasts. Running hands through his tawny hair, the simple sensation sent a new shudder of delight coursing through me. I'd been doing this wrong or with the wrong kind of man because I had no clue orgasms could be so intense or a lover so giving.

I'd shattered against him but now his exquisite petting built a new need. I tugged on his hair and he grinned up at me. "You tasted sweeter than honey."

My heart stuttered again at the tenderness in his expression. "You tasted like salt and earth." I'd loved his taste. "But I need it all, fuck me now." He said all I had to do was say what I wanted, and I might combust if he didn't take me soon.

The boyish grin spread wide, displaying the dimples I was becoming addicted to. Damn sexy. "Thought you'd never say those words," he teased.

He picked up the foil wrapper from beside me. I'd totally missed that move, but I didn't miss his hard cock jutting up as he covered up. "Like what you see?"

"Like to feel it inside me, now," I demanded with the same playful tone.

"How though?" The stubborn man stared down at me with that one eyebrow cocked up.

I frowned at him. "You've done this before, right?" I sassed.

"Baby, you got to use your words." He stared me down as if he wasn't dying to slide into me. "At least tell me who's on top?"

Frustrating man. I'd never, ever put desires like that to words. Did I want to be on top? Nope, I wanted Rebel in control, he'd proven his prowess. One I couldn't even pretend to claim. "You on top in your favorite position."

His eyes darkened. "Flip over."

Mouth dry, anxiety choked me. What did he plan to do? Or more to the point, what had I just agreed to? Unable to make myself move, icy fingers of dread chilled me.

He smacked my hip. "Should I move you?"

I looked up at him. I'd trusted him all night, resulting in the best orgasms of my life. With a bravado I didn't feel, I flipped over.

"You have a succulent ass." He smacked my ass cheek before he pulled my hips up. "On your elbows."

I complied, curiosity drove away my worry. Anticipation overcame my earlier fears. No doubt this experience would be world altering.

He slid his cock through my wet folds. "Damn, baby,

so ready for me." He jerked my hips back into him making the head of his cock butt against my already sensitized clit.

A moan escaped.

"That's it." He stroked me again and again until I rocked into him needing the brief jolts of ecstasy more than my next breath. My breasts rubbed the bed, his cock teased me, but I needed more.

"Please fuck me," I moaned.

"Good girl." His words a soft caress before he pushed deep into me.

"Yeah, Rebel." I thrust back, needing every bit of him buried inside me.

His fingers dug into my hips, setting the rhythm, even if it was too slow. I wanted hard, fast, all of it now. I tried to move faster, but he held me steady, refusing to be rushed.

"Rebel," I pleaded.

"Love hearing you say my name." He swiveled his hips and my eyes might've crossed from the intense pleasure bursting inside me.

I gave over and let the sensations drag me under. Lost to his mastery, I succumbed completely to our intimate exchange. Instinctual, primitive and perfect, I soared higher unable to contain the force inside me. Chanting his name, my muscles clenched and I quivered on the edge before I flew apart with a soul—wrenching climax that consumed me.

"Fuck, baby." I felt him follow me over. "Elle." His name on my lips when he came was the sexiest sound I'd ever heard.

I fell flat onto the bed and he followed me down. His delicious heat covering the back of me.

I definitely needed to let my wild side out more. Tonight had freed me and I hadn't known I was caged. How could I know this plane of pleasure existed? Now that I did, I'd never settle for less. Rebel had broken through every lock I'd hidden behind and my new reality excited and scared me.

I just didn't know which would win out. Fuck that, I knew myself better than that. I would never cower behind those walls now that I understood the payoff for the risks I'd been afraid to take.

Control. That's what I'd named my prison. That was my past. Would Rebel fit into my future? Right now, I couldn't imagine him not being there. But deep down, my instincts said he wasn't the staying kind. Even if it was just this night, he'd give me a gift I could never repay, awakening something I didn't even know I'd missed.

Rebel smacked my ass before he rolled off me to head to the bathroom. When the door shut, I rolled over and sat up. Endorphins swamped me giving me this sated satisfaction I'd rarely felt. The idea of curling up to sleep sounded perfect. My watch read two-thirty.

How long before Stone moved? Maybe there was time for a nap. Relaxed, I closed my eyes but my thoughts returned to Stone and his capture. How would we intercept him? I'd loved riding on Rebel's bike, but that wasn't really the vehicle to apprehend the bounty. And he'd make my truck. Shit. I needed one of the company SUVs.

When Rebel opened the door to the bathroom, I snapped my jeans while I searched for my discarded top. The one I'd so hastily cut earlier tonight. This one day felt like a hundred and the sexy naked biker staring at me was a trusted ally. I didn't understand how we'd come so far so fast, but it was true, at least for me.

"Where you going, Blondie?"

"You see my shirt?" We spoke at the same time.

He pointed to a scrap of cloth tucked under the edge of the bed.

"I was thinking…"

His lips tilted in this sarcastic half smile.

"…That when Stone moves, we won't have a good vehicle to capture him. Your bike isn't a good option and he knows my truck."

"You have been thinking." He chuckled. "All I'd thought about was another round with you."

Damn that sounded perfect, but not worth losing two hundred grand.

"So I was going to call a cab, since you need to monitor the app, and pick up an Escalade so we're ready when he moves." I grabbed my phone from the table, flipping through for the taxi number.

Still in his birthday suit, the handsome hunk of manhood strolled across the room making me wish this wasn't a work night or better that my father hadn't turned into my enemy. He sat on the edge of the bed and nodded his agreement. "We need the transpo, if he moves before you're back, I'll follow and text you where we land."

So much more than a sex god, the man had great hunting instincts. "That's a plan." I placed the call and the taxi dispatcher said a car would be here in ten minutes.

When I hung up, Rebel crooked a finger at me. "Come here, baby."

Despite knowing this was a bad idea, I moved to sit

beside him, but he situated me on his lap, again. "Is this a biker thing?"

He cocked his head at me in question.

"The lap thing? I usually sit in my own seat." It was a thought that had bugged me all night. I hadn't been the only woman in a biker's lap. In fact I don't remember any of the women in their own chair.

Throwing back his head, he laughed in that deep timbre of his. I loved his laugh. "I guess it is. We like our women real close."

"For protection?"

"And pleasure." He leaned forward and kissed my chin then sucked in my lower lip.

I lost myself in our kiss, my body, remembering the pleasure, was on board for another round right now. My phone pinged—the taxi. I pulled away from his kiss despite wanting to stay all night and for many more nights until I was beyond sated. However, I had a feeling I'd never be done with his brand of lovemaking.

"See you soon, lover boy." I stepped away.

"Stay safe. You need cash for the cab?" He moved to his jeans.

"Nope, got it covered." I hurried out the door before I never left again.

After I paid the taxi, I stepped out in front of the darkened building of Jackson Bonds. A two—story building in downtown, it wasn't a new building but it wasn't as old as some. I punched in the code that let me inside and hurried to get the keys. I wanted to be back there as quick as possible.

I drove into the lot of the Sleepy Time Motel in less than an hour from the time I left. Good time considering I'd stopped by my place for a few necessities—a bra, shirt and my gun. I'd hated to leave the Brotherhood shirt behind, but if I didn't want to stop Stone with my boobs hanging out, I needed real clothes. My biker girl fantasy time was at an end, which sucked, however it'd always be my favorite undercover experience.

Rebel opened the red door to room seven before I knocked. He'd put on his jeans but he was possibly sexier like this. A man with bare feet and chest that screamed sex and Rebel's decibel level was off the charts.

He spoke into his phone while he closed and locked the door behind me.

"I don't give a fuck what time it is. I own your asses. Get up and get down here, pronto. I'll text the address. You got two hours." He hung up, closing the distance between us. He kissed me and I forgot my name.

Before I knew what was happening I was flat on my back on the bed. He leaned over me with a naughty smile tugging up his lips. "Why do you do this?"

True my mind was muddled but I don't think his question made sense anyway. "What?"

"Strap down your sexy tits?"

I laughed and swiped his chin. "So I don't get a black eye," I joked but it was true in its own way. "Running, let alone fighting, without this kind of support hurts like a motherfucker."

"Interesting. You fight a lot?" His finger traced my lips.

"More than most of the other bail enforcers. Something about being a woman makes guys think they can take me out before I take them in." It's why I held a black belt in both hapkido and karate.

"Your gun doesn't convince them?"

"Nope." I sighed. "Besides shooting one of them is a real pain in the ass and can get my license revoked."

Rebel nodded with a serious demeanor that didn't match the fact he was raising my shirt. He flitted his fingers across my breasts sending shockwaves through me. "No hooks?" He pulled me up to sitting and removed my shirt then tugged up my sports bar.

He grinned. "Damn that's better than a pop-up book."

I laughed at his asinine comparison. "You like pop-up books?"

"I like surprises." He purred in my ear.

"We need to be ready for Stone." My breathy voice didn't inspire confidence.

"My phone will sound and we can be out of here in minutes, but it'd be a shame to waste this time." He trailed kisses down my throat.

"Don't want a nap?" I played with the hair on his chest. A Jericho Brotherhood tattoo covered his left chest where his heart was and another spread across his back but I hadn't noticed any other tattoos. I wanted a tattoo in a bucket list kind of way but nothing had ever compelled me to mark my body.

"I can sleep when I'm dead." His mouth covered my breast.

I lay back more than willing to spend more time in bed with him.

He undressed me before he set another condom beside us. Once he discarded his jeans he lay down next to me. "Your turn to ride me."

"I can get behind that." I straddled him and he tugged me down until he feasted on my breasts. I liked that a lot. I rocked against his erection, letting the intimate contact reignite the fire inside me. When I couldn't wait another minute, I slid the condom in place before I showed him how this Texas cowgirl could ride her man.

We lay panting on the bed after yet another round of play when his phone rang. He grabbed it from the bedside. "Not Stone," he said before answering.

"Good work, stay the fuck out with my bike until I'm ready to leave."

He listened as someone spoke on the other end.

"If you're cold get a damn room." He hung up. "Damn whiners." He tossed his phone back on the bedside table.

I wasn't sure about the boundaries of our friendship but my curiosity won out. "Who was that?"

He turned on his side to look down at me. "Prospects. I'm not leaving my ride in this shitty neighborhood without protection."

I couldn't believe what he said. "You just called guys in the middle of the night and they came to watch your bike?"

"Yeah." He didn't volunteer more so I left it alone. The guys who'd fought Rebel had talked about prospects but I didn't know what they meant either. "Now what were we doing?"

"Again?" I'd never met a man who'd been interested in more than one round of sex, this would be our fourth.

"All night, baby. We're making memories."

That sounded like a well-used line. Cold raced down my spine. Memories, as in past tense. He'd said it in every way that mattered—this was just about tonight. I shook free the disappointment that tried to plant itself inside me. I'd take every minute of my fantasy night and find someone who wanted a more regular kind of relationship. Because having awakened me to this kind of pleasure, I wasn't going back to my mostly sexless existence.

Rebel grinned down at me, his cock covered in another condom, when an alarm rang on his phone.

"Fuck." He growled and stood to grab his phone. "Time to go, Elle. He's moving."

I shot off the bed dressing in under two minutes and still Rebel beat me. He held out his hand. "I'm driving."

I opened my mouth to argue.

"Easier for you to jump him." He pointed out a key fact.

I wanted the first stab at Stone, needing to get some of my own back for the way he'd floored me yesterday. I handed over the keys.

We rolled out of the lot in less than five minutes. He punched a key on his phone and growled into it. "Guard duty starts now." He hung up and mounted his phone to the holder all of our vehicles were equipped with.

We stayed back but we caught up and followed him with no problem. I needed to invest in some of those tracking things, they worked well.

"Man, she must have a golden pussy," Rebel grunted.

"What the hell?"

He nodded to the map on the phone. "He's going back to the woman's house where you clocked him yesterday."

"Really?" I studied the map. "Can you get there ahead of him?"

"Yeah." He sped up and took the next left. "What you thinking?"

"Slow down so I can jump out, wait for him to pull

in the drive and you back me up. He won't expect the attack from the side."

"Solid plan. Have your gun out." He whipped around the corner. "Looks like he's still a few blocks away, we'll be there in thirty seconds."

I nodded and pulled my gun out of my bag along with my brass knuckles. If a Taser didn't take him down, I'd need all the extra power I could get. No way I'd end up under his knife a second time.

"If we're wrong, you need to haul ass to the vehicle so we don't lose him." He eyed me. "If you hear me whistle run for the SUV."

"Deal." It wasn't a great plan, but it was better than the one I'd had earlier. But then I'd seen Rebel in action, I had no doubt between us we'd have Stone down. I grabbed plastic cuffs from my bag and he pulled up in front of the same house. I jumped out. He sped off, whipping around in the street and parking close by, he shut down the headlights, I hid in the dark by the garage.

City sounds were dampened at night, but in a city it was never silent. The sound of the bike put me on alert. Gun tucked into my waist, I placed the brass knuckles on my hand. The night suddenly got louder, brighter as the adrenaline kick-started all my survival instincts. The bike slowed and I got my first surprise in the early morning hours—he had the woman on the back of his bike. The bike stopped and the garage door shot up. I considered trying to hit him now, but I'd wait and follow him into the garage. After this morning a contained area would be an advantage. The bike rolled in and I ran in after it. The bike went silent.

"Stone. Hands up, bail enforcement," I shouted, gun

pointing at his back. Hands up, he stepped off the bike. The sound of the garage door going down made me jerk.

"Drop it, bitch, you're in my sights, straight through you to him works for me."

"Do it, Stella," Stone growled.

Stella dropped the clicker then turned and fired a gun. I hit the concrete floor but felt the bullet graze the edge of my arm.

Rebel rolled under the closing door and kicked the gun out of the woman's hand before I found my way to my feet. Stone's hands went low and I fired, the shot whizzed past his ear and his hands moved out. Apparently he wasn't ready to risk death.

Rebel pushed him into the wall. "Don't move."

I quick stepped over to where the woman lay on the floor, unconscious. I handed the cuffs to Rebel. He secured Stone. "Don't even think about fighting. She's got the Glock centered on your back."

"I knew I'd seen you." Stone spit out the words. He seethed with anger. "You turn on your own kind?"

"I hunt bounties. You wouldn't take a contract for the 200 large to end me?" Rebel glanced at me. "Grab the remote."

Stone looked over his shoulder to see me bend for the remote. I held the gun steady on him, my eyes not leaving him as I pushed the button to raise the door. "I won't kill you, but prison will suck worse if you're maimed."

He growled out a string of curse words but he stayed still. "My woman, she okay?"

"She's breathing, more than you were going leave her with." His head pointed in my direction. "Move it." Rebel didn't let him out of his grasp as we walked to the SUV. He'd put up the glass partition we had in all our vehicles.

He jerked Stone into the back and shut the door. Just like cop cars, the windows and door handles wouldn't work from the inside. "I like your Escalade, it's got cool toys." He handed me the keys. "Drop me at the motel before you take him in."

"You aren't coming?" I wasn't ready for this to be the end of our association.

"This is your contract." He walked around to the passenger side and got inside.

I started the Escalade. "I'll need your license number and some other information."

"You still have my card?"

I nodded.

He pointed a thumb to the glass. "It's not sound-proof?"

I shook my head.

"Then call me tomorrow. We'll work out the details." He stared ahead and didn't say another word.

I knew he didn't want Stone to have any information but the silence still stung and I didn't know why. He'd done everything, even more, than he'd agreed to yet I felt the bitter ache of disappointment churn in my gut. Now my ulcers decided to act up.

I dropped Rebel at the Sleepy Time lot, he didn't even bother heading back into the room. He just threw his leg over his bike and started it up.

I drove away.

Pain I was used to ignoring, but the new emptiness hurt worse. One day, not even twenty-four hours and he'd carved out part of me and taken it with him. How long before the ache went away?

Chapter Eleven

Elle

I'd turned over Stone to the Dallas PD before six and headed into the office to finish up paperwork. I stared at the card in my hand. A simple black card said Brotherhood Bonds with two numbers on it. They weren't big on information but then in jail a phone number was the only thing that mattered.

I called the first number and it went to voice mail, the office number apparently. He should have someone answering that line 24/7 but that wasn't my business.

I stared at the second number a long minute, remembering all that had happened in the last day. I picked up my mobile phone and punched in the number. It rang once and my apprehension grew. It rang a second time and I almost hung up. Why did I feel like a nervous teen calling a boy for the first time? A third ring and I waited for voice mail.

"Yeah?" A sleepy-sounding Rebel answered the phone.

My heart did this silly flip-flop before I cleared my throat and spoke. "It's Elle, I wanted to wrap up this contract before I head home."

"Hey, baby." His sleep-roughened voice made my stomach do mad somersaults.

"Sorry to wake you, you want me to get the info later?" I hated the idea of getting off the phone with him. After this I'd have absolutely no reason to call him again. He wasn't interested in more hot sex and we were competitors, so there was that.

"Nah, I'm good."

I heard sheets rustling and had to bite my tongue to stop from asking if he was naked.

"You had breakfast?"

"No, but I'm going to hit the sack soon." I yawned, it'd been too long since I'd slept.

"Don't tease me." He paused. "Come on, sexy, let's have breakfast, we need to talk, but I wasn't doing it in front of the asshole."

So that's why he'd acted like I was no one, nothing to him. "Look if you want, just email me your contract information." I was too tired to play this game with him.

"You aren't getting me. You and me are going to talk, now, in person." He made it clear this wasn't an option.

Why was I fighting this? *To protect your damn heart, stupid.*

I wasn't that frightened girl anymore. "You want to talk, come to my place. I'll have breakfast."

"Are you breakfast?" His sexy growl made my lady parts wake up.

"Come and see." Who was I and where had the Elle I knew gone? Up in smoke after one night with the bad boy biker.

"Text me your address."

"Give me at least thirty minutes to get there," I told him, already planning to stop and pick up breakfast at

my favorite deli. I was too beat to cook and my cooking was marginal at best.

"See you soon." He hung up.

He didn't wait for me to say goodbye. Who did
that? Apparently Rebel did. Shaking off my wander-
ing thoughts, I texted my address before I called the
deli ordering too much of everything because I had no
idea how much he ate.

I stood to go when my office door opened and Daddy
strolled inside. He was the last person I wanted to see
right now, or maybe ever. I headed for the door having
no time for more of his bullshit.

"Sugar dumpling," he called and stopped me outside
the door. "Good job bringing Stone in."

Maybe it was sleep deprivation or maybe it was my
new attitude, but I turned and smiled. "Fuck you very
much." I had never said fuck in my daddy's presence
let alone aimed one his way.

"That's no way to treat your father," he blustered, as
surprised as me at my new sense of rebellion.

I stalked back to him, inches separated us. "I'll treat
you like my father when you start acting like one again."

I stormed out of the building and jumped in the Escalade. The anger tried to take over but I was done with
that. I had a sexy man on his way to my place and I'd
taken down one of the most dangerous bounties in the
state. No, maybe tomorrow I'd have time for anger or
regret, but not today.

I pulled into my townhouse drive and packed the
bags of food into the kitchen then ran into my bedroom and changed. I shrugged off all my work clothes,
dropping my gun in its safe before I dressed in a tank
top and shorts, no bra. So maybe I'd misread what he

wanted from me, but I wasn't going to make saying no easy on him. Even one more day would be enough, I lied to myself. I was a greedy bitch who would still want more. More orgasms. More intimacy. More everything.

Chapter Twelve

Rebel

I stared up at the townhouse a minute before I lowered my kickstand and got off my bike. If I were in my right mind, I'd already be back in Ardmore. But insanity had me in its grips so I walked up to the door and rang the doorbell.

Elle opened the door looking good enough to eat. Her long blonde hair loose, a tank top showed those nipples that drove me wild, and her legs were framed in shorts that rode high on her thigh. Definitely having more than one taste of her.

"Breakfast is in the kitchen," she told me as she closed and locked the front door.

"No, it looks like you're my breakfast." I closed the distance between us.

She pushed hands into my chest, stopping me before I could get in tasting range. "Food. Business. Sex."

No, that wouldn't work, business had to be last because I didn't want to miss the good parts if my proposal pissed her off. And there was a good chance she'd kick my ass to the curb. "Food. Sex. Sleep. Business."

"Deal. This way." She led me down the hall, a living room was to the left and a home office to the right. She had an eye for color and the place felt warm and cozy, a home. I had a house but it wasn't a home, but then I liked it that way.

"I like your place. Great colors." I followed her into the bright blue kitchen

"Thank you." She opened the cabinet and brought out two plates, handing me one. "Breakfast from Tessa's Deli. I'm not much of a cook."

I kissed the top of her nose. "I'm starved." I dug into the food, piling my plate full. I cooked at my place all the time and was better than average, not that I told any of my brothers that. The mooches would be on my doorstep every meal.

"So how did it go at the police station?" I yawned starting to feel the lack of sleep.

She told me about the processing and the shit Stone got when a woman brought him in. She rambled on telling me about her office, then about the fucked-up scene with her father. It pissed me off that the guy was making her jump through hoops.

"I blame you. You're a bad influence," she teased me.

"Sounds like he deserved it, and I like corrupting you." I waggled my eyebrows.

She lost it, laughing so hard she could barely breathe. "You're terrible."

"I'm fucking awesome." I scooped up more eggs. "You can admit it, I already know it."

Once she brought her laugh fest to an end, she looked me straight in the eyes. "You are awesome at fucking." She didn't blush or crack a smile.

I threw my head back and laughed. "You read my mind. Show me to your bedroom, baby. I need to maintain my rep." I stood and pulled her to me. "I want to taste you, but if I do that now, I'll take you right here on your table."

"Exciting as that sounds…" And by the smile on her lips she was considering it. "I'm going to crash and my bed is so comfy."

"Like I said, lead the way." We made our way upstairs.

Her room was all deep greens and browns, I liked it. I threw back the bedspread before I picked her up and tossed her in the middle of the bed. "Just where I want you."

Shedding my clothes, I climbed into bed on top of her and asked the question of the day. "Tell me you have condoms, I'm out." I should've stopped on my way here but my brain short-circuited and I'd forgotten.

"What if I don't?"

"Say you do," I pleaded because I didn't want to drag my ass out of bed and go get some.

"I do. In the nightstand drawer."

Inside was a box of condoms, barely used. I brought out a whole string.

She giggled, a sound I'd never heard from her before. "I'll be unconscious before we make it that far."

"Baby, you never know." Then I kissed her. It was like coming home.

I'd wanted that kiss since I'd arrived. With the condom stash replenished I might never leave this bed.

I woke before her and watched her sleep, but her naked body made me want to do other things, and I'd have to leave before too long. I nudged her legs open wider so I could taste her again.

"I thought I was dreaming." Her sleepy voice was so sexy.

I grinned up at her before returning my mouth to her. She thrust her hips unable to remain still. I could see the orgasm building. When it hit her, I lapped it up along with her sweet cream before I moved up to take her again.

I was addicted to Elle calling my name when she came. I hadn't meant to see her again, but I couldn't stay away. Besides what was the fun of rules if I didn't break them. My one night and done rule was history where she was concerned. Maybe it should worry me, but I couldn't be bothered when Elle climbed atop me. While I wished we could fuck our way through the whole box of condoms, I had to head home for a council meeting tomorrow but before I left we were going to come to an understanding.

Her small hands rolled the condom down my length. She straddled me sliding her tight pussy around me and my thoughts scattered to the wind. I let her set the rhythm at first, content to watch her beautiful body bounce atop mine.

"Fuck me harder, baby." I wanted her wild, to let loose of all the passion she'd bottled inside.

She dug fingers into my shoulders and rode me hard but too soon I needed to set the pace. I gripped her hips and pushed her to go faster. Her sexy noises flipped a switch inside me. "That's it, girl, come for me," I coaxed her.

An image of her on her knees at the party flashed through my mind and I was a goner. Trying to hold back was no use, she was kryptonite to my control. Gone was the jaded master who could fuck for hours before I came, with her I was someone different and I had no fucking clue why.

Knees tightening I called her name and let go. Her tight pussy squeezed my cock as she came undone for me. I lived for the moments she climaxed—passion fierce and primal transformed her face. Elle Jackson did nothing in half measures, when she came for me her orgasm reached all the way down to her soul, and she shared it with me like it wasn't the most precious gift in the world.

I held her tight while the shudders of her release tore through her. I'd have to guard my heart close or she'd end up stealing it, and it'd fucking suck to live the rest of my life without it. No matter how much I craved her now, it'd pass, because I didn't have it in me to love. My family had cured me of that stupidity.

She glanced up with a lazy smile. "Shower and then we need to talk or sleep," she yawned. "You have worn me out, again."

After we made it out of the shower, I dressed quickly to avoid the temptation of taking her back to bed. No matter how many times I had her, I wanted her just like it was the first time all over again.

"Come on, let's talk downstairs." She motioned for me to follow her.

We left her very orderly bedroom, and she called me a neat freak, and ended up in her living room on a couch that had flowers all over it. I mean as far as couches went, it looked good in the room, but who the fuck bought a couch with flowers on it. Not understanding the mystery of that, I turned my attention to what I wanted to say. Would it piss her off? Likely, it's why I'd put talking last on the agenda.

She grabbed a notepad and pen from the end table

and tossed it to me. "Write your license and stuff down so I can process your half of the bounty."

"About that." I set the notepad aside. "I don't want it. In fact, I want you to keep the entire thing. It was your contract."

Her eyes narrowed and nostrils flared—she was getting ready to give me hell.

"Look, Elle, I know it wasn't the deal we made but I want to make a new deal."

With hellfire in her eyes she crossed her arms. "Why?"

"The way I figure this, even with the cash from Stone, you'll be doing the impossible to earn 500 large in…what…how many days do you have left?"

"Ten days and a few hours." She clenched her jaw tight.

Damn I wanted to kiss away the mad. "Without sharing the history of my fucked-up family, let's just say I understand the suckiness of family betraying you."

Her eyes softened.

"So let me do this for you, and add to that the offer of being your backup, no fees will be accepted, so you can shove this fucking deal down your father's throat." Anytime I thought of what her dickhead of a dad was doing to her, I saw red.

"So that's it? You want to help me even though you don't think it's possible to do." She assessed me. "Or just not possible for me to do?"

I clasped her hand. "So you get I'm an arrogant bastard."

"I get that." She almost smiled for me.

"I don't think even with your company's resources behind me that I could do it, that your father could in his day, and the prick tricked you into the corner you're in because he thinks he knows better than you. That kind of arrogance just pisses me the fuck off." My jaw ached from clenching as I tried to hold back harsher words she didn't need to hear.

"Why not take the cash if it's so hopeless?" Hurt echoed in her question.

"Because maybe you'll do it. I want you to do it, no matter what I think or anyone thinks."

Now she did smile. "So that's the deal?"

"The work part of the deal." I ran my hands through my hair not even believing I was saying this shit. "Whether we work together or not, I want to see you again, see you often." I stood and walked to the far side of the room before I turned around and said the rest. "I'm a bastard, haven't even had a girlfriend since I was 16."

Her expression was blank.

"Until you, right now, I haven't spent two nights with the same woman since I joined the Brotherhood." I couldn't look at her face because I didn't want to see the disgust or judgment there. Best to get the rest out.

"How long have you been in the club?" Her quiet question almost undid me.

I was a breath away from walking out the door and drinking myself into oblivion until this crazy idea couldn't raise its head ever again.

"Twelve years, I joined when I was 20." Of course that didn't count the two years I'd been a prospect and my father had rained down hell on the Brotherhood. I had been sure they'd kick me loose just to avoid his wrath, but they had stood by me. "I'm laying this out clear as I can because while I want more, I'll never want it all, that's just not in me. I'll walk away sooner or later because that is me." Because I wasn't a coward, I met her gaze.

I couldn't read a damn thing in her face, if some emotion had been there it was gone now. It was the same look she'd had when we took down Stone—her poker face was a damn good one.

"So you're telling me you want to come back and fuck me, give me more of those mind-melting orgasms, but not to get too attached because you'll bail sometime?"

I nodded.

"And what if I'm done first?"

The idea hadn't even occurred to me. I truly was an arrogant son of a bitch. "Same thing, no harm, no foul."

"Would I go to more biker parties?" Her lips quirked up.

"If you wanted to, I'm all about fantasy fulfillment." Maybe this wasn't the big deal I'd made it out to be. If she was a biker chick or one of the regulars at the club, I wouldn't have felt compelled to spell it out. This was the norm in our world, but Elle wasn't part of that world and honestly, I couldn't ever picture her being part of it. As I thought it, the picture of her on my lap with my club shirt on fucked with my mind.

"Since you shared, perhaps a little of my sexual history would help you understand."

Fuck. I didn't want to know about her lovers or boyfriends. Hell maybe she'd even been married. That idea pissed me off for some unknown reason.

"I have had four, count them." She lifted one finger at a time until four fingers were raised. "You make number five."

Holy fuck, he'd had five women in one night. They could never talk numbers again.

"Until this badass biker showed me what I'd been

missing, sex wasn't something I was ever interested in, and it sure as hell wasn't satisfying, at least now that I know what the really good stuff is."

I grinned at that comment. My ego loved to be fed.

"I'd never given a blow job until last night."

"What the fuck?" I stormed across the room pissed off all over again.

"No man had ever gone down on me." She ignored my outburst. "So I think I'm due for some just sex, no emotional bullshit about now."

"You sure?"

"Did I fucking stutter?" She threw me attitude, the same kick-ass attitude that she'd shown at the diner and when she'd taken down Stone.

"Baby, you don't know how happy that makes me." I knelt before her. "You make me break my rules."

"Well back at you. I had a ton of rules about sex, relationships, all that stuff, and so far you've broken every one of them. I have to admit, I've never been more satisfied."

I threw my head back and laughed. What the fuck else could I do? Down deep, we might be copies of each other in most of the important ways. As soon as I thought it, I shoved that thought away, locking it tight. That kind of thinking led to the dark hole where I'd buried all my emotions.

"So only one blow job?" I teased her. "And you decided to do that in front of all those strangers?"

She nodded. "I probably need some practice, I mean, if you need to go right now, I understand."

"I have some time." For her, I had all the time in the world, and if I were brutally honest with myself, the very notion had me shaking in my boots.

Chapter Thirteen

Elle

Four days to go and I was still 150,000 dollars short. Today, I had four mid-ticket guys on my cleanup list. If I apprehended all four, I'd be down to 50,000, but I had no idea where that income would come from. One hour at a time, one contract completed then the next until I made my goal.

I pulled up in front of the flop house, Maurice missed his court date. Normally, he showed but no one had seen the guy in a week. Last night a tip had come in that he was back in his familiar haunts. I shrugged on my BEA jacket to hide the shoulder holster I'd been wearing the past few days. While not subtle, it had been easier since I'd been taking down so many contracts. Maurice would be my fifteenth.

I pushed open my truck door and forced myself out, I was bone weary and heart sore. The deadline grew closer while Daddy and I grew further apart. I think he'd expected me to give up by now, but I hadn't. However, I had made it clear what I thought of his manipulations. We couldn't be in the office together without a shouting match starting.

I opened the off-kilter wooden door on the run-down building. I stopped at the front desk. "Where's Maurice?" I asked the woman behind the desk.

"I ain't—"

I pointed my Glock at her triple chins, no time left for bullshit. "Where?"

"Room 31. Don't shoot me," she pleaded making those chins quiver.

Nodding, I moved upstairs one floor, then two. The third floors held the thirties, I'd been here too many times to count. Maurice's flop was the first door past the stairs. The stench of the stairwell amplified once I stepped into the hall. I didn't bother knocking, just kicked his door open. Maurice lay sprawled on the floor. Dead. The smells of death assaulted my nose making me gag.

A needle lay beside him, an overdose. I backed out of the room and pulled out my phone to call the police. If I waited on the manager to notify the police, weeks might pass. After reporting his death, I hung up without giving my name or waiting on police as the operator advised. I was out in my truck in minutes but the smell hung on me. I pushed the buttons to roll down both windows before I drove off.

Time for the next bounty. Normally, I didn't do prostitutes because I figured their life sucked enough without being tracked down for missing court, but Lisa had been bailed out for $50,000 and the bonder was paying $10,000 to bring her in. While I didn't know why, it was a lot more than her kind of case normally paid.

Walking up another set of steps, this time in public housing, the sound of crying echoed off the walls.

Kids, babies, and pregnant moms filled up Dallas's section eight housing. Shit. I hoped she didn't have kids.

I knocked on the door, and Lisa opened up. Not only did she have a toddler clinging to her jeans, her belly was round with pregnancy.

Sticking my foot in the door, I glanced behind her, no one else around. "Bail enforcement, you're coming with me."

"My kid," she whined. "You don't need the five hundred bucks I bring."

"If that was the bounty, then you'd be right, but Johnny is pissed, put a ten thousand dollar reward on your capture." I shouldered into the room. "Get someone to watch the kid or I'll call in a uniform to take care of it."

"No…" She backed up from me. Her door still wide open. I heard neighbors milling in the hallway. "He put 10 G on me?"

I nodded. "Give me your hands."

Tears streamed down her face and she kind of crumpled, defeated. I brought her hands together in front and restrained her.

"I'll take Micah." A small Asian woman hurried into the room and snatched up the toddler.

"Thanks." Lisa sniffed. "Take good care of him for me."

The woman nodded before she rushed out like she was afraid I'd restrain her next.

It took me two hours to transport and process Lisa downtown. The woman cried the entire time making me feel about two inches tall which pissed me off. Her problems were not my responsibility.

By afternoon, I was ready to move on the first of my two big targets for the day. Jasper was a mule who spent his afternoons on a corner not far from where the Angels held their party. The kid was young, hot-headed and fast on his feet. I'd brought him in one other time and the punk had given me a black eye.

Parking a few feet away, I shed the BEA jacket for a hoodie that I pulled up to cover my blonde head. Shuffling down the street past junkies and the homeless, I tried to look as pathetic as they did. Jasper glanced my way but dismissed me until I was within a few feet. "Man, can I buy a hit?"

His face screwed up into a snarl. "You want to score that's two blocks over, stupid damn junkie." He went to push me.

I grabbed his wrist and flipped him down to the sidewalk, pressing him face-first into the concrete. "Jasper, you missed court again." I secured his wrists with my disposable restraints.

"Fucking bitch." He tried to buck free, but he was down.

I jerked him up. "You can walk or I can shock the shit out of you."

"Don't tase me, I hate that shit." He moved forward bitching the entire way.

The desk sergeant shook his head when he saw me coming again. "You almost live here these days."

I gave him a fake smile. "A girl has to eat." I jerked Jasper forward.

"Really eating well then." He came around the desk and took possession of my guy. "I'll put him in holding. It'll be a bit on the paperwork, someone just brought in Harry Long."

My carefully constructed plan for the day crumbled in ashes at my feet. The hundred thousand had now been reduced by half. Harry had been my next target.

We had an exclusive on Harry so I'd been beat out by one of our people. As much as I wanted to shout for no else to capture bounties, I knew I couldn't do that because most of their income came from the people they brought in. While I waited my phone buzzed, a text from Doris. Business dinner tonight at 7 p.m. at Domino's. Not optional.

Dammit my bad luck continued. I typed a sparse *K* and stuck my phone back in my pocket. My phone buzzed again, I almost didn't look at it, but it could be real business.

In town. Want to see you tonight. Rebel had been the only bright light in my life. Work sucked, my father was my only family, so family life sucked, and Jess kept pushing me to get married. He was the only one that didn't have a comment on my crazy race to meet the stupid goal. Well, at least not since he'd told me the first day he thought it was impossible. Why did I even bother?

Because there wasn't a single quitter bone in my stubborn body.

Got a business dinner. Don't know when I'll be done. I thought about typing more but regrets seemed too personal. This was just physical, so I guarded my emotions carefully—not that it'd do any damn good—but I tried.

Come by after. I'm staying at Best Western downtown.

I typed out a quick note to agree when the desk sergeant called my name. Distracted, I almost ran smack into Dale Jenkins, one of the newer agents at the company. Stopping short, I pasted a smile on my face. "Great job, catching Long."

He glanced away, uncomfortable. With a mumbled thanks he hurried away. My father had made the whole office scared to talk to me. No, that wasn't right. Together we'd scared the shit out of the office. Our instability at work had to make others worry about job security. Most people avoided both of us.

I let the valet park my truck and walked through the door of my father's favorite Italian restaurant. We'd eaten here so much growing up, it was almost like a second home. Georgio, the floor manager, kissed my cheek before taking me to the table. When I was a little girl, he'd been Daddy's favorite waiter, now he managed the place. Too bad Daddy didn't see the value in promoting talent. Discounting I was family, I was the best damn bail and bond agent in the company.

We turned the corner and shock stopped me cold. Chaz Carter, owner of bail bonds businesses all over Texas, sat next to Daddy. No one else was here. What the hell was Daddy planning and why was I here? I wanted to turn and walk out but I needed the intel.

Georgio held out the chair for me like he had when I was a child, and I sat down.

"Sugar dumpling, glad you could make it." He patted my hand like we weren't at war.

"Daddy." I managed a neutral tone.

"You know Chaz?" He patted the guy on the back.

"How are you doing? A little far north for you." Most of his businesses were located in the southern half of the state.

"Your daddy is a persuasive man." He took my outstretched hand but didn't shake it. He kissed the back of my hand.

I jerked my hand away. "What the—"

"Elle." Daddy cut off the curse word on the tip of my tongue. "We need to discuss the merger."

Merger. A cold sweat broke out and my ulcers doubled in size and my stomach shot pain through my middle. I didn't move a muscle, trying hard not to blow my top until I knew his devious plan. I could do this.

"Not that I mind the bargain. Between us we know more about bounty hunting than any two people in the U.S. of A. That's more than most have to base a marriage on." Chaz's gaze skimmed my face before landing on my breasts.

Daddy's face paled.

"So you marry me and get the business?" I asked.

"No, you manage this one and together we add more and more to the kingdom, so to speak. Jack told me how you wanted to expand Jackson's to more locations. You're dead right, that's the way to make real money in this business." He gave the whole speech to my breasts.

The cold sweat had evaporated with the fury coursing through my veins. I'd heard all I cared to hear.

"Did 'Jack' tell you I'd agreed?" I used my sweetest voice.

Chaz glanced over to the traitor who called himself my father. "Of course. This was the first step to our merger." He made the word a double entendre.

"Now, Chaz, you may want one more look at my breasts because it'll be your last." I spoke in the same sweet voice.

Confusion wrinkled his brow. He glanced from Daddy to me.

I stood up, throwing the napkin down to the table. I

narrowed my eyes on my father. "Despicable. As if I'd marry this worm. You are delusional."

Anger turned Daddy's face beet red. "No way you'll make the deadline. Ella Jane Jackson, I will sell this company to Chaz and there is nothing you can do about that."

"You're right, I cannot stop you from selling Jackson Bonds." Spitting those words out sliced me deep and I felt the bleeding in my soul. "But you cannot sell me too, you arrogant bastard."

I spun away and marched out of Domino's. Unwilling to wait for the valet, I tipped him twenty bucks to just give me my keys and ran for my truck. I had to be away from Daddy, from Domino's, from everyone before the tears fell.

I found my truck and squealed the tires speeding out of the lot. I drove like demons pursued me until I had to park because of the tears obscuring my vision. I pulled into a lot and pushed the truck into park.

A low keen escaped me as I sobbed. This truly was the end, technically I had three days but there was no way I'd raise 100K unless something crazy happened. I refused to marry—if I had to earn the company that way, then what was the point in having it?

Eventually the tears stopped and a hollow ache was all that remained. I'd never felt hurt so deep, in fact, I had no idea hurt like this existed. Somewhere deep in me, a place I'd taken for granted, I was now broken, and I didn't think anything could heal the rip. Maybe I could forgive my father for being stubborn, but ripping me apart like this, I would never forgive this. He'd betrayed my love on every level, if this is what trust and love got you, I wanted no part of it. Ever.

I started the truck and backed out of the empty parking lot. I drove, no destination, no plan. My plans were done. I was finished. My future a huge black hole for the first time in my life. After another loop downtown, I headed up on the interstate, maybe I'd just drive until I was too tired and stay there. Get up and drive again until I was as far away from Texas as I could get.

But I didn't. I found myself back downtown, pulling into the Best Western. Comfort lived here, at least for tonight. I spotted his bike first, and without looking at my text, I knew his room was the one right in front of that bike. I got out of the truck and trudged to his door, each step so hard to make. All I wanted to do was lie down and never get up again. Soon, I told myself. Just a few more steps, then I'd find oblivion.

Knocking on the burnt-orange metal door made my knuckles ache. I looked at the red spots on them with a distant curiosity. Elle had left the building, so to speak. I was watching everything from afar because I couldn't face the fact that this shitty reality was mine.

Rebel threw open the door, a scowl on his face. "Who the fuck—"

He stared down at me then stepped aside without a word. I took the final steps of my journey, forcing each foot to move until I made it to his bed and sat down. I managed not to curl into a ball, but just barely.

"Whiskey or sex?"

A dry laugh escaped. "Yes."

He dug in his duffel bag and brought out a bottle of Johnnie Walker. Taking off the cap, he handed it over to me. I drank deep from the bottle, welcoming the burn of the liquor on my throat.

I took a breath then downed another long swig before thrusting the bottle out to him. He tipped the bottle up. While he drank, I shed my flats and tore off the dress I'd worn to Domino's. I'd burn it later because I'd never wear it again.

I dropped my bra to the ground and slid back on the crisp white sheets before I lifted my hips and shimmied out of my underwear.

I still felt like a voyeur watching this scene. This wasn't me, not my life. I couldn't be the pathetic girl with puffy eyes and no future. Maybe this was just a dream.

He tossed the empty bottle to the floor without a word before he stripped off his own clothes. I closed my eyes unable to deal with reality at the moment. My head swam and stomach churned. The whiskey was working on me.

Rebel smacked my thigh. When I didn't open my eyes, he flipped me over as if I weighed nothing. I needed this. All of this. I hurried onto all fours and without a single stroke of foreplay, he plunged deep inside me.

I loved it. Moving to meet him our bodies smacked together and the numbness turned into a pressure building harsh and out of control.

"Give it to me," he growled.

His sexy voice penetrated my haze, my body came alive under his touch. My mind shut down and my body crashed down with the orgasm, emptying out all the anger and hate I'd bottled inside. Rebel didn't even slow while the sensations tore through me, he pushed me on and I went with him. My head swam and body sang as release after release crashed through me, making me new again.

My body quivered and exhaustion rolled through me, I couldn't keep going. There was nothing left inside me. He'd purged the poison.

As if he'd read my mind, he pulled out. Emptiness crept back and the rip inside me pulsed with each beat of my heart, but now I could breathe through the hurt it caused.

"Turn over, baby." His soft voice almost broke me, but I refused to cry again.

I turned over, meeting his eyes for the first time since I'd come inside. The intensity of his gaze locked me to him in a way I can't explain. He was all I could see, all I could think about. He was my universe and I was a tiny speck drawn to him.

He covered my body, his stiff erection pressing into my stomach, he lowered his head to kiss me. The kiss, too sweet for words, started soft and tentative. I pressed into him, needing the heat of him, not his gentle side. But he refused to give me the hot bad boy that had just rocked my world. With a slow seduction, he claimed me, drawing me into him and holding me tight. Body and mind consumed by his ministrations, I let my control fall away.

For a reason I couldn't name, I trusted him in a way I did very few. Instinct said he wouldn't let me fall, not tonight anyway. He caressed me and his lips made love to my mouth. More intoxicating than the whiskey, he drew me into his spell.

Magic surrounded me as the weight of the day lifted, replaced by his brand of bliss. I willingly gave it away and fell deeper into the depths of ecstasy. He moved back and his cock skimmed over my sex, back and forth, building the need in me again. Then he glided inside me, swiveling his hips to move deeper inside me.

Moaning, I gave over, letting him set the rhythm. His mouth reconnected with mine. Yes. He owned me in that moment. Snaking my arms around his neck I pulled him down until his body rubbed mine with each movement.

All that was left was my primal responses; I had no defenses and honestly wanted none. Rebel cherished me and I ate up every bit of it, hoping I gave him at least some of what he gave me. His circling movements became frantic. I moaned into his lips and clung tight.

He broke our kiss. "I need you to come for me."

I shook my head. "Never stop," I mumbled unable to make sense.

My head tossed back and forth as the sensations ricocheted through me, leading me to a place I'd never been. I gripped his shoulders, digging my nails in so he stayed close then before I could think to stop it my body exploded, sending shock waves of ecstasy bouncing through me, lighting me up.

I screamed his name and pushed up into him. Driving into me, he came deep inside me. I held on to my universe as pleasure consumed me, dragging me into the oblivion I'd sought.

Chapter Fourteen

Rebel

When Elle gave me her last orgasm, she'd shown me her soul, not just the glimpses I'd gotten before, but all of her inner beauty. Had she fallen asleep, passed out, as we came together? Whatever you called it, my sweet girl was out, exhausted from whatever trauma had sent her to me looking like her world collapsed.

I pulled out and cursed, no condom. Dammit, another rule broken. Tonight she'd stripped away every bit of armor I used to protect myself, leaving me exposed. When she'd bared herself to me, I had no choice but to do the same, and it had changed me.

Not wanting to think, I left her sleeping and headed for a shower, needing to clear my head and find perspective. *You mean distance, coward.*

Hell yes I did. Opening up only led to the worst kind of heartache. Sure she was special, but no one was special enough to make me risk my heart. I'd learned my lesson the first time, I mean, if my family couldn't love me, no one could.

I pushed down all the feelings our lovemaking, because fuck me if that wasn't what we'd done, opened up, but they wouldn't stay down. I stepped out of the shower and stared into the fogged-over mirror. The ghost reflection reminded me I wasn't capable of a real relationship, too much damage and too many scars. Wrapping the towel around my waist, I stepped out of the bathroom to find Elle awake, staring at the stained white ceiling. This crummy motel room, like a thousand others, was no place for someone as special as her.

"How are you?" I asked, though if she started crying I was seriously fucking someone up. I didn't do tears.

She sat up and her soft blue eyes settled on me. "Much better, thanks to you. I've never been fucked unconscious before, so another first." She gave me a small smile.

"Baby, I aim to please." Comfortable with the familiar ground, I relaxed, dropping the towel before I climbed into bed next to her.

"You want to tell me?" I wished I could take back the words as soon as I said them.

"No, yes. I don't know." She sat up, fidgeting.

"Spill it, Blondie." I knew if something ate at me I'd want to spit that shit out, not that I did, but I'd wanted to.

"The business meeting..." she turned toward me in bed, "...was with Chaz Carter. Dad offered him me and the company in some kind of merger."

"Damn that had to sting."

She snorted a laugh. "A bit. I told them both off and marched out of there."

"Good job, he deserved a beat down for that level of stupid." I hated to see her family hurt her because I understood too well what it was like.

"The part that sucks worse is I admitted to myself, I'm not going to make it." She blew out a breath. "Leaves me marriage or I'll be out in the cold."

"What are you going to do?" I wanted to beat her father black and blue.

"I have no damn idea." She pulled a sheet up before she sat back against the bed. Her tits were still on display, distracting me. But she didn't need sex, she needed to talk.

"What do you have against marriage, besides the obvious shittiness of your dad making you get married?"

Elle glanced away and didn't look back for a long time. I was sure she wasn't going to answer. Besides, it wasn't any of my business why she didn't do the simplest thing to get the company.

"Part is pride."

Damn that was honest.

"Part is fairy tales. Under all my protests, I always thought if I married, which I didn't really plan to ever do, it'd be because I was so in love I had to get married." She laughed. "That doesn't even make sense to me."

"I get it. You either wanted the real thing or nothing." My parents had the real thing, right down to both agreeing to cut me out of their lives.

"I guess so, but if I walk away for pride and fairy tales, then maybe this isn't my passion. Shouldn't I be willing to sacrifice everything for what I'm passionate about?" She stared up at the ceiling for a long time.

I didn't interrupt her. She had a lot to sift through.

"I never accepted, until tonight, this choice was real. My dad loves me in his own misguided way, so I was sure he'd back down because he loved me." She turned her head to me and her expression stole my breath.

Her normally sunny expression was weighed down

with sorrow. "Tonight, I finally understood no matter what happened with the business, I've lost my father because he's pushed me too far, taken this too far. He might think he can come back from here, but he can't." She hit her fist against her chest. "He tore something deep in here tonight and nothing he says will ever fix that. You don't do that to people you love."

Her words drove me from the bed. Pissed off in a way I had no right to be, I prowled the room wanting to plant my fist in the white wall again and again until the fury faded.

"What's got you so worked up?" she teased.

Her story wasn't my own. This situation wasn't mine, yet I craved to set shit right for her. She couldn't have her family back any more than I could, but I had my brothers. She deserved to have something at the end of this fight, or what was the goddam point. She wanted the company, and I wanted to give it to her.

"Listen to me, okay." I sat on the edge of the bed, her face cupped in my hands.

She tried to nod even though I held her face.

"All the way to the end." I stood and paced again, unable to believe I was going to say this.

"You should marry me, now before the first deadline passes."

She opened her mouth to speak but I held up a finger.

"You promised to wait."

She clamped her mouth shut.

"I don't want your company, we can have a lawyer draw up whatever papers you want. In Oklahoma, we can get married without waiting. We just need to purchase the license and reserve time with a judge."

"You're crazy," she interrupted.

I put my finger to my lips to quiet her again. "This is a get-your-business-only kind of marriage. And when the requirements are met, we get divorced. Shove his terms down his fucking throat and get what's yours." I growled the last part when my anger got the best of me.

"Now you can speak," I said when she was quiet for a long time.

"You're serious?" She reached for her shirt.

"What are you doing?" I had no idea why she was dressing.

"Putting on clothes. I can't have a serious conversation while you're naked." Her face turned pink.

I found my jeans. "Why not?"

"It distracts me." She pulled on her underwear and pants before grabbing her phone.

I had to smile, we were discussing her future and she was distracted by me. I was so focused I hadn't even thought about her delicious tits on display, well not much, anyway.

"Yes, I'm serious."

"Aren't there repercussions in the club for marrying me?" She bit her lip, making me want to bite it too.

"In my club, we have a ceremony to make a woman belong to us." I picked my words carefully. "It's the one that matters." I pushed a hand through my hair. "Marriage means next to nothing in the club—in fact only a handful of my seventy-some brothers are married but maybe a third of them have an old lady, maybe even more."

"An old lady?" She wrinkled her nose.

"It's just words." It wasn't, but we were doing this to secure her company, not because of something real. The idea of Elle wearing my property patch made my pulse spike. I wasn't sure if that was because of fear or excitement, either way, I wasn't looking for an old lady, ever.

She scrolled through her phone before glancing up. "The worst condition—we have to live together from the time we're married until at least September 1. He requires we live together sixty days after he signs over the company, and he doesn't have to do that until June 30."

The idea of Elle in my bed for the next four months didn't send me running—it should have, but it didn't.

"I can live with that. Some of the time here; some time in Ardmore works for me."

"I wouldn't work for him." She shuddered. "I have some savings, but I'd need to work."

"Work for Brotherhood Bonds. You probably already have an Oklahoma license." We needed her experience even if it was only for a few months.

Excitement shone in her eyes then she scowled at me. "Not as your secretary, right? Even if you need one."

I laughed. "No way, but how did you know I needed one?"

"I called your business number and no one answered."

Cursing, I planned to rip JoJo a new asshole when I returned. He was in charge of the office which included forwarding the line when he was out.

"So this sounds like a go?" I needed her commitment before she overthought the deal.

"You're good with the terms?"

"I need to add two." I was crazy for doing this.

"First, I go with you when you deliver the marriage license to your father."

She clapped her hands together. "Yes. I was afraid to ask you to go with me. Let's say you're the last guy he'd expect me to marry." Her smile dropped away and her head bent. "You have to know something, even if you don't want to know."

Shit, no love words. Please no love words. I don't know what would happen if she said she loved me.

"I wouldn't trust anyone else to have my back, but not be after more. I considered this idea, but couldn't think of anyone who wouldn't try to take my company or take me. But, I trust you."

Her words rocked my foundation. My brothers trusted me, but no one else had ever put total faith in me, not like she was. "Well, I still plan to do wicked things to your body, but that's a totally separate deal between us."

"Agreed, now what was the second thing?"

"We do this, it's only me and you together while we're doing this." My skin crawled. Uncomfortable didn't begin to describe the sensations roiling through me. I'd never proposed any kind of exclusivity to another person. However, I knew I didn't want her in another man's bed and I wasn't stupid enough to believe she'd agree to a one-way exclusivity. Maybe after four months of her, I'd be ready to walk away.

She opened and closed her mouth. "You sure?" She squeaked the words out when she finally spoke. "I can live with it the way it was before."

"You been screwing other guys?" Anger sparked inside me.

She rolled her eyes at me. "No, but I assumed you'd been, you know…"

"Fucking other women?"

Anger flashed across her face then was gone. "We never said otherwise."

I was an asshole of epic proportions. I knelt in front of her. "Just you since we started this, and that's the way it's going to stay, yeah?"

"Yeah." A sexy smile graced her face, making her look like her old self for the first time tonight.

Then she shot up almost knocking me on my ass. "Oh sorry, but I gotta go. I have stuff to do if we're getting married the day after tomorrow."

"What's wrong with tomorrow?" Confusion had me glancing her way again, but she only searched for her shoes. "Under the bed."

She grinned at me before digging them out. "I want it on April 17, the day of the deal."

My girl was ferocious and I liked it. "Got it. Be ready to head north with me tomorrow night."

"I can meet you there." She stood on tiptoes and kissed my lips with a quick peck.

I held her in place for a thorough kissing. If she hadn't made me get dressed, I'd have had her again and again tonight. "You'll be going up with me. Got it." I swiped her nose.

"Fine. But only because I like your bike." She stepped away and hurried out the door.

I stood in my empty room laughing. I was marrying the first girl I'd let on the back of my bike. Thinking about bikes brought me to the club. The marriage had nothing to do with the club, but I still picked up the phone to call my Prez.

"What?" Jericho growled into the phone.

"You got a minute."

"I answered didn't I?"

"Fine, just letting you know I'm getting married in Ardmore the day after tomorrow." I hung up.

Fucking ass anyway. See how he liked the sarcasm.

My phone rang a second later.

"Explain."

I told him about Elle, her father, and the deal.

"She going to be your old lady?"

"No." She couldn't be my old lady even if I wanted one.

"You're protecting her like she will be."

"Can't ever happen." Shit, why those words. Now Jericho would be all up in my business.

"Why? She too good for us?" Anger tinged his words.

"I don't want a fucking old lady, and what's the point of doing all this shit to get her the company with no strings, to put even bigger strings on her shit."

"That made no sense." Jericho spoke to someone on the other end and then shut a door. "Explain in a way I understand."

"You get I don't want her as an old lady."

"I'll agree to that for now, but if you did, what would stop you?"

"She'd be my property, meaning we'd own her business. Remember that shit?" I wasn't pissed, and honestly it was one of the reasons I liked being with Elle. She'd never be a forever kind of girl because nothing was more important than Jackson Bonds. It gave me comfort knowing it was impossible.

"Good point, that's a big chunk and we couldn't just exclude it, but you know we'd only take a small percent." Jericho was being lenient.

"One percent would be too much and that's part of what I like, she's not permanent. Get me yet?"

Jericho chuckled. "I get you, but you don't get it, not yet." He hung up. The bastard always liked having the last word.

Chapter Fifteen

Elle

Today I was getting married for all the wrong reasons, but I couldn't squish this giddiness bubbling in me. The little spark of emotion had blossomed into this fragile love that I'd live to regret. This wasn't a real marriage, and Rebel didn't love me back. Even repeating the cold hard facts didn't dim my happiness.

Hopeless romantic, that's me.

Right now, I needed to change clothes again. Rebel's cat, his purr on high, slipped between my legs, wrapping a tail around me. While Rebel had warned me Harley was mean, the cat and I got along fine, maybe he was a ladies' man like his owner. I stroked Harley's sleek fur before digging through my bag for a new shirt.

Rebel walked into the room. "Damn, baby, you look hot."

I glanced up from my bag into appreciative cinnamon eyes. I wore the Jericho Brotherhood half shirt I'd made with a denim skirt with cowboy boots. Every Texas girl wore cowboy boots with skirts, it was practically a state law.

"I was about to change." I tugged on my skirt.

"Don't you dare." He stalked to me. "I love what you're wearing."

He clasped my hand. "Let's go."

"Wait." I grabbed my purse, slipping the ring in my pocket. I'd bought his ring yesterday afternoon on impulse even though I wasn't sure if I'd even take it out, but it didn't feel right not having one.

The drive to the courthouse took less than five minutes, small towns had some advantages. We parked in front of the building that looked like every courthouse in small-town America. It even had a bell tower.

I tried to settle the bubbly feeling inside me by reminding myself for the thousandth time this wasn't a real wedding. The happiness remained. Yup, somewhere down the path, I was in for some long nights of ice cream and sappy love stories because he'd break my heart. On the plus side, at least I loved the man I'd marry. And if I felt this way now, it could only get worse. I feared living with Rebel for the next four months would turn my love into this wild, uncontrollable garden that took over my life. How lonely my life would be when he's gone.

Stop borrowing trouble, Jackson. I wiped all the sappy thoughts from my mind and focused on the plan. Get married. Get my company. Get on with my life. I had no room for love, let alone loving a wild biker who didn't do love.

He held my hand and we walked inside the brick building and up a flight of steps to the second story. Courtroom was written on a brass plaque over the two wood doors. Rebel pushed the door open and we walked inside. One person sat in the bench seats, dammit, it was Jess. What was she doing here? I'd expressly forbid her to come since it wasn't a real wedding. Our fake wedding didn't need guests.

"Jess," I hissed.

She turned to me, a huge smile on her face.

"You're not supposed to be here."

Rebel laughed and let go of my hand.

She teetered to us on impossible high heels. "Hey, introduce me to handsome biker guy."

"Handsome biker guy." I pointed to Jess. "This is my crazy-ass best friend who isn't supposed to be here."

"You're hot and chivalrous. I like you." She held out a hand.

"Jess, this is Rebel."

"Nice to meet you." Rebel shook her hand. "I'm glad my girl has good friends."

Jess let her gaze travel up and down him before she turned to me. "He'll do."

Rebel threw back his head when he laughed. I loved the rumble of his laugh, it lit me like a winning slot machine. I glanced at my watch, ten minutes until wedding time. When would the judge come in?

The back door swung open and five huge, tatted guys walked into the courtroom. The room shrunk, and suddenly, it was crowded in the courtroom.

Whoa, every one of them was hot, not as hot as Rebel, but still, damn hot.

"Oh my." Jess whimpered. "Please let them not all be taken," she whispered.

Rebel chuckled and I smacked her arm, even if I understood the sentiment.

"Dude, say it ain't so." The youngest one had a grief-stricken look on his face. "You're all falling so fast."

Shit. Did they think this was real? I tugged on Rebel's

hand until he leaned down. "They know this isn't like a love thing?" I whispered.

He nodded before turning to the biker horde. "Zero, meet Elle and her very available friend Jessica."

Zero took one look at Jess and smiled at her like a boy on Christmas morning. "Hey, beautiful, I might need some consoling. My brothers keep dropping like flies."

I didn't hear what Jess said because they already were walking away heads bent toward each other.

Rebel drew me close. "Elle, meet my family. This is Viper, Jericho, Thorn and JoJo, who is supposed to be covering the office." He growled at the last one.

"Don't blame him, I made him tell me." Jericho's voice echoed in the quiet room. "Once he knew we were coming—"

"Man, you know I got your back, especially in a courtroom." JoJo winked at me and sauntered off to sit down.

"Hello, everyone." I gulped. "Nice of you to come."

Jericho focused on me for the first time and his grin widened in a scary way. Not many people were scarier when they smiled, but this guy was. "Like that shirt."

Shit. Yeah, here I was wearing their name on me like this was a real thing.

"And she blushes, how cute," the black-haired one said. "I'm Viper," he reminded me.

"You guys have interesting names." I heard noise from the front of the courtroom. I glanced over my shoulder to see a woman judge sit down, peering over reading glasses at all of us. A bailiff and court reporter stepped into the room as well.

"I read my docket right? This is a civil ceremony, not a bail hearing?" She looked back down at her notes.

Did these guys get in trouble a lot? Or was that some kind of judge humor? I didn't know Rebel or his friends well enough to guess.

"Yup." Rebel and I stepped forward to the judge's bench.

With a dry mouth and anxiety clutching my throat, I stared up at the judge.

"Will there be rings?" the judge asked.

I shook my head and Rebel nodded. I frowned over at him because this was turning into a lot of real, which only increased my struggle not to freak the hell out. With friends and now rings, my delusions of love were being fed when I needed to starve them.

The judge looked confused, so I spoke up. "Yeah, to the rings."

The judge began the ceremony by asking for two witnesses to step forward. Jess clicked up beside me and Jericho stood beside Rebel. I had to blink back tears.

"Do you, Kevin Jacob Johnson, take Ella Jane Jackson to be your lawfully wedded wife?"

Kevin. I'd never thought that Rebel had to have a real name, I hadn't even asked what it was.

"I do." He looked into my eyes.

Oh holy mother of all that was sexy, every girl part of me lit up. Sincerity rang in those two words and echoed in my heart. Yup, this was one hundred percent real to me, even though it was one hundred percent not real for him. I had dove into a deep pool and sooner or later I'd sink.

"Do you, Ella Jane Jackson, take Kevin Jacob Johnson to be your lawfully wedded husband?"

"I do." My voice rang clear. I might be going down one day, but today I met Rebel's gaze and swore to be his wife. Guilt tugged at me, but I locked it away. I'd feel guilty for swearing marriage vows I intended to break another day.

"You may now exchange rings." The judge smiled down at us.

He held a princess diamond cut on a gold band in his right hand.

I will not cry, I reminded myself.

Rebel slipped the ring on my third finger—it fit perfectly. Of course it did, because he did everything just right. He started to turn back to the judge, but I tugged his left hand. He glanced down then met my eyes with a bright smile while I slid the titanium black ring onto his finger, pride swelled when it fit snugly on his finger.

"Truly shackled," Zero called from the gallery.

He squeezed my hand and we turned to the judge. "By the power vested in me by the State of Oklahoma I now pronounce you man and wife."

It was over.

"Man, you better kiss that bride," another of the bikers called out.

Rebel kissed me. The emotion of the ceremony had to come out, so I snagged his neck pulling him closer, pouring every bit of my confusing feelings into him. We finally separated when cat calls started from the bikers.

"The very reason I don't say that bit," the judge grumbled. "You and the witnesses need to sign this." She pushed the marriage license to me first. I signed my name, then Rebel signed his followed by Jessica and Jericho.

Legally married, yet when I turned toward our

friends unease slid through me. Jackson Bonds would be mine, but what would it cost me in the end?

With ruthless determination, I squished down every happy feeling and attempted to lock down my heart. *Get it together, this is a short-term, get-my-business marriage.*

No matter how I lectured myself, my heart refused to cooperate.

Jericho squeezed Rebel in a back-slapping hug. "Always got to be different."

What did he mean by that? I wished I knew a lot more about Rebel's club but I had no clue what questions to ask. I hadn't even thought to ask his name.

The judge banged her gavel, giving us all a stern look. "Clear my courtroom, I got more business to conduct."

I don't think she was fond of bikers, but I was, especially the redheaded one holding my hand. We walked out of the courtroom and stopped in the hallway outside.

Jess embraced me in a big hug. I tried to free my other hand to return her hug, but Rebel held on tight. While awkward, I lapped up the warmth and acceptance. Rebel and I were on a crash course, but Jess would be there when I picked myself up after our sham marriage ended.

"…the party starts at five, be there." I heard the last part of the conversation.

"I said no parties," Rebel growled.

"Last I checked—" Jericho looked down at his cut. "Yup, I'm still the Prez, so when I say party, we party."

Jericho sounded a lot like Rebel. Tell you first, ask you never.

"We got to go to Dallas for business."

"We can be back by five." I squeezed his hand.

"That work for you?" His eyes said more than the words.

He was worried about me which was all kinds of sweet.

"I'm dressed for a party, my second biker party should be more fun than the first." I grinned up at him.

"Second?" Viper glanced between us. "Tell me more."

"Later." Rebel pushed Viper out of his way.

"You should stay for the party," Zero told Jessica.

I glanced back to see her big-ass smile. "But what will I do until it starts?"

"I've got an idea." Zero led her away.

The bikers all hugged Rebel, which was weird to me because the men I knew didn't touch each other let alone hug like they did, but what did I know.

We left the courthouse behind. Outside the smell of spring was heavy on the air. Trees had new green leaves and tulips bloomed along the front of the courthouse. Five bikes were lined up next to Rebel's. The guys moved to their bikes, and Jessica straddled the back of Zero's bike. I couldn't wait to hear this story.

"I need to call the office before we go," I told Rebel.

He nodded and headed over to talk to one of the bikers while I called Doris.

"Where you been?" She sounded grouchy. "Your daddy—"

"Needs to meet with me at one. Just have him there," I snapped, not ready for any lectures. "Did you know about Chaz?"

"I got you down for one." Ignoring my question meant yes.

"See you then." I hung up.

Rebel sauntered back to me. "Everything straight?"

"One o'clock." I wished it could be now so it'd be over. Anxiety and regret tried to find holds inside me but I shook it off. Daddy started this and now I'd end it, but not in the way he wanted. Worse, I know he hadn't faced the fact his decision to try to control me would end our relationship. It was my turn to ambush him.

Rebel revved the motor before taking off, the other bikes fell in line with us. When we hit the on ramp outside of Ardmore, they turned left down a side road.

I was married to Rebel...the line repeated over and over in my head worse than the catchiest song lyrics. Our marriage didn't matter to him. Then why did he buy a ring? Let alone an expensive, beautiful ring. I didn't understand the way he'd acted today, and while I tried to deny it, down deep it mattered. He took our marriage ceremony seriously—I'd seen it in his eyes and heard it in his voice—and it tripped forever fantasies in my mind. No matter how I lectured myself, the kernel of hope had rooted deep in my heart.

I focused on the passing scenery, letting my senses become immersed in the feel of the sunshine on my face, the scent of spring in the air, and the sight of green grass and budding trees. Add the excited rush of being exposed as we sped down the highway, and I understood the taste of freedom. Addicting.

About halfway to Dallas, Rebel slowed and took a ramp down to a blacktop highway. He traveled down the road a couple of miles before turning on a dirt road that ended in a field.

What were we doing here?

He turned off the bike and set the kickstand.

"Why did you stop here?"

He slid off the bike and turned to me. "Need you, right now." His low, sexy voice made my body hum.

"Right now?" A heady rush made me light-headed. Hell yes, I wanted him, but then I always wanted him.

"This needs to be extra legal, consummated and all." He grinned in a very naughty way that lit up his cinnamon eyes.

"Oh, well we better be legal." I stood up next to him, looking for a spot we could spread out.

"No, baby, you don't understand, right here, with you bent over my bike." He positioned me at the back of his bike. "Now lean forward onto the seat."

I bent forward, excited by another new experience. With Rebel, I gave up even trying to guess the wicked, way his mind worked. He positioned my feet further apart before his hand slid up my leg to discover the second surprise, I wore no underwear.

"Fuck, you didn't have panties on all day." He was breathing heavy. "Not going to last long, wanted you all damn morning."

"Yeah? You like your club name on me?" I didn't know why, but I was sure that was at least part of it.

"You know I do." He hiked up my skirt.

I heard foil rip then his covered dick probed my sex.

"And you want me too. You're so wet, baby." He thrust into me, pushing me down on the bike seat and filled me in the best way. I gripped the seat, unable to move while he drove into me faster and faster.

"Please," I moaned when his thumb found my clit.

"Elle," he panted, making the sexiest noises.

He tried to be controlled, but I wanted him wild. I pressed back into his groin again and again. He pounded into me, all control gone. I felt him go, the first time he'd come before me.

"Come with me." He urged and I fell over, unable to deny him anything.

Satisfaction filled me from tip to toes, I'd made Mr. Control lose his control. I liked knowing I affected him like he did me. He drew me up and flipped me to him, claiming me with a wild kiss. I fisted hands in his hair giving all I had to him. This time. Every time.

He pulled away from me then came back for a second, slower kiss, making me melt into his arms. By the time he let me go, I barely remembered my name. The man had skills on top of skills and he gave me pleasure time and again.

He'd given me so much, saving my business while asking nothing from me. I owed him so much, and somehow I'd make sure I paid him back because his kind of loyalty was a rare gift. I promised myself, somehow I'd give him as much as he'd given me. Even if all I could give him was his freedom when our time was up.

We left the field behind and headed back to Dallas. The wind on my face and Rebel in my arms, I was pretty sure life didn't get better than this. When we hit downtown Dallas, my nerves sprang to life. My ulcers sent little volcanos of acid up my esophagus, my stomach acted up anytime I had to confront someone. Ignoring my stomach I focused on the upcoming confrontation. How should I play it? Angry? Satisfied? What did I want from this exchange?

The answer depressed me—I wanted nothing from this, not even vindication. I just wanted it over and done with so I could start rebuilding my life, filling in the blocks where Daddy used to reside. Walling him out was the only way to keep my sanity. I couldn't forgive him, so we both deserved a clean break.

Rebel parked in front of Jackson Bonds and we both got off the bike quickly.

"You good?" He tilted my chin up to look in my eyes.

"I just want it done."

He grasped my hand and together we walked in the front door, upstairs and directly to Daddy's office. I closed the door behind us.

Doris looked up and did a double take. "Girl, what fool thing did you do?"

"Come on in with me, you know what he knows, right?" I couldn't keep the hurt from my voice.

Doris grimaced but followed Rebel and me into Daddy's office—the last time I'd be here when he was.

"What the hell are you wearing?" Daddy stood up and stormed toward me, only noticing Rebel when he stepped up beside me.

I put a hand out to stop Rebel from doing more. This was mine. Tension radiated from him but he stayed beside me.

"Daddy, this is Rebel, we were married today." I handed Daddy my marriage license and the pre-nuptial agreement Rebel had signed. "I plan to fulfill the terms of the marriage portion of the contract you offered me."

He glanced from the marriage license in his hand up to me and back down. Red crept up his neck and filled his face. "He's using you, to get my company." He staggered back, sitting in his captain's chair.

"No, he's signed away all rights to Jackson Bonds. You have a copy." I was dead inside, nothing. Anger, fury, hate, anything would be better than this numbness. He'd been in my heart since I was born, but I'd cut him out and cauterized the wound. Scar tissue was all that remained of my relationship with my father.

Daddy spent a few minutes reading over the contracts, the red receded and a tentative smile spread across his face. "Son, you're not what I expected, but welcome to the family." He walked forward, hand held out.

This was the part where he expected a reunion. I would be quick, and maybe brutal, but that was best.

"I have fulfilled the terms to date. I also tender my resignation. I won't step back inside Jackson Bonds until I own it." I steeled myself for this last part. "We won't ever work together again, or see each other again."

Color drained from his face and his hand went to his chest. "Wait, you can't do that." He blustered. "I'll—"

"Do nothing." I spat out the words. "You won, and lost it all in the same moment because that's what you made me do, and you don't fucking do that to people you love." I turned to walk from the room. Rebel fell into step beside me.

Doris hurried to the door blocking my path. "You can't do this to him."

I stared Doris down. "Don't you see, I didn't do any of this. He did it all, now he has to live with the consequences."

Before me, Doris deflated, looking old and worn down for the first time. She moved aside, looking to Rebel. "Talk to her."

I don't know what Rebel did but Doris didn't say anything else. I walked out of the building and hurried onto the back of his bike. Rebel said nothing as we drove away. In just a few minutes we were at my place. I was proud, no tears, nothing. I was still numb.

I got off the bike and grabbed my purse. Rebel snagged me and turned me around to him. "You good to drive?"

I stepped away from his touch. I needed space now. "Yeah, I don't feel anything, just empty." I hated saying the words. What kind of monster felt nothing when she'd just kicked her only living relative out of her life?

He nodded and I bet he knew exactly how I felt. One day maybe he'd tell me his story, but if not, that was okay. He'd been there for me when I needed him, hopefully someone had been there for him.

He leaned forward and gave me a quick kiss before nodding for me to get into my truck. I'd put all the stuff I was taking with me in the cab yesterday, so I didn't need to do anything but drive away. Hopping up into the driver's seat, I waited for Rebel to back out. He did but didn't go ahead of me. Okay, I backed out and headed away from my home.

Bittersweet. I'd be back, but for now, I wanted away from my father and anything he might do to try to mend our relationship. I didn't have any more confrontations in me right now. I drove north, trying to find some of my earlier happiness. It had blown away, gone. A tear slid down my cheek, then another. I shut those down because Daddy had already used up his tears. I'd cried that night I ended up at Rebel's room and I was done with tears.

What was done was done. Over. The end.

I breathed deep and turned up the radio, loving the heavy rock blaring through my speakers.

We made it to Rebel's place by three thirty. I needed the time to recover and find something to celebrate. I couldn't be a downer at my second biker party.

He unlocked the door to his place and I carried in my big duffel. I dropped it inside the door, exhausted.

He opened his arms wide. "Come here, baby."

I fell into his arms, needing the comfort I'd been too shell-shocked to want earlier. He swept me up in his arms and carried me upstairs.

"What are you doing?"

"The only thing that stops the hurt, at least for a little while." He gave me a sad half smile.

Chapter Sixteen

Rebel

During the ride home I worried about Elle. She'd been harsh with her father and I knew it would rebound on her. Nothing I could do to make the hurt stop, but maybe I could distract her a while. Every day would be easier than the last, and eventually it'd be her new normal. And that fucking sucked.

I had to give credit to the old man, he'd been willing to put the whole thing behind them, more than my family had ever offered. Everybody had a limit where the hurt was too big to forgive, and her father had earned her scorn for good damn reason.

"Strip, baby." I tossed her into the center of my king-size bed.

An angry growl came from the fur ball as he shot out from under my bed and out of the room. While Harley liked Elle fine, he was still pissy with me.

I stepped back to shut the door, not wanting to share my woman with the cat. When I looked back, Elle was naked spread across my bed. Perfect.

Shrugging out of my clothes, I knelt between her thighs ready to make her forget everything, even her own name.

* * *

"I can't believe you let me sleep so long." She smacked my arm before she slid off the back of my bike. Her eyes were wide as she surveyed the club compound. "There's a lot of bikes here."

"We have lots of brothers." I brought her close to me. "Stay with me tonight, always, just like at the Angels' party."

"Why?" Her confusion made me want to kick myself.

I should've explained the rules better but I wasn't looking forward to that conversation. Our world was unique and male-dominated, something my kick-ass wife, that word blew my mind, wouldn't like. I scanned the crowd searching for Zero and her friend, Jess. Maybe they would distract her from any more questions. I cursed when I found Zero sitting with Bear, Dare, Viper, and Jericho. I had bad luck all around. They lived to fuck with me, and I'd deserve it. I'd given all of them enough shit over the years they were likely itching to return the favor.

When she saw Jess, she flew from my side, the two hugged and Jess asked her something that Elle waved away. A chair appeared, but that ass Zero moved to it, leaving one open between Bear and Viper. Fucking great.

"Where's Marr?" Jericho's lap was empty.

"Had a client, she'll be around soon." He smiled wide. "Trouble getting out of bed?"

"Fuck you." I flipped him the bird.

Mama stood and hugged me. "Congratulations."

"You know, we did it to save her business." I spoke low.

"But still, that's a stand-up move and she's hot. Might

make a great old lady." She elbowed me in the ribs. "Introduce me."

Dare stood and walked the few steps with us to where Jess and Elle talked. "Hey, baby." I brought her back to my side. "I want you to meet Dare and his old lady, Mama."

"Heard you had a crowd this morning." Dare cracked a smile.

"Why didn't we go?" Mama demanded, narrowing her eyes on her man.

"Shit, Red, not going nowhere near a marriage ceremony, not giving you any ideas." He smiled as he spoke.

She rolled her eyes. "Go, take Rebel with you."

"I'm not going anywhere," I told her.

"Fine." Mama looked up at her badass biker. "Shoo, you scare people."

He laughed and headed off to the bar.

"Glad to meet you." Mama hugged Elle.

Elle watched Dare move away. "Do you always tell him what to do?"

"I wish, but no, not often."

I coughed, afraid to laugh.

"You shut it, Rebel." She frowned before focusing on Elle again. "You need anything at all, want to get lunch or just go shopping, you holler and we'll go have some fun."

"That's a plan," Elle agreed.

Before someone else could get to them, I pulled her down into the chair with me.

"So, Kevin, how was the ceremony?" Bear raised a brow.

"Fine, Jason, how was the porn-making business

today?" The asshat knew my name, I'd used it all the time I was a prospect. He just wanted to yank my chain.

"Elle, meet Bear." I introduced him.

"But you called him Jason." She looked between us.

"We all have nicknames, and don't use our given names, ever." I shot Bear a dirty look.

"So you're the one that makes porn movies?" She tilted her head. "Do you like doing it?"

Bear laughed. "I do. But the question is do you?"

I'd told her about all our businesses before we left, so she wouldn't be too surprised. She'd been most interested in the porn business, not that she'd told me why.

She frowned. "Like what?"

"Making a porn video," Bear offered. "I always need new stars."

Mama frowned over at Bear. "Feel free to tell him to fuck off."

"Just because you won't, doesn't mean everyone is a prude," Bear shot back.

Elle watched the interaction, then glanced up at me. "Is he serious?"

"Hell yeah, I am." He nodded his head to Rebel. "You have how many under your belt? Four?"

"Five," the guy next to Bear said.

"You made porn movies?" She looked to Bear. "Where can I see them?"

"Write your email here on my arm and I'll send them to you." He handed her a pen.

Elle quickly scrawled her email on Bear's arm before she looked up at me. "You have so many secrets. Were they good movies?"

"Hell yeah, I was in them." I was good at everything I did.

Dare tossed me a bottle of whiskey before he sat and positioned Mama on his lap.

"You haven't said no." Bear drew her attention back to him.

"I haven't," the minx said.

"Only porn you'll be in is with me," I growled, not sure how I felt about her enthusiasm to do a movie. Part of me thought it was hot as hell and the rest of me wasn't sure I wanted the world looking at her.

"You'd be in another movie, with me?" She gave me a huge smile. "That sounds fun," she whispered in my ear.

"No answer?" Bear prodded.

"I'll check out the videos you send then decide." She winked at me.

Shit, I was even less sure I wanted her watching me fuck other chicks. Maybe I should escape now, there was a lot she didn't know about me. We really didn't do the whole get to know you thing, and my world was far away from her very vanilla one. I drank whiskey and contemplated escape routes.

"Heard you're going to work with Rebel at the bail bonds business," Viper spoke up. "You don't look like any bounty hunter I have met."

She laughed. "That's an advantage, don't you think?"

"You should've seen her take down DeRulo, she was slick. Hit him before he even knew what happened." I couldn't help bragging.

"You watched me take him down?" She frowned up at me.

I nodded.

"Oh, yeah, he was all kinds of pissed you beat him to the punch," Viper, the ass, volunteered.

"You were?" She frowned, then smiled. "That's why

you were at Lucky's. I never thought about it." Her smile widened. "You snooze, you lose."

Viper and Bear laughed. It smarted a bit, but she was right. She'd beat me out and had done a great job with Stone.

"So is this your first biker party?" Viper grinned wide. The bastard had heard her say it wasn't earlier today.

"No, I went undercover with Rebel to an Angels of Death party." She beamed. "I had a great time, at least until the other bikers decided to fight Rebel."

Shit, I hadn't told this story yet.

"Really? Makes sense, I often want to punch him." Dare spoke in the suddenly quiet group. "Tell us about it." He met my eyes but Elle had already started talking.

"We were staking out Stone, and we were leaving when five Angels—"

"Two Angels and three looking to make prospect," I corrected her. This wasn't a story I wanted blown out because we already had tension between our clubs.

"Who threw the first punch?" Jericho added.

Fuck. Good thing I'd kept it legit.

"The prospect guy, he was nasty, and Rebel made me promise not to fight, I only got to call backup, if needed." She still sounded pissed that she hadn't gotten to kick ass.

"Who was backup?" Viper asked low.

"Charlie." She grinned. "I liked him. Anyway, there were five of them and one as big as the other guy who came this morning." She looked up to me for a name.

"Thorn," I told her.

"Yeah, as big as Thorn. But Rebel knocked them all down and out. Not one was still conscious when he was done." She frowned. "I called Charlie for no reason, but when he went down I got worried."

"Only to my knee," I protested.

"I need to be a bounty hunter," Zero chimed in. "I never get to kick ass like that."

"You're a sensitive artist," I shot back.

"True." He laughed. "My hands are precious."

Jessica said something that made Zero laugh harder.

"Rebel, I need a word," Jericho growled.

"Later," I told him, looking to Elle.

"Bear, watch her for Rebel." Jericho stood, already walking away.

"Should I sit on his lap?" She frowned at me.

"Nope, you're fine in this seat." I left her there and followed Jericho and Dare away from my woman.

"You didn't tell me about a fight." Jericho poked me in the chest. "Those fuckers keep pushing us, and then lay hands on you."

"Look, I was with Charlie and scouting Stone." I didn't want my shit to cause any more tension with the Angels. "They haven't been back around trying to sell, have they?"

"Not after Thorn ran them out," Dare snarled. "But they want their drugs from Dallas to Oklahoma City. They don't like us standing in the way."

"Well then, fuck, I also helped Elle take down Stone, but I didn't collect the bounty—it was her contract."

Both guys raised eyebrows at my admission. I never gave up a bounty because I was competitive as hell.

"You did that and married her, all to help her out?" Jericho's disbelief was obvious.

"So what if I did." I clenched fists ready to go a

round with him if he as much as batted an eye over my decisions.

"Nothing, brother, just trying to understand." Jericho gave him that cocky grin of his. "Hurry that other thing up." He eyed Dare who just nodded back.

"We done?"

"Yeah, go get your woman." Jericho walked away with Dare.

I wondered what they were planning, but Jericho never tipped his hand until he was ready, so I headed back to Elle who was sitting on Viper's fucking lap.

I eyed Bear who just grinned wider. "She went willingly." He pointed to Viper. "He's telling her what a master is. Appears you left a few details out."

Fuck me.

Elle glanced at me wide-eyed. "You need to tell me more about this master thing." She climbed off Viper's lap without a second glance his way.

"Come with me, baby, and I'll show you." I put my arm around her waist and directed her away from my brothers who were hooting behind us.

"You really know how to do all that stuff?"

We moved into the clubhouse and down the hall to a room. My control was about to snap. I needed her to myself before I said another word.

I locked the door behind us. "Now exactly what did Viper tell you?" I stepped closer and tugged off her shirt, tossing it to the ground. "Naked now."

She did as commanded. "Good girl," I crooned.

"Are you being a master now?" She gulped.

I nodded. "Does that scare you?"

"No, just want to know what you are master of?

Viper didn't really say." She scooted back on the bed, and looked up at me.

"Do you really want to know? Or do you want this?" I cupped myself.

"Both." She stared up at me, propped on her elbows.

I couldn't resist, no judgment, only curiosity reflected in her eyes.

"You know what BDSM means?"

She shook her head.

I was so screwed. I stripped off my clothes and got into bed with her. I brushed her hair from her face trying to decide how to explain. "Forget that for now. A master trains in forms of sexual pleasure for years, I studied for four years to become Master."

"In a school?"

"No, in our sex club, Bound. Dogg was the master who trained me. Lots of us in the club have reached master status."

Confusion still clouded her face.

"You're a black belt, right?"

"Yeah, in karate and hapkido. It took me seven years to earn both of them."

"So being a master is like being a black belt in sex. You can teach, demonstrate, or provide sessions for others once you become master."

"So that's why you are so awesome at sex?"

That smarted. "No, I was awesome before, but now I know a lot more about all kinds of sexual pleasure."

"So Viper said he was a master in bondage and dominance, but didn't tell me what that meant. Do you have a thing?"

"I am a master of control. People came to me to lose control, for me to strip away all but the sexual core of who they were." I wish I had better words to explain it. "Most people have layers of shit between what they experience and what they could experience. I used to do that in my sessions."

"Used to?"

"I don't have a dungeon, don't work at Bound anymore, not since I opened my bounty hunting business. It's what I've wanted to do for years now, but I had to work my way up in the club first." I traced a finger down her stomach. "I managed the sex club for several years, it was a headache."

She reached up and kissed me. Soft and seductive, the kiss held promise of more to come. I moved on top of her, unable to take more of her sweet torture.

Pushing my chest, she frowned up at me. "I want to be on top. I have ideas."

I liked the sound of ideas, a lot, actually. I rolled over and she straddled me. "Condoms?"

I pointed to the nightstand. Once she covered my shaft, she straddled me, my tip just inside her before she sank ever so slowly over me.

"You're going to kill me."

She swiveled her hips and I lost my ability to think. I was close, my body already tightening in anticipation, I moved to tease her clit but she captured my hand with hers.

"No touching," she whispered.

"Touch yourself." I clasped my hands behind my head, making my hips stay still.

Fingers in her mouth, she let them trail down her until they circled her sweet spot. I wanted this to last forever but it wouldn't, maybe not even another minute if she kept making that keening sound. Beautiful, erotic and mine.

Primed to explode, I bit back the desire, searching for the control I'd told her about. I'd wait her out even if it killed me. Lost to her own sensations, her eyes closed but stark pleasure played across her features. We soared together, but I didn't know how much further I could go before I crashed back down. Her body quaked and her muscles clenched me tight. I was about gone, only my need to see how far she could take herself held me back. My woman wasn't afraid of anything— she pushed boundaries without even knowing where it would lead her. Courageous.

My hips rocked and I couldn't stop moving, no matter how much I wanted to wait, my body had other plans. She drove me beyond my control, something no one else had ever done. I moved faster, our rhythm surged together.

"Rebel." She screamed my name. Her orgasm consumed her totally, the raw beauty of her undid me and stripped me bare. I had no defense against her brand of honesty. Clasping her hips, I pressed up and spun out of control with her.

She lay sprawled across me, and I hated to move her, but the condom had to go, now. I moved her over, she still panted, recovering from her own release. I hit the bathroom to flush the condom and splash water on my face. I'd never found anyone as intense as Elle when she set her mind to a task, like fucking my brains out.

Nothing. No one. I had no point of reference for where we'd ended up. Sex, while always great, had never been this intimate and I was a damn addict. I couldn't get enough, then she went and upped the game.

Did she even know how special she was? I don't know if I was brave enough to tell her, but I wished I was.

When I walked out she sat up on the bed, looking sexy as hell. "Baby, that was beyond awesome."

"Yeah?" She glanced up at me, something bothered her.

"What's wrong?"

"Nothing." She looked away.

I sat on the bed before I dragged her up to my lap. "You don't rock my world one minute and hide from me the next. Tell me."

Chapter Seventeen

Elle

I wasn't telling him because it was embarrassing and stupid. My self-doubts were not his problem, so I'd just get over myself. Knowing he was truly a master of sex had changed something between us, or maybe, in me. What could I offer him? He'd had the best, knew how to make it the best, and I'd had nothing like him in my life. I wanted to release him from the "only me" clause, but I didn't know how to say the words.

"Elle, you're pissing me off." He turned me to face him. "Spill it."

I stood and strode across the small paneled room. "You know so much, and I know nothing. You shouldn't be limited to just me, why would you even have done that?" I covered my mouth with my hands. I hadn't planned to say any of that. Now I just needed to run away, but I stood frozen in place. My body and mind locked in battle for control.

Rebel growled and closed the distance between us before I made my body obey. This was fight or flight and I totally wanted to fly away.

"Look at me."

I didn't want to, but I couldn't stand here staring at the frayed carpet forever. Own it, I told myself. I shut down all the doubt and crap in my head and met Rebel's stare. Damn, he was really pissed.

"I never want to hear you talk bad about yourself." He barked out the words.

I stepped back.

He got even closer then scooped me up and carried me back to the bed. He sat, holding me on his lap. "I have tasted everything under the sun." His harsh words hurt.

I flinched away, staring at the shabby dresser in the corner of the room. In fact the entire room looked as if it had been furnished by discarded remnants from a thrift store.

He turned my face to his. "And you're the only one I ever came back to, and I can't stop coming back."

"Do you want to?" Another thing I hadn't planned to say aloud.

"Hell yes, I want to stop." He scraped a hand through his hair. "But more than anything, I want another taste because, baby, you give all of you every damn time we're together."

I did? "Only with you," I whispered. "I can't hold anything back. I have no control."

"Exactly, and that makes me so hot, baby, I'm the moth and you're my flame." He kissed my forehead. "It scares me to want you so much."

"Why?"

"Because I'd mastered control until I met you, and you stole it without ever trying." He bent his forehead to mine.

"Are you breaking more rules?"

He lips tipped up in a hint of a smile. "I'm so far beyond my rules, I have no idea what I'm doing."

"Me too." I held him, not knowing what else to say.

"Rebel." Pounding on the door. "We need to fucking race." A voice sounded outside the door.

"Fucking Dare, here's more payback," Rebel grumbled.

"Payback?" I didn't understand.

"Sometimes I can be an asshole, and now that I brought you around, my brothers are paying me back."

"Only sometimes?" I laughed and stood, looking for my discarded clothes. "Better get dressed and pay your debts."

He laughed, the worry lines gone. "Give me a minute," he yelled to Dare.

"Shit, you are going to hell, bro, if it only takes a minute." Dare chuckled.

"Fuck you," he shouted back.

I was dressed and opened up the door. "He's all yours." I started to walk by the blonde biker but he grasped my arm. "Wait, you need a keeper."

Rebel hurried to the door. "Where's Mama?"

"Out with Bear and Marr." Dare gave him a flat stare. "I'll take your woman there, meet me in the lot."

"Go with Dare." Rebel pulled on his socks, a totally adorable picture, but I didn't say anything.

"He's different with you," Dare said as we walked out of the clubhouse.

"I wouldn't know. This world isn't mine." I stared around at all the people in small groups.

"Could be."

I glanced up at Dare. Had he just said Rebel could really be mine?

"That's not our deal."

"Deals change."

"So this is Rebel's girl." An old guy who looked a bit like Santa Claus stood in our way.

"Dogg, this is Elle," Dare growled, stepping around the old guy.

Dogg fell into step beside them. "You treating my boy right?"

I smiled over at the man who had trained Rebel. Did that mean they were close? "Did you help him when his family walked away?"

Both men stopped and stared at me.

"It's why he's helping me." I didn't see what the big deal was.

"He tell you about it?" Dogg crossed his arms and gave me a nasty glare.

"Nope." I blinked my eyes fast to keep the tears from falling. "I guess I just hoped someone helped him like he helped me."

Something softened in the biker's face. "Yeah, I helped him." Dogg pulled me in for a hug. "He's a good man."

"Come on," Dare called. "I need to get you settled so I can race that bastard."

"What did he do?" I caught up to Dare.

"When my old lady and I were working shit out, he liked to poke at me, so now I'm returning the favor." Dare grinned. It made the handsome man, almost devastating with a harsh beauty. Not that I was telling this big biker he was beautiful, but he was.

"Mama, Marr, you two are on guard duty." Dare nodded for me to join them.

I sat down beside them at a table, no men were around. "Why is it okay for you to be alone but not me?"

"We're old ladies," Mama said.

"I'll kick their ass," Marr said at the same time.

"I could totally kick their asses," I countered, liking Marr.

"You must be the bounty hunter, nice to meet you." Marr grinned at me.

"Women don't fight bikers." Mama scowled at Marr. "That shit caused you no end of trouble."

"You fought bikers?"

"Only my old man, Jericho. He won't let me fight with the others." She crossed her arms with a pout on her face.

"So explain more about what women can do in the club." I eyed the two women.

"You don't want to know." Marr waved away the question. "What did Rebel tell you?"

"To stick by him." I looked between the two women confused when they started laughing.

"What?"

"At least Dare told me more, no it was MJ who told me more. Men suck." Mama sighed. "I keep having to tell this, Marr, you do it."

Marr looked at Mama as if she'd lost her mind. When Mama didn't speak, Marr grimaced. "See the ones running around with no cut." She pointed to a few girls.

I noticed for the first time both she and Mama wore cuts like the bikers.

"Those ones, any guy can have if they want them. And if they don't have a woman who carries knives..." She pulled a knife out of her thigh-high boot.

"I didn't wear my gun or knife tonight." I'd remember to bring my knife next time.

Mama rolled her eyes but didn't challenge Marr's description.

"Girls, a demeaning term, are women who are with one biker for a night or for a while." She pointed the tip of the knife at me. "You are a girl. I was never a girl."

"Not the best idea ever," Mama interjected. "A girl has the least protection and other bikers can screw with you if you're not with your guy. Even cause problems between members."

"Old ladies," Marr picked up the conversation, "are sworn to the club and their man in a ceremony, no one but the biker can touch you, and you're part of the family."

That didn't sound so bad.

"While that's true, you're considered property. Marr is Jericho's property and I am Dare's property."

Marr growled at Mama but didn't contradict her. Mama turned her back to me and I read her patch, it said property. That sounded a lot less appealing.

"Why would either of you be property?" The question was out of my mouth before I could think better of it.

Mama whipped around with a warning look, and Marr's dark look made me realize that might sound insulting, so I zipped my lips shut before I made things worse.

"If your biker owns your heart, then what does it matter?" Mama looked directly into my soul when she spoke.

Did she know I loved Rebel? Surely, I wasn't that obvious.

"It's protection, status, not a bad thing." Mama patted my hand.

"If you say so."

"So you're trained with a gun and knife. How about hand to hand?" Marr inspected me like she was sizing up a cut of meat.

"Black belt," I answered.

"Bloody great, we could spar just like the fucking men." Marr grinned wide.

"No, don't ever take Marr up on that." Rebel stepped up to me.

I'd been so absorbed in the conversation I hadn't seen him come close.

"Marr is also a master." He glared at Marr. "Of sadism. You know what that is?"

I glanced at the grinning woman. "Would you do real damage?"

"Never, not in the dungeon and definitely not sparring." She shot Rebel a defiant look. "Your woman can decide on her own what she wants to risk."

"I'll think about it." I stood up, glad he was back with me. "Did you win?"

Rebel didn't respond.

"Dare always wins the races, pisses Rebel off." Mama waved, heading to her man.

He shrugged. "She's right." He hugged me to him. "You ready to go?"

I wanted to know more about his club, but that wasn't part of the deal. "Whenever you are."

"Drinking contest, Rebel, get your ass over here." Jericho yelled loud enough everyone turned to him.

"Dammit, baby, this will be boring for you." He

kissed my head. "It takes forever for us all to pass the fuck out."

An idea hit me. Did I even want to suggest it? Was I brave enough? Maybe his club wasn't like the Angels that way. I worried my lip and debated whether to say it.

"What are you thinking?"

I jumped, surprised when Rebel spoke because I'd been wrapped up in my internal debate. "I have an idea, maybe a really bad one."

He walked me away from the others. "What's your bad idea?" He gave me his naughty smile.

"What if you add blow jobs to the equation? Whoever comes or passes out first?" I blurted it out then shut my eyes tight, afraid of what he'd think of me.

"That's an awesome idea, baby, look at me."

I opened my eyes and met his gaze.

"You really want to do that?"

"Um, maybe I've even fantasized about it." I scrunched my face up worried. I mean I'd just admitted to a thing for public sex, there was probably a name for that.

"So that's a yes." He laughed.

"Yes."

Rebel grabbed me and threw me over his shoulder.

"What the hell are you doing?" I protested as he loped across the ground until we were right next to Jericho.

He set me down. "New game." Rebel eyed the guys assembled. "If you dare, let's mix it up. Whoever comes or passes out loses, until only one dick remains."

Marr appeared next to Jericho. "You better agree." She gave him a look that had Jericho grinning wide.

"New game," Jericho thundered in his loud voice. "Gotta have a girl and a bottle, last dick standing wins."

Whoops went through the group and a half dozen other bikers showed up.

I noticed tension as words flew between Mama and Zero. Dare stomped over to Zero who had Jess beside him. "Give me your fucking jacket," the man snarled at Zero.

Zero shrugged it off and threw it to him. "Won't help you win."

Dare gave him the finger and stalked back beside his woman. I was guessing that Dare wasn't keen on people watching his woman, but maybe it was Mama wanting to cover his cock.

Young guys hurried over and set three boxes on the table. Jericho opened up the first box and passed out bottles of whiskey. The young guys did the same. Soon each of the guys had two bottles of whiskey in front of them on the two long rectangular tables that had been pushed together. "May the best man be left standing," Jericho shouted. "Girls, to your knees. And drink."

I unfastened Rebel's pants, he lifted his hips so I could slide them down before I sucked him down. He glanced down at me and guzzled whiskey at the same time. I didn't know how they drank, straight chugging or what, but I had something more important to focus on, I didn't plan to make this easy for him.

I rolled down my bra and brought my breasts out of my shirt, his cock hardened but I didn't look to see if he appreciated his view. I had a man to defeat.

Each time someone fell to booze or their woman, someone shouted the name, but I didn't know the bikers well enough to know who was who or how many were left. I lost myself to the rhythm, loving it when he pushed up into me, but then stilled, soon his hips rocked again. This time I was sure I had him and then he came hard, shuddering as he thrust up again and again. He pulled me to standing and hugged him to me. "We won, baby."

What? We'd been the last ones. Suddenly I didn't want to turn and look to see if everyone watched me, but I couldn't really hide in his chest forever. He tucked my breasts back into my shirt before he bent to pull his pants on and fell back in the chair laughing. My bad boy was drunk off his ass.

Chapter Eighteen

Rebel

I had dreaded living with Elle because I liked my solo routines and was set in my ways. We had been together three weeks and she'd meshed with my routine right away. In fact, I liked coming home with her, knowing I'd cook for both of us before we relaxed for the night. She read and I surfed channels or worked out. We both worked out in the morning but I liked hitting the weights at night if I spent the day in the damn office. Even the damn cat had mellowed with her there.

Not only did we mesh at home, but I liked working with her. We'd started teaming up on bigger bounties and Gus had been sending all those contracts my way lately. I think he might've been pissed at the elder Jackson or maybe he just liked Elle. I knew it wasn't me.

"You ready to roll?" I hollered in the bathroom.

"Yeah. Give me a minute." She walked out dressed in a T-shirt, jeans and boots like she did every day for work. The boots held two knife holders and she kept her Glock in the car but rarely carried it. She preferred her Taser, I think she liked shocking the hell out of the bounties, it was her cruel streak.

Her boobs were captured behind that tight bra she insisted on, but it just made it more fun to set them free every night. "We heading north today? Or is that tomorrow?" She took the coffee I handed her and drank half of it.

"Today, we're taking the SUV. Greg Parks isn't one we want to take chances with."

She held her hand up and I quit talking. She refused to talk cases before she drained her supersized cup of coffee. We were thirty minutes out of Ardmore before she looked over at me. "Now what were you saying?"

"You're a grouch when you wake up," I teased her.

"Someone shouldn't fuck with my morning routine," she growled back.

"Not even for really awesome fucking."

She smiled at me. "Tell me about Greg Parks."

"The hundred thousand dollar bounty." I handed her the folder. "We'll start with the bar at the top of the list."

She read the file as I drove, commenting occasionally. "You think it'll take three days?"

"Maybe two, depending on how lucky we are in the information department."

"You know better, I don't do Oklahoma City much." She yawned. "I need more sleep." She gave me the stink eye.

"You were the one who insisted on round two last night." I'd underestimated the benefits of having a woman in my bed every night. And I have to admit, I'd been greedy. We were heading toward two months and it was like the first time every time. I had no fucking idea what to do with that, so I tried hard not to think about it.

"Do I get to question the guy at the bar?" She put her gun in the glove box.

"Yup, and I get to beat him if he doesn't answer."

"You always get the fun jobs," she quipped as she got out.

"You get to Taser them," I pointed out.

Inside, I assessed the lunch crowd. A few regulars and in the back corner, that would be Jack, the guy who knew how to find Greg. Elle swayed her hips as she walked. Jack was so focused on her that he didn't even notice me until I scooted in beside him.

"Now, Jack," Elle crooned. "We're here for Greg and we can do it the easy way." She pointed to herself and thumbed through a stack of cash. "Or the hard way." She pointed to me. "Either way we're leaving with all you know."

"Don't know nothing," he growled.

"Now that's a lie." Elle nodded.

I popped him in the nose with the back of my fist.

"Motherfucker." His nose began to bleed.

Elle handed him tissues. "Now that's strike one, on the third strike, we take you out back and work you over."

"What's it worth to you?"

"A hundred." She tossed it to the middle of the table.

"Three hundred," he countered.

"If you have a location, it's a deal, otherwise only a hundred."

He eyed the money and scratched his arms. Junkie, that meant he'd take the cash and rat out his friend.

Elle leaned forward. "Buy lots of good shit with three hundred."

"He's staying over at the Boardmont on the third

floor, last room in the hall." Sweat broke out on his forehead.

"What ain't you telling us?"

"He's got eyes watching for your type." He nodded to me.

"He ever go out?"

"Not much, and never out the front door, he uses the fire escape." He looked at the money then up to Elle.

She glanced at me. I nodded. He'd told us all he knew. She flipped the other two bills on the table. "Happy score." She slid out of the booth and I followed behind her.

Elle had a touch with questioning, maybe rats liked telling her their secrets better than me. I'd always had to beat it out of them, but she flashed her smile and a few bills then most of the guys turned talkative. I'd asked her about it, but she'd said she had to beat people more before we'd teamed up. It must be the winning combination.

I cruised past the flop twice. Not an easy penetration if he had eyes on the street or in the lobby. Was he paranoid enough to have eyes on his fire escape?

"You know what we need to do." She was matter-of-fact.

I didn't want to send her in there alone. Greg was dangerous.

"I can look like a prostitute, you can't look like a junkie."

I stayed quiet even though I knew she was right.

"We need food, planning, and a change of wardrobe. I need to shop."

I drove to a diner I liked and pulled into the parking lot, figuring we could talk it through while we ate.

"They have great pie here."

"As if my ass needs another slab of pie on it." She rolled her eyes.

"Your ass needs pie." I smacked her ass as we walked into the diner. "It told me so last night."

She elbowed me. Once we ordered two cheeseburgers, fries and two slices of apple pie, I was ready to talk logistics.

"You wait to go in," I started, doodling on a napkin as I laid it out. "I'll get a visual and if he's there, I tell you and you knock, do your working girl bit. I cover the fire escape, you cover the front door. And you take your damn gun."

"It doesn't fit with the outfit," she protested. "I'll have my Taser."

"Don't take a Taser to a gun fight."

The waitress brought the food and I dug in. Elle messed with it, cutting the sandwich in half, before she began to eat.

"I take the gun," she agreed as she wiped her French fry through her pile of ketchup.

"Okay. Where do we need to shop? Whores R Us?"

She threw a fry at me. "Any sex toy shop."

I waggled my brows. "Can we buy toys too?"

"Are there any you don't already have?" She shook her head at me.

"We'll have to see." This trip was already sounding better.

We hit a store a few blocks away. I didn't find any toys but Elle got a great vinyl skirt, halter and boots. I wanted to play dress up later at the motel and she didn't say no. Instead of driving across town to change, Elle changed in the dressing room of Candy Cane's Adult

Store. She was hot as hell when she stepped out of the dressing room.

She refused all my attempts to convince her to detour to any motel. We drove the block around the flop again, seeing no one in the alley by the fire escape. I parked a street over, apprehension settling into my gut. Greg had a reputation for brutality, which was why the contract was so high. I'd considered leaving her in Ardmore and bringing JoJo instead, but there was no way she'd forgive me if I dissed her that way.

I put the small Bluetooth device in my ear and Elle did the same. It'd allow us to communicate through our phones.

I left the SUV first, heading to the alley. "You are too sexy for this joint."

"And?"

"Don't stand out," I warned her, not sure what kind of surveillance Greg had in place.

"Got it, boss. You know, I've done this before."

Her sarcasm made me smile. "Don't forget your gun."

"Yeah, yeah." Then I heard her boots echo on concrete.

"Where did you put that gun?" I was to the fire escape, no eyes watching me that I could see.

"You'll just have to wonder," she quipped. "Going silent, heading in."

I heard the chatter of a television in the lobby, her boots on wood steps. I climbed the last flight of the fire escape, then pressed myself to the wall beside the window.

"In position," Elle whispered.

I bent low and peeked into the window. Greg lay

sprawled on an orange couch with the TV on. I couldn't see his face so I didn't know if he was actually awake.

I moved back against the wall. "Go."

She didn't respond but I heard her boots echo on the floor. She pounded on the door. I heard Greg move inside.

Another pound. "Come on, already, you called me."

The sign, I moved to cover the window, seeing Greg staring through the peep hole. He turned, moving toward the window. I opened it, and he turned back throwing open the door.

I heard the sound of fist hitting flesh and looked up while I whipped through the window. The bastard had knocked Elle to the ground, but she'd caught his leg. Not expecting her move, he fell just beyond her, kicking his leg out to shake her off. She let go, springing up to stand, her boot connected with his ribs. He'd turned her foot and sent her to the floor, she was on top of him.

Then I was there. "Don't move or you're dead," I told Greg, but he was already very still. I stepped forward to see Elle, Glock pointed under the bastard's chin with a grin on her face.

Anger surged through me but I kept that shit in check. I positioned the gun so it was pointing dead center to his forehead. "Move away, Elle."

She moved off him, but didn't move away. "Roll over, hands out," she commanded.

He rolled over, not causing any trouble. Then one hand disappeared and a knife appeared. I kicked the fucker in the head, knocking him out. "Restrain him," I ground out. She slid the knife away before reaching for his hands and binding them behind his back.

Then she stood. "Now what?" She sucked in deep breaths trying to catch her breath from the fight.

"You cover him and I'll drag him in his place until the wagon arrives."

She pointed the gun at him before I grabbed his feet and pulled him into the room. Elle closed the door, her phone out to call the duty officer. She identified herself and requested a pickup. I stared at her quickly swelling left cheek and eye. "Go to the SUV and treat that."

"I'm fine."

"Do it." I stood in front of her.

Greg groaned and tried to free his hands.

She stepped around me. "Don't even think about it."

"A fucking woman," he spat, staring up at her gun. "Thought you were just a distraction."

"Your mistake." She grinned at him.

The police arrived about fifteen minutes later. Elle stood beside me, letting the fucking cops get an eyeful before they led Greg away. The duty officer had sent the paperwork, so we were able to sign everything without having to go down to the station.

"I wouldn't even be mad if you arrested me." One of the cops stared at her tits as he spoke.

I growled and the cop moved out of the room real fast.

"Down, boy," Elle joked but I wasn't in a joking mood.

"Let's go," I ground out, trying not to say the shit in my head. Part of me realized that if JoJo had been clocked on an apprehension, I wouldn't think twice about it, but he wasn't my woman. No one fucking hurt what was mine.

I held my silence, started the SUV and headed across

town to our motel. I wanted that face treated now, and I wanted inside her. I'd never needed to possess her as much as I did right now.

I retrieved the first aid kit and our bags while Elle got the door. I walked inside and set the bags down then turned to Elle to find pissed off staring right back at me.

"What the hell is your problem?" She stalked toward me. "Why were you all up in my business?"

"You're pissed at me?" I clarified before I lost my damn mind.

She jerked her head.

I threw an ice pack to her. "On your face."

"My face is fucking fine, but we aren't fine." She stood inches from me, anger lighting up her blue eyes. "You order JoJo to the fucking car when he takes a hit?"

"You didn't go," I shot back, getting pissed off all over again. "He fucking knocked you down. Hurt what was mine."

"I'm yours?"

"Fuck yes you are and I wanted to kill that bastard for touching you." She had to be fucking with me. Of course she was mine.

"So this is some guy thing because we're together?" Her chin tilted up in that stubborn way of hers.

"Hell yeah it is."

"You wanted retribution?"

I nodded. "Kicked the fucker good."

"You did." She rubbed my chest.

"You were magnificent taking that bastard down," I admitted. She'd been perfect.

"Yeah?"

"Yeah." I grinned down at her.

She pressed against me. "I need you, inside me, now."

"Goddammit." I picked her up and laid her down on the bed. "You don't fight fair."

"Not even a little bit."

I left Elle sleeping at home while I headed to the club for another Council meeting. My phone buzzed but I couldn't answer as I rode out to the clubhouse. As soon as I parked, I pulled out my phone, expecting it to be Elle checking on me.

It wasn't. I hit redial and Shorty picked up. "Rebel, glad you called me right back."

"Hey, how's the whiskey business?" Shorty distilled whiskey in a little town about forty minutes from Barden.

"Awesome, man, you still paying for information on Gerald?"

Tension filled me and I wanted to reach through the phone and make Shorty appear in front of me.

"Yup." I kept my voice calm. "Paying big."

"He's been showing up in Driscoll, the next town over, now and again. Likes lunch at that diner, at least that's what a friend told me."

"Is that so?" This was the best lead we'd had in months.

"You got more?"

"Word is he's got eyes all over that town, knows you boys want him bad." Shorty paused. "Maybe even has eyes in Barden, counting you guys, so to speak."

Fuck, no wonder we hadn't been able to get close to him.

"When does he show up at the diner?"

"Days vary, according to Janice, she's my sweetie and a waitress there, so keep her out of this."

"My word on that." I'd never breathe a word.

"So she says when he comes, it's at 11:30." Shorty spoke quickly. "What kind of cash for that information."

"You get $5,000 now and if I get him, another $20,000."

"No shit?"

"No shit. And I owe you big, I've been hunting that bastard a year."

"I told Janice we had to call, but she's scared. Gerald has friends that have people spooked."

"I appreciate the call. Cash work for you?"

"Cash works for me, get it my way whenever works for you."

"I'll do that, Shorty. Thanks." I hung up. Looked for the number to call Jericho when he pulled into the lot.

I walked over to him. "I got a lead on Avery's father."

His eyes lit up. I gave him a quick rundown of what Shorty told me. "I gotta work this, I'm missing the meeting."

"Get the fucker," Jericho told me before he walked inside. I called JoJo, Delta and our three prospects and told them to meet me at my place in twenty minutes. Then I called Elle and woke her up.

I sped down the road to Ardmore, adrenaline pumping inside me. I had him if I could arrange it all the right way. Elle would be our secret weapon.

I walked into a house full of people. Elle had coffee in her hand and grinned when I walked inside. Her face was barely bruised now and when she wore makeup it was gone. That was good because I needed her in Driscoll today. We had thirty minutes to arrange the plan before I sent her south.

I laid out the information Shorty gave me.

"So that's why we've gotten nowhere." Delta nodded. "At least that makes sense."

We'd ridden through every small town from here to Austin and heard nothing about Gerald but the barest whispers. Those whispers vanished anytime we got close.

"So Elle goes in as what?" JoJo asked the question of the day.

"I'm going to have to go more than once, so I need a story that stands up." She tapped a finger on the table. "How about if I'm house hunting, looking to move from Dallas to a small town. I could even get an agent if I need to go back a couple of times."

"Good idea." I grinned at her. "You could drive all over with that story."

"Exactly. And we use your little trackers to tag his truck, then I follow and direct you guys in. No way you won't want to be the guy taking him down."

God I loved it when she got me. She understood me better than I did myself half of the time.

"I want Dan to be your backup. He looks like every kid when you put him in street clothes and a cap."

"Thanks," the kid groused.

"You're a farm boy through and through," Elle crooned.

Dan turned red, exactly the reason he was perfect backup.

"The three of us—" I pointed to Delta and JoJo "—will wait in the SUV outside town, only moving in when we know where he is."

"We should put a tracker on Elle's truck, that way we can mobilize faster." Delta stood. "We ready to roll?"

I grabbed some trackers to give Elle and we headed out. If I was real damn lucky, I'd have Gerald Townsend in jail tonight.

Chapter Nineteen

Elle

Rebel activated the tracker on my truck while I found directions to Driscoll, Oklahoma. Google gave an ETA of fifteen minutes, putting me at the diner by 11:15. Perfect. I climbed up in my truck and started it.

Rebel walked toward me, so I rolled down my window.

"Be careful, he put his own daughter in the hospital and has evaded us for a year." He leaned in and kissed me.

"I'll be careful. Let's get this bastard."

I drove hard to Driscoll, it was 11:12 when I turned on to Main Street. Halfway down the street, I saw a sign for Millie's Café. I parked beside three other trucks and checked my pocket for a tracker then pulled up the mug shot of Gerald, memorizing his face before I pocketed my phone and headed inside.

The place was run-down with worn chairs and faded booths. I sat at the counter because it was easier to monitor the door from there. An older lady came over and smiled at me. "You're new here."

I grinned wide. "Maybe not for long. I'm looking to move to a small town around here."

"Where you coming from?" She grinned at me. "I'm Millie by the way."

"Nice to meet you, I'm Elle. And I'm living in Dallas, but I'm tired of city life." I opened the menu she had set in front of me. "What do you recommend?"

"The tenderloin. Clyde makes a damn good tenderloin and fries."

"I'm sold. Give me a sweet tea too."

Millie nodded her approval and moved off. The door opened four times but Gerald wasn't among them.

I checked my watch—11:25. If Rebel's information was correct, then I had five minutes until Gerald showed or didn't.

Millie dropped off my sweet tea and lingered. "Why would you want to move away from the city? I always wanted to move there."

Nosy people were the main reason I didn't like small towns. "I guess you want what you don't have, and my job lets me work anywhere."

"Must be nice." She blew a lock of gray hair off her forehead. "What do you do?"

Nosy had just gone personal, but I remembered my purpose before I told her to mind her own business.

"I write those *For Dummy* books. You know *Computers for Dummies*, et cetera." I made it up on the spot.

"I need that." She laughed. "You working on a book now?"

The door jingled and Gerald walked inside. Millie's eyes went to him and the woman he was with.

"I'm working on *Online Dating for Dummies* right now. I have finished my interviews and need to start writing." I chatted on even though Millie wasn't paying attention anymore.

She focused back on me.

"Interesting."

"You know any good real estate agents?" I sipped my sweet tea.

A bell rang and Millie turned and retrieved my plate. It smelled delicious. She set it down in front of me. "I'd try Nancy Phillips up in Ardmore, she's good."

Millie hurried toward Gerald's table. I bit into the sandwich and almost moaned. Millie was right, it was delicious. I glanced out at the trucks lined along Main Street, focusing on the old GMC Gerald had arrived in. Where to plant the tracker? The grille would be the easiest. An antique shop was right in front of where Gerald parked, so I could always stop and window shop a moment while sticking the quarter-size device in place. Satisfied with my plan, I finished the huge sandwich and pushed my plate away. Millie dropped off the check so I left a ten on the counter and headed out the door.

I strolled down the walk, stopping to look in a shop window, starting and stopping until I was in front of the GMC I needed to mark. Tracker in my hand, I stuck it in the grille as I looked at the antique rocker in the antique shop window. Then I went into the shop to ask about it because I wanted to be sure I covered myself. The lady at the register asked me a lot of the same questions as Millie although not quite as pointed. Millie might be one of Gerald's spies, but it was too late, he was in our net. Telling the lady I might be back after I found a house, I walked down to my truck. I noticed Millie watching out the window when I drove away.

Once I turned off Main Street, I called Rebel. "We're a go, he's in the restaurant now, tracker works."

"He's there?" Disbelief echoed in his words.

"With some woman. The owner of the diner, I'm sure she's one of his spies, she all but interrogated me."

"Did you pass?"

"Yup, because I planted the tracker and I'm gone, but she missed her calling as an interrogator." I pulled into the driveway of an abandoned house with a for sale sign planted in the scraggly grass.

Rebel laughed. "Gerald's time has run out. We were talking about the next step. Once you follow him to ground, stage a breakdown right in front of his drive, blocking his escape. I'm almost positive he'll end up out in the country in a hunting cabin kind of place."

"Why?"

"All our early leads pointed to those type of places but he was never where people said he'd be." Rebel and I talked for another fifteen minutes then the app beeped, Winston was on the move.

"Gotta go, see you soon."

"Be careful." He hung up.

Backing out of the driveway, I drove through town where I turned onto a gravel road. I made sure to stay back, so he wouldn't see me, even stopping once beside the road when I was afraid I might drive up on him.

Finally, the dot turned up a drive and stopped. I drove past, then did a three-point turn out of sight of the drive before I drove back, stopping in the middle of the road at the end of the drive. I dialed Rebel, my Bluetooth in my ear.

"I'm here, you got my location."

"We do, you see anything?"

I opened my hood and loosened a battery cable just in case someone came out to help. "Can't see his truck or the house, it's a long driveway."

"We're close enough to see you, it's a hunting cabin about a mile back. I hit this place twice but he wasn't there and there wasn't any sign he'd been there."

"Did you have a tip?" I frowned down at my truck motor then went back to try the key again.

"Yup. We're stopping about a half mile down the road, around the curve, so you can't see the SUV. We'll go in from the woods."

"Got it. What do you need me to do?"

"Stay there, and stop anyone who tries to leave. I'll let you know once we have him." He clicked mute, I stayed on the line, ready if he needed me.

While in the truck, I grabbed my Glock from the holster under the driver's seat and stuffed it in the waist of my jeans.

Under the hood, I fixed my cable, just in case I needed to move fast. Minutes passed, I hated waiting. "We're going in," Rebel said in my ear.

Chapter Twenty

Rebel

Elle had done her part, now I'd take the bastard down. He'd fucked with Pixie, Rock and our club. Today would be sweet justice, even if it was too long in coming.

Delta moved around the back of the cabin so he could come in from the left, I hurried to the cabin until I leaned against the wall, right beside the porch, while JoJo covered us with a rifle from the woods. We were ready.

Delta began his approach, he'd gotten about halfway to the cabin when Gerald stepped onto the porch. "Stop there." He held a shotgun with shaky hands.

"Gerald." I hopped on the porch and clocked him. He fell to the floor, gun falling from his hands.

I turned my gun when I heard noise from the doorway. Gretchen, Pixie's mom, laid down the knife she held. Son of a bitch. No wonder we'd never gotten close, she'd been telling him everything. Delta joined me on the porch with his gun aimed at Gerald. I stepped inside and kicked the knife away. "Get out here."

She stepped around her husband and stood shaking

on the front porch. I clicked the Bluetooth to talk to Elle. "Bring the truck up."

I nodded to Delta. "Restrain him."

"We need to talk." I grasped Gretchen's arm and marched her away from the others.

"You will move within the month. I don't care where or what you tell Pixie, but you'll be out of our housing and you won't go to Chet."

"I'll have nothing, nowhere." Her voice trembled.

"That or I tell her and Chet the truth."

She tried to step away from me but I held firm. "You abused our trust and that ends now."

"Okay." She started crying. I walked her back to Gerald who now stood upright. I pushed his wife next to him and snapped a picture with my phone. I wanted proof. She hid her face and cried harder.

Elle stepped out of the truck then opened the back door of her truck.

"You were in the diner," Gerald snapped. "You, you did this."

"No you did this." Elle glared at him.

Delta manhandled Gerald into the back before he shut the doors. "What about her?"

"Let her take the truck, she's out of our lives."

"You telling Pixie?" Delta looked between husband and wife.

I shook my head. "I'll let Rock know, he can decide from there."

Delta nodded.

"I'm going with Elle. You two let the club know. I don't want that fucker hearing a word."

"Got it, boss." He jogged over to where JoJo stood, and they both disappeared into the woods.

Elle met me halfway to the truck. "You driving?"

"Yup. And don't say anything he can hear, got me, not even your name."

She nodded. "You did good work." Then she headed for the passenger side.

It would've been good work if I'd caught him a year ago, but at least I'd closed the case. A small redemption for the way I'd failed my family.

I turned the truck around and drove away. Thoughts raced inside me, and I kicked myself for not realizing the problem months ago. We'd all thought Gretchen a victim because Gerald beat her, but she'd helped him from the beginning. And I'd bet Pixie told her mom anytime I updated her, trying to reassure her mom that Gerald would be caught. The Winstons had been good friends with my parents, and they were just like them.

By the time we reached Barden, my bad mood had settled into my bones. I needed a fight, whiskey, and fucking in that order. I glanced over at Elle, she sat silently staring out the window. When we got to town, I parked in front of the police office.

"I'm going to head over to the tattoo shop, pick me up there."

Before I could ask what she was about, she was gone. I opened the truck door and pulled the bastard down from the truck. He stumbled and I kept going. I walked him into the police station and silence descended when they saw me and Gerald. "I need to turn in a bounty."

It took me an hour before the idiots finished the paperwork, three different guys tried to congratulate me, but I couldn't talk because I wanted to smash my fist into someone. These fuckers had arrested Rock and me but let Gerald escape. I had nothing but contempt for Barden's finest, but then we had a long history.

Once I'd turned Gerald over to the police, I drove two blocks to Marked Man. No one manned the front counter. When I heard Elle's laugh, I stormed to the back, anger still fucking with my head. Rock and Elle had smiles on their faces until they looked at me.

"You're right," Rock said to Elle. "He's got it all wrong."

I stared from one to the other. "What?"

"I told him you were pissed off, not happy to have caught the scumbag." Elle drank from a bottle of whiskey. I stalked over to her and took it from her, downing half the bottle.

"So I owe you." Rock met me with a calm determination. "If you need to beat on someone, you know I like that shit."

Fuck. I drank more whiskey and felt some of the anger drain away. What the hell was wrong with me?

"I should've caught him sooner. I fucked it all up."

Elle had started for the back door.

"Where are you going?"

"I'll be in the truck when you're done." She kept going.

"Get your ass over here."

She turned and cocked her head in question.

"Stay with me."

She rushed to me, I squeezed her tight.

I sat in one of the barber chairs the guys used to tattoo then settled Elle onto my lap. "I'm only telling this once. Wait, Pixie's not here?"

"She's with Mama." Rock sat across from us.

"So I found Pixie's mom with Gerald at the cabin."

Rock's face turned stony. "Fuck."

"She was with him at the diner too," Elle added.

"Anyway, I told her she had thirty days to clear out of our space without going to Pixie or Chet."

Rock nodded.

"I'm not telling this story to anyone else. What you do with it is up to you." I sent him the picture then deleted it from my phone.

"What would you do?" Rock asked, looking a bit lost.

"Fuck, you know I'm the worst for that shit. You do what you'd want Pixie to do, that's my best advice." I stood up and Rock clasped me in a hug.

"Brother, it's worried us both. Thanks for putting it to bed."

"Should have been sooner," I told him.

"It's done and behind us." He stepped away. "We got a party to go to. Jericho says he'll drag your ass there if you try and duck it."

A party was the last thing I wanted tonight. If only I'd thought it through, realized the problem was inside our circle of trust, then I'd have had him a lot faster.

"Pixie took my truck out to the clubhouse, give me a ride?" Rock grinned, knowing I was stuck.

"Let's go." I threw the keys to Elle. "I need more whiskey."

"I can help you there." Rock grabbed two bottles from the back room before we left.

Elle stayed quiet on the drive out to the compound, and I wanted to know what bothered her, but I didn't ask in front of Rock.

Rock left us as soon as we'd parked the truck, on the search for his woman.

Elle got out and stood there, just looking at the clubhouse. I walked around the truck until I was in front of her. "What is it?"

"We need one of those rooms." Her words were hard.

"This way." We walked in the back of the club and I took her to the first room, a different one from the last time we were here.

Once we were inside, she closed and locked the door. "You told me you strip the crap away." She shoved me back onto the bed. "Now, you'll tell me how to do that for you because your head is all kinds of fucked up."

"Elle—"

She held up a hand. "The only words you can speak are ones that tell me what drives you insane, what pushes you beyond."

I stared up at her, she wasn't being a Domme, but she'd committed to helping me, even if I didn't want help. Fuck me. Why would she even care?

"You don't know what you're saying. You don't want to go there," I warned her.

She stripped off her clothes and climbed atop me. "You can have all of me, anything you want."

No one had ever offered me so much. "What if I want to share you with one of my brothers?" I was the worst asshole for saying it.

"I trust you, so bring it." She leaned down and kissed me. Her soft lips on mine were too much, or maybe it was her words. *I trust you.* She had no idea what I might want, yet she gave herself to me without hesitation.

"Even if I say no condoms?" I baited her.

But she grinned up at me. "Even then."

I should resist, walk away, but the darkness in me wanted out, craved her offering. I flipped her over, so I was on top, then moved off her to grab the whiskey.

I needed more whiskey, maybe I'd find what I needed there.

She moved to the edge of the bed where I stood and undid my belt before releasing my fly and tugging down my pants. No words, no eye contact, then she sucked my cock into her mouth. I was lost, a goner. In that moment, I knew I'd take everything from her, all she'd promised. I just hoped it wasn't too much.

We were on our third round of balls-to-the-wall sex and she embraced it, maybe even more than me. The weight of my failure felt lighter—how could I feel anything but high when she gave me more every single time we came together?

"You got more, give it to me." She spoke with a staccato rhythm as I pounded into her.

And I did have more, she might regret challenging me once I gave it to her. I pushed harder, stealing another orgasm from her, each one made me stronger, cleaner, renewed.

When her pussy clenched around me, I fell with her, again, loving the wild freedom of her release. I smacked her ass before I moved away, needing to find supplies for what came next.

The sounds of her deep breaths filled the room, I glanced over my shoulder to my sexy goddess, hair tumbled and sweat glistened on her body, but the wide grin on her face made something right inside me.

"You have a fine ass," she wheezed.

"Back at ya." I found an unopened set of anal beads and new container of lube.

Her eyes widened when I set them on the bed. "Flip over." I wasn't going to tell her about this, only show her.

She hesitated and I thought I'd reached her limit but

then she turned over. Not even a question, when I knew this was virgin territory for her. My body thrummed with anticipation.

When I rubbed lube over her pucker she shivered, tensing a little, before she tensed more I slipped the beads in with a single thrust.

"Oh," she breathed, wiggling a minute before settling.

"Feel good?" I purred, stroking her leg.

"Different, not bad."

"You'll tell me if anything hurts, even a pinch," I commanded.

"I will." She spoke in a small voice.

A prickle of conscience bothered me. "We don't—"

"I'm yours."

"Oh, baby." My heart broke wide open with her admission. "On your hands and knees."

She hurried to comply, excitement and something less sure sparked across her expression.

Words failed me and need filled me, so I took what she gave me, pumping into her tight pussy again. Rocking into me, her sexy sounds drove me crazy. I pushed her, driving her to the point of frenzy, needing her totally open to me. She didn't disappoint, rushing headlong into another orgasm. When she convulsed, I slid out the beads.

"No, I need, fill me again," she groaned.

I rolled on the condom, added extra lube, before I pressed against her pucker.

"Please."

I inched inside with slow precision while I held her hips still. She gasped.

"Did that hurt?"

"Not hurt," she panted, "need more. Something more."

I pressed fully inside, moving in a slow slide, in and out. Sensations swamped me and my body tensed, I was already on edge.

"How do you feel?" I needed to be sure she was feeling what I did.

My thumb found her sweet spot and she tried to move, but I held her firm. "Tell me."

"Good, really good."

Her sexy noises increased, and I felt the pressure build inside her. "Yes, Rebel," she shouted as she came. I loved feeling the tension unravel and her body sag. I moved faster, careful not to hurt her, and felt my own driving need thunder through me. She pressed back and I lost it, spiraling out of control yet again.

Pulling out of her, I disposed of the condom in the bedside trash then rolled onto my back totally spent. We'd fucked my dark mood away. I felt lighter than I had in, I don't know when, but longer than I could remember.

Elle climbed atop me, nuzzling my neck. I liked her cuddled into me and held her tight, savoring the moment of complete relaxation.

She nipped my neck, wiggling down my front until she held my stiffening cock in her hand.

"Baby, I'm done." I grinned up at her. "You did it."

Seductive, hooded eyes met mine. "But I'm not."

I groaned and my body woke up, ready for whatever my woman wanted, unsure what she had in store for me.

After a few teasing licks, she straddled me before pushing my cock deep inside her. Leaning forward her body covered mine. Her softness pressed into me as her hips circled in a slow, seductive dance. She sucked my neck as she writhed over me. Pure torture and pure bliss wrapped together. I had no shields left and each stab of emotion, each slice of pleasure, dug deeper into me, until I was filled with so much I felt adrift, unable to find a single solid thing to grasp to keep from falling under her spell.

Sweetness. She made sweet love to me with all she was bared on her beautiful face. I shuddered when she bit down on my neck grounding me with the pain, letting all I felt become even more real—a living dream turned to a reality.

Before I even took a breath to steel myself, Elle plunged deep and shattered, drawing me into her maelstrom of ecstasy. Lost and loving it, I held tight to her and let go completely.

We lay entwined and silent for a long while until I remembered the party outside. I had to make an appearance. Glancing at the bedside clock, I groaned. We'd been in here two hours and couldn't hide anymore although partying was the last thing on my mind. Even the need for booze had fallen away, all I wanted was to lie here and hold her forever, but soon, someone would pound on our door if I didn't get my ass out of bed.

"We got to go out there," I murmured into her ear.

"I know." She tried to roll off me, but I held her to me.

"Thank you, I have no words for tonight, nothing that even comes close." I kissed her cheek afraid if I touched her lips we wouldn't leave this bed for another hour.

She squealed when I smacked her ass, jumping off me. We dressed and headed outside. My brothers glanced from me to Elle with smirks on their faces.

They should have looks of pure jealousy because my woman was the hottest.

A scream was the only warning I got before Pixie launched herself at me. Elle must've been paying attention because she'd stepped clear before I caught Pixie in a full-body hug.

"Thank you, thank you, thank you." She squeezed me tight.

I set her back down.

Hands fisted on hips she glared at her man. "Rock wouldn't let me knock on your door to thank you."

I laughed at her knowing smile and ruffled her fire engine red hair. "You should meet Elle."

Elle stepped forward with her own smile. "You must be Pixie."

Pixie ignored Elle's outstretched hand and gave her the same big squeeze she gave me. "Thank you too. I'm glad he's behind bars." She shivered.

Rock walked up and put his arms around her and the four of us walked through the party, eventually settling by Viper and JoJo.

"We're getting close to the grand plan, boss." JoJo grinned wide. "I got two more military guys ready to jump over when you say the word."

"It's cleared with Ringer?"

"What?" Ringer called from another group of guys.

"That we can snare two more of your guys," JoJo shouted back.

Ringer gave a thumbs up and turned his attention back to his wife.

"Is that the grand plan?" Elle frowned, looking between the two of us.

"A step in the right direction." I tucked her tight to

me in the chair, liking how close she was. "We want to be able to buy other bail bonds companies, expand that way. I've looked at the business models and that promises the fastest growth."

She scooted away from me. "Exactly. I've been telling…well anyway when I'm in charge of the company, I plan to do the same, picking up more shops and expanding our footprint."

I cocked an eyebrow at her. "So I'll be competing with you for bounties and businesses?"

"Are you heading to Texas?" She gave me a smug grin.

"Still working that part out." I wanted to be in Dallas, but I wasn't sure how some of the bigger clubs would take our expansion, although Charlie thought it'd be okay.

"Do you two share a brain?" JoJo shook his head. "I'm headed north tomorrow, so I need some beauty rest." He gave a two-finger salute and walked away.

"You two are scary, you're so alike." Rock grinned. "Maybe it's a bounty hunter thing?"

"Like you and Zero are twins?" I shot back.

Rock laughed. "Well, not even a bit."

I pushed on my girl so she'd stand up. "Let's follow JoJo."

We were back in Ardmore before midnight, but I wasn't ready to sleep because a restless energy had settled into me on the drive home. Elle had changed me, changed our relationship and I didn't know what to do about it. I wanted more but surely that would go away soon because more wasn't possible.

Once home, I dropped my cut on the leather recliner before heading back to the bedroom to change into workout clothes. I needed to rid myself of this energy and some time with my weights and punching bag should do the trick.

Elle had curled into one end of the couch with her book, she didn't even look up when I passed through on my way to the workroom attached to the garage. Strange. Maybe she was as unsettled as me because it was unlike her to be so quiet. I'd converted the workshop into an exercise room with a treadmill, free weights, punching bag, and speed bag. I'd added a pedestal bag for Elle to practice her kicks on.

After an hour with the weights, my muscles hurt but my body still buzzed in that uncomfortable way. What the hell could I do to get rid of it? No way could I sleep, and the idea of vegging out on my couch sounded worse than sleeping. Maybe a ride on my bike.

I wiped the sweat off with a towel that I dropped in my washing machine as I passed through the garage. I needed to change clothes if I planned to ride tonight, but I didn't want to wake up Elle. However that wasn't a problem because she was still up, reading in the same place I'd left her.

"Why aren't you asleep?" The question sounded sharper than I'd intended.

She laid her book on the end table. "Not tired." Questions simmered in her eyes.

"What's bothering you?" I was drawn to her even though next to her was the last place I wanted to be. My insides were too raw to be near Elle.

She turned so her back was against the black leather arm rest of my couch. "You."

Damn. Why was she playing coy? "What's the deal with the short answers?"

"I don't think you want my questions or my long answers." She slumped when she said it as if it was some kind of personal defeat. "So, I was trying to give you that."

As if I'd turned into a masochist, suddenly I had to know what she was holding inside and why she wouldn't tell me. Maybe her words would be the impetus I needed to push away, find the distance I longed for. What an asshole thought, but I was a desperate man.

"What questions?"

Cocking her head to the side she studied me a long moment before dropping her head. With her hair covering her face, I couldn't see her expression.

"Why do you think you failed them? Why does that eat at you so much?" Her gaze met mine. "Who made you fear that you'd lose them if you failed them?"

Son of a bitch, she'd nailed it on the head. I stood and walked away. "I don't want to talk about that shit." I stormed into the bedroom to find my riding clothes, but her questions had slipped under my defenses, gnawing on me. Or maybe it was what had eaten at me all damn night. I collapsed on the bed, sitting with my elbows on my knees. I let my head fall into my hands, trying to silence the doubts her questions had unlocked.

No one stood by me, not my girlfriend in high school, not my family, not the Old Man even though he'd brought me into the club. Dogg stood by me but then he'd left. Did some maggoty part of me think my brothers would turn away from me if I hadn't found Gerald? That I had to prove my worth to them, over and over, to earn the trust they gave me? No, I wasn't that fucked up.

I was tight with a lot of my brothers, but none of

them were close to me, not like Jericho, Dare and Bear were, or Delta and JoJo for that matter. In fact few of us formed real tight bonds, but maybe that was because we were too fucked up. There'd been a time Jericho had tried to bring me into his circle, when I was just a prospect, but I'd craved the Old Man's approval too damn much.

My restlessness grew until I couldn't stay still. I paced then found myself back in the living room, anger simmering under the raw edges. "You don't really want to know those answers."

She marked her place and closed her book before looking up at me. "I told you all that festered in me that night. You need to do the same." No heat or judgment, just the raw truth. "I'd thought maybe you'd share with one of the guys, but it's clear you didn't."

"We don't talk about shit like that," I scoffed, starting to turn away.

"You can tell me anything." The sincerity in her voice stopped me cold.

Yearning for something I'd rarely had tugged me backward until I'd crossed the room to her. Staring down into her somber face, I knew I could talk and she'd listen, but some shit couldn't be unheard or unsaid. It was a risk I hadn't taken since the night I'd told Dogg my whole sorry story. Of course, I'd been drunk, which made everything easier. Too easy. That had been the last night I'd been drunk for four years.

I sat on the other side of the couch and stared forward, remembering the past. "Fear drives me.

"I get that because I spent years fearing I'd disappoint my dad because I wasn't the son he wanted." Her quiet words held the ache I felt. "Turns out he disappointed me worse."

"Betrayed you." Anger sizzled in me. "My parents walked away from me, didn't ever really believe in me."

Her jeans made a sound when she slid across the leather seat, until her knee touched my leg. I liked it there.

"I drank my first beer on my sixteenth birthday." I remembered how freeing it was to be drunk, all the thousands of expectations gone. "Six months later, I was drinking as soon as I woke up, and I had two DUIs, both of which my dad swept away." I glanced over to her. "He was the sheriff in Barden, had been since I was ten."

"Sucks to be you."

"There are a lot of expectations of the sheriff's son, and they drowned me until I drowned them with booze." I remembered the blurred months when I was never quite sober and often drunk on my ass. "I was out of control, and my parents put me in rehab."

"Sounds reasonable." Her words were just a way to let me know she was there.

"I thought so too, until they left. It was an extreme treatment center where aversion therapy was a primary tool."

She gasped and clasped my hand. "What did they do?"

"Fed me alcohol and shocked me every time I drank it." I hadn't been a fan. "I was too stubborn, I drank until either the shock or the liquor knocked me out.

"One night I broke out of my room, the first night they'd denied me liquor, and broke into the room where they kept the hard stuff. By the time a nurse found me,

I was passed out, they had to take me to the hospital to have my stomach pumped."

"You should never have been treated like that." The warmth of her hand in mine comforted me.

"When I was back at the treatment center, they decided to go the other extreme—straight detox, no meds or anything to help me through it." I hurried on hating to think of the horrible week where I'd have gladly killed myself if I'd had the strength. "It worked, I guess, six weeks later I left clean and sober."

I hadn't even wanted to contemplate a drink, fearing to ever go through the hell of detox again. "I stayed sober almost a year, then on my eighteenth birthday, I got hammered, first time." I remembered the high, how sweet it had tasted.

"Mom and Dad cornered me, told me they were shipping me back to that place." The remembered fear raced through me now, making my pulse spike. "I knocked my dad down, and ran out the door. I moved to Ardmore, I mean, I was 18, they couldn't make me go as long as I didn't live with them, but I wasn't sure about that. The fear chewed me up and turned me paranoid. I was afraid to leave my apartment to go to work.

"I'd always had a thing for the Brotherhood, I mean, they were the only ones who did whatever they wanted. All my life I'd grown up seeing them as an idea of freedom, chaos and freedom really. My dad hated the club, but they didn't do illegal stuff so he had to put up with them."

"Your club is totally legitimate?"

I frowned over at her. "Yeah, none of our businesses are illegal, not saying there hasn't been any of us do something illegal, but we don't earn our living that way."

"Sorry, so is that why you joined?"

I nodded. "And I wanted to piss my dad off, shove his nose in it. I mean, if you're from town, you're against the club, not a single person from Barden had ever joined the club until I did, not in the twenty-five years they'd been in town."

It had been the best feeling in the world when the Old Man had put my cut on me. "Anyway, they accepted me as a prospect, it takes two years to earn your membership in the club. Jericho's dad, we all called him the Old Man, ran the club then, and he put a bottle in my hand and kept me close to him. Now I know he was shoving my dad's, the whole town's, face in the fact that I'd chosen the Brotherhood. My dad went bat-shit crazy and tried to find any way to arrest the members. Hell, he had me in jail at least once a week."

"How was that for you?"

"I was too drunk and too pissed off to really care." I honestly remembered little of that six months of my life. "Then one night we were at the sex club and I'd been up and drinking for days. Next thing I remember, I'm in the hospital and Dogg is beside my bed. The Old Man had left me there, to die maybe, but Dogg found me and got me help."

"What the fuck? I thought they were—"

"The Old Man is cruel and a rotten bastard, that's why he doesn't run this club anymore. I just had to learn that lesson the hard way. I was so busy looking for approval, I didn't care about anything else." Those words hurt to say, but it was the truth.

"Is that when you started training to be a sex master?"

I grinned at her choice of words. "Yup, Dogg took me in and made me follow his rules, one of which was I couldn't drink again until I'd become a Master. He helped me through the worst of the withdrawal, then began teaching me. Hell for a solid year, I didn't even step foot in Barden, hoping that'd cool things down between my dad and the club. It didn't."

"So that was the end of your family?"

I nodded. "After I earned my cut, after my dad had lost his job as sheriff, I went to them, but my parents met me with a shotgun at the front door, told me never to come back." I hadn't expected a warm reunion but their reaction had cut me deep.

"Dogg left later that same year, he retired from the club, and I started managing it." I had learned by then how to manipulate the Old Man into doing whatever I wanted. Dogg had taught me that and so much more.

"Then, I got the go-ahead on the bounty business, right when Pixie's dad skipped on his bail. It was my first case, and I couldn't catch him. It ate at me bad. I'd failed my family, and now my brothers. I never once considered that Gretchen was telling him things, probably others too. I mean we're a pretty easy group to spot." That pissed me off to have been blinded by such an obvious thing. "Most of the time our status as members of the Jericho Brotherhood unlocks doors, but not this time."

"You think you're God?"

"I *am* almost perfect, but no, not him."

She scowled at my attempt at humor. "I didn't see one person there looking like you had screwed up. They

were thanking you, happy for you, glad you got someone who'd hurt one of your own."

I shook my head.

She smacked her hand over my mouth, climbing onto
my lap. "Do you agree I read people well?"

I nodded.

"Am I a good judge of character?"

I nodded again. She was a helluva lot better than me
at reading the people she bonded, in fact, I wished I was
as good as she was.

"Do I lie?"

I paused, then shook my head. She'd never once lied
to me even when it would have been easier for her.

Removing her hand from my mouth, she stared up
at me. "Then believe me when I say what you're feeling is just your past trying to fuck with you. No one
thought you'd failed, or that you were too slow. It was
truly a celebration."

I hugged her to me, unable to form words. The restlessness disappeared along with the anger, and all that
was left was some deep feeling for Elle, one I refused
to examine let alone name. Normally, all this crap was
locked down tight, not even a passing thought, but since
I'd met Elle, too many of those locked-down parts kept
surfacing.

Once she had her company, then I'd be back to normal. My life could continue uninterrupted. A hollow-
ness opened inside me because I wasn't sure I wanted
that life anymore.

Chapter Twenty-One

Elle

Our relationship shifted after Rebel had told me about his past, we'd grown closer in intangible ways. After spending six weeks under the same roof, it seemed like a year. I liked living with him and working with him even more, which was why I planned to spend the next two days in Dallas without Rebel. I just had to tell him.

We enjoyed a late breakfast before we headed to the Brotherhood clubhouse. He had a meeting and I planned to spar with Marr. I hadn't told him that part either. He placed a stack of pancakes in front of me that I would never finish. "Eat up."

"You know I only can eat two of these." I poured hot syrup over the four pancakes. I'd never thought to heat up syrup when I'd had pancakes at home. Of course, those were frozen pancakes I reheated, but still, hot syrup made a difference.

"Trisha, the new office assistant, starts tomorrow. You plan to be in the office?" I started, hoping to work my way to the trip to Dallas.

"You show her."

"I won't be here, I'm going to Dallas for a couple of days."

His head shot up. "I'll go with you."

"No, I need to do some house maintenance and want to spend some time with Jess." There, I put up a strong boundary. We'd spent too much time together. If this continued, I'd never be able to leave his side.

"Is this to get out of training Trisha?" He glared at me.

"Partially. It's your damn office, you train the help." I pointed my fork at him. "You aren't so sneaky. I know you've been using me to fix the stuff you've messed up there."

"I'm new, and you're not." He grinned at me with both his damn dimples. I was a sucker for his dimples.

"Now Trisha is new, and you can train her," I reminded him. "I'll be home, I mean back up here, by Saturday at the latest."

His grin widened. "You could take Marr or Pixie with you."

"I am capable of going to Dallas on my own, besides I'm seeing Marr today." I filled my mouth full of pancakes.

"Why?"

"For a visit," I said once I'd swallowed.

"What kind of visit?" His voice darkened. "She didn't convince you to try out her dungeon?"

"God no," I squeaked, not even sure what a sadist did in a dungeon. "We're going to spar, we're both black belts, and you go too easy on me."

He looked much more interested. "Sparring? Where?"

"None of your business. You have your own meeting." I crossed my arms. Truth be told I didn't know where because Marr said we'd figure it out when I got there.

"Be careful." He kissed me before he picked up my plate to rinse.

"Why don't you eat breakfast at the club?" Mama had told me about breakfast and had hinted I could cook, but I told her she didn't want me to cook.

"I don't like biscuits and gravy. It's what we have on Thursdays." He placed both plates in the dishwasher, rinsed out the sink then dried it. I liked his neat streak. "Ready to go?"

Riding on the back of Rebel's bike was amazing. I loved it, just another thing I'd miss once our save-my-business marriage was over. We parked next to a bright red bike. Walking down the row of bikes, I wondered how many of them had women who rode tandem. I was jealous of Mama, Marr and the others who had their biker for real. Even being Rebel's property would be worth it if he really loved me.

I blew out a breath, trying to dismiss my stupid thoughts. The inside of the club was as eclectic as the bikers eating there. Every table appeared different than the next, no color scheme or theme tied the place together. But the bikers looked even more different, some had the typical long hair and full beards I expected, others looked military, and even more defied definition. Rebel, for example, looked like the boy next door more than a dangerous biker, not that I'd ever tell him that.

Marr stood beside a table of food talking with Mama. I gave Rebel a peck on the cheek and tried to pull away, but he held my hand, walking me over to Marr.

"Keep her safe, and don't bruise her too bad." Rebel basically handed me over to Marr, like I was some kind of child. I didn't like this part of the club because it made me feel incompetent and somehow weak.

He gave me a much deeper kiss before he strolled away. Arrogant man, anyway.

"So where are we going to spar?" I asked her.

"You're really doing this?" Mama frowned at me. "She's mean."

"Why doesn't anyone think I'm mean?" I was frustrated by the way everyone treated me. I could kick ass and did so on a regular basis.

"Let's go out in the grass on the side of the building." Marr arched an eyebrow at me. "Unless you want to go to my dungeon?"

I gulped. "The grass is great." I wasn't sure what a dungeon looked like, but I pictured the medieval kind and decided to stay far away.

Staring down at her wicked boots, I added another condition. "No shoes."

"Of course. Jeans give you enough flexibility?" She eyed my clothes. I wore what I did all the time—jeans, T-shirt and boots.

"Yup, sure you won't fall out of that?" I pointed to the leather bustier she wore with jean shorts.

"Will it distract you if I do?"

"Not really." I laughed. "Let's go. I haven't had a decent workout since I left Dallas."

"Who do you spar with there?" Marr led the way through the kitchen, a huge industrial deal, and through a side door. There was a wide lawn and toward the back a porch swing hung on swing set poles. I leaned against the concrete block wall to remove my boots and socks.

"My sensei in Dallas doesn't pull his punches, unlike Rebel." I tried to spar with him but he always went easy on me, and then we'd get sidetracked once we started touching each other and ended up having sex on the workout mats. That was fun, but not the workout I craved today.

"No broken bones, torn muscles, or dislocated joints. I'm game for everything else." Marr's confidence was an area I could exploit.

"Works for me." It was how I sparred at my dojo. Blood and bruises were the price of training.

We bowed to each other before we moved forward and Marr kicked out and I blocked, we moved back and forth in a quick dance of karate strikes, almost equally matched there. She struck my lip and blood trickled from the cut.

"I love first blood." Marr stepped back, breathing as hard as I was.

I licked my lip. "We need water."

"Here," Mama called.

I turned and she threw me a bottle. Pixie threw one to Marr.

"How long have you been there?" Marr asked the question I'd been ready to ask.

"Since you started. We want to see this." Pixie grinned wide.

"Ready?" I focused on Marr, planning to focus more on my hapkido moves this round.

Marr and I bowed again and moved together, this time I deflected the kick, moving close to take hold of the pressure point, slowing her before I kicked. A solid hit, and better, I'd thrown off the rhythm she'd thrived on last time. A hit to my face, a kick to the stomach but I deflected the sweep that'd take me down instead flipping Marr to the ground with a thud. She lay there a minute and I backed up to grab my water bottle. Marr groaned and stood, shaking her head, before drinking her own water.

A door slammed and I turned to see a group of bikers, Rebel among them, headed our way. Marr frowned and put hands on hips.

"Don't you bloody think to stop us—"

"Never, just want to watch the ass kicking." Jericho grinned at his woman. "Who's kicking whose ass?"

"It's really even," Pixie volunteered.

The nine guys made a wide circle around us, a few others joined from the front. The young guy that Jess had spent the day with was among them. "How long you been out here?" he groused.

"Twenty minutes," Mama said.

"Hate missing the good stuff." He filled in the circle along with a handful of others.

Marr glanced my way and I shrugged. An audience didn't matter to me because once I began to spar, I only focused on opponents.

We bowed before we began the third round, Marr struck my nose and it bled, I wiped it away as I kicked up, smacking my toes into her chin. Her teeth chomped together with a satisfying rattle. While neither of us said anything, we both knew this was the last round. The guys would be interfering as soon as we stopped. Moving back to karate, we traded quick strikes before I accepted a kick to the chest in order to get her foot for a throw. She twisted out before I could fling her on her ass but she dropped to a knee to regain balance. I struck her chin with a kick, drawing blood from her.

Part of me was aware of the noise in the background, but no one moved forward—no attackers but Marr to focus on. She shot up, trying to grab my foot for a hold, but I moved away. We slashed and kicked, but most of our attempts were blocked by the other. Her left arm drooped, which could be a trick, but I decided to try for one more throw. Moving in with karate, we traded fast strikes until I saw my opportunity, kicked her knee and grasped her left wrist right for a joint lock and flip. As she flipped in the air she somehow caught my kicking leg, and I flew back. We both ended up on the ground panting.

I heard Marr laugh as she sat up. "You're a good match for me."

"Back at you." I grinned and sucked in air, trying to calm my breathing.

"Forty minutes," Pixie shouted over the noise. "Forty minutes of awesomeness."

I pushed myself to standing and wiped a hand under my nose, the bleeding had stopped.

"We gotta do this every week." Marr came toward me.

"I might not be up here, I'll be in Dallas a lot."

"Then I'll come there." She frowned at me. "Bloody hard to find a good sparring partner."

"I'll introduce you to Master Ken, he's wicked to spar with." Something lightened in my chest. Maybe I didn't have to lose all the friends I made when Rebel and I were finished.

Pixie and Mama came up to me and Marr. "You should teach the women self-defense," Pixie chattered away. "That'd be awesome."

"Marr can teach it." I deferred to her since I wouldn't be here.

"Marr is mean," Pixie grumbled. "I should know."

"Why do you think she'd be easier on you?" Marr grinned.

"Because Elle looks nice." Pixie smiled up at the tall dark-haired woman beside me. "You look mean."

When Pixie and Mama turned expectant looks to me, I wanted to crawl away. "Not my thing, besides I'm gone a lot."

"We could—"

"Leave it be." Rock came up and collected Pixie. "You don't need to be any more dangerous."

A knowing look passed between the two but I had no idea what he meant. Rebel, Jericho, and Dare joined us while the other bikers faded away, now that the match was over. "You know more than karate." Jericho stared down at me.

"I have a black belt in hapkido too." Rebel wrapped his arms around me, feeling way too good. His erection pushed into my backside.

Jericho nodded. "You happy, now?" He looked at Marr.

Marr smiled wide. "Hell yeah, we get distracted before we make it half that far."

"We need to get distracted right now, woman." He tugged Marr's hand and she went with him.

Soon it was only Rebel and me left. He flipped me to him. "You're lethal with your hands."

"In more ways than one," I teased, wanting my hands on him in a very personal way right now.

"Let's find a room to talk about that." He led me into the clubhouse.

I pulled into my driveway in Dallas around three that afternoon, already missing Rebel. Jessica and I had plans for dinner, but first I needed a couple of hours to decompress. Life had turned messy and I had no idea how to fix it, and worse I had no desire to fix it. Burdened with my Rebel problem, I headed inside. I walked around my house, but it felt strange now, not like my home and I couldn't settle anywhere. Just as I'd decided to run a bath, my doorbell rang. I checked the clock, but it was still two hours before I met Jessica. Luckily I hadn't undressed, so I turned off the water and hurried downstairs. Looking through the peephole, I saw Doris on my doorstep. Dammit, she wouldn't go away, so I opened the door.

"About damn time." She marched through my door to the living room.

"Hello, Doris." I sat on my couch, wishing I had some whiskey. Already Rebel's habits were becoming mine.

"Don't hello me, missy. How long are you gonna tear your daddy's heart out? You got the man, the business, everything." She pointed at me.

What the hell? "How do you know what I have or don't have?"

"Really?" She rolled her eyes. "Your daddy hired a PI to follow you, and I had one of our guys watch your house."

Red-hot anger filled me. "And what do you know?"

"You love each other, it's obvious from the pictures, and he's another bounty hunter." Approval tinged her words.

"We love each other?" If only that were true, but it wasn't. Her gall to assume anything about my life angered me, but to jump to that conclusion heaped hurt on top of my anger.

"I do love him." Sadness swept away the anger because this was my reality, a horrible reality to have given my heart to a man who didn't want it.

Satisfaction gleamed on her face.

"He doesn't love me. Bikers don't do marriage, they do other ceremonies, live differently." I didn't fully understand and unfortunately I never would. "But once Daddy's conditions are met, I promised him a speedy divorce. And that hasn't changed." I held back the tears, no use in crying for something I never had.

"No, that can't be true." Doris sat on a chair. "You two…"

"We get along well, when no one had my back, he did. He helped me capture Stone, offered to marry me, because he hated to see my family turn their back on me. To see you turn your back on me."

Doris blanched. "Why would he do that if he doesn't love you?"

I lifted a shoulder. "Because he understands being backed in a corner by family, but that's all there is." I wished I could work up some rage, even indignation would feel better than this horrible ache inside me. "Every day I stay I fall a bit more in love and nothing changes for him. That's what Daddy's scheming did."

"Oh no, he never thought… I never thought…what has he done?" Doris stood with a devastated look on her face.

"Welcome to my world."

Doris stared at me then she turned and hurried out. I heard the door close. I have no idea how long I sat there, but my phone pinged and brought me out of my stupor. Jess had texted me. Be there in 20.

I picked up my phone and hit the call button.

"Hey, girlfriend, we are going to have serious girl time. I have so much—"

"I can't do it tonight, can we do lunch tomorrow?" I barely recognized my voice, so wooden and forlorn.

"What's wrong?"

"Tomorrow, I just can't do this tonight, okay?"

"Yeah, I'll be there at eleven and you be ready because that's all the time I'm giving you to be all sad." Jess had a forced cheeriness.

"Deal." I hung up. With mechanical motions, I turned out the lights, locked the door and trudged up the stairs to my bed. Crawling under the covers, I curled into a ball and let silent tears fall. I was beyond screwed.

I woke up at seven, and sat up to start my day. After a long run, I showered and resolved to be done with tears and self-pity because I wasn't that girl. I was tougher, stronger and whatever else it'd take to survive my heartbreak in one piece. When people said to be careful what you wish for, I hadn't truly appreciated the wisdom of that advice. Rebel gave me exactly what I'd wanted, and I was miserable, which was bullshit.

Attitude adjusted, I'd taken extra time getting ready. Looking in the mirror, I spoke to my reflection. "I kick ass and take down bad guys. I don't whine and complain."

When Jess knocked I had on my brave face.

"You okay?" She gathered me in a hug.

I sunk into the warm embrace, treasuring her comfort. "Yeah, Doris visited me yesterday and threw me off my game."

"Oh no." Jess grimaced. "Trying to play peacekeeper?"

I nodded. "I'll tell you about it at lunch."

"And how it's going with hot biker guy." She winked at me.

"Only if you tell me about your night with Zero," I shot back.

"You mean nights." She sounded very pleased with herself.

The doorbell rang and I considered not answering it because I couldn't think of anyone I wanted to see. The bell rang again. Jess glanced at me but my gaze skittered away. "Oh my God," she huffed. "You can't pretend not to be here. Your damn truck is in the drive."

When I didn't move, she marched toward my front door and swung it open. I heard her speak a minute, then the door shut. Who had been at my door? When had I turned into a coward? The answer to the second question was easy—I'd turned yellow the moment I'd had to stare Doris down. Imagine if it'd been my father, I couldn't handle seeing him now, maybe ever.

Jess walked into my living room opening a bright yellow courier envelope. She slipped out a sheaf of paper, thumbing through it.

"What is it?" I moved to her and read snatches of the pages as she flicked through them. ...*becomes sole owner... Jackson Bail Bonds...no condition to owner- ship.* Other words registered but those words slammed home.

I snatched the papers from Jessica's hands and flipped back to the first page.

My dearest Elle,
I am sorry for everything, as if that makes any of this okay. I have signed the company over to you, all you have to do is sign the last page and

*send them to the lawyer. I will retire May 30, and
you can take over June 1. There are no conditions attached to your ownership, and I'm sorry I
ever thought there should be. I hope the company
brings you the happiness you seek.*
Love You Always,
Daddy

A strangled cry escaped, but I tamped down all the
emotion trying to drown me. Unable to settle myself
enough to read the legalese word for word, I scanned
the pages three times—everything appeared legitimate.
I owned Jackson Bonds.

"What made him do that?" Jess stood at my elbow.

I glanced up but had no words, nothing.

Rebel and I were done. The thought stuck in my mind
on repeat. There was no reason to go back to him, other
than to pack up and move home. My stomach hurt, my
throat burned and I wanted to cry. How come I felt like
my world ended when I got the only thing that ever
mattered to me?

Suck it up, I commanded myself, internally shaking
off the morose feeling trying to smother me.

"Doris came by yesterday and it's complicated, but
I'm sure that's why." I cleared my throat. "Shake your
ass, Beaumont. We need to celebrate." I dropped the
papers into my purse, planning to drop them by the
lawyer's office on my way home.

"Sign that." Jess nodded to the papers. "We'll drop
them off and then celebrate. I don't want your daddy
to change his mind."

After dropping the signed document off at our lawyer's office, Jess and I headed to Franklin's, a posh kind

of restaurant for dedicated foodies. Jess loved fine dining and fine everything else, too.

Decorated only with glass windows for walls and sleek black tables and chairs, Franklin's was the definition of chic. While not my style, it fit Jess perfectly. We both ordered and Jess insisted on a bottle of champagne to celebrate Daddy coming to his senses.

Once the waiter had left, Jess leaned forward in her stunning red dress. "Tell me everything."

"The part where I told Doris off or the part where I fell in love with Rebel?" I sipped my water, wishing the champagne was already here.

"You can't be that stupid, tell me you're not that stupid," Jess huffed.

"I'm that stupid. He's funny, sexy, and naughty in the best ways. Do you know he's a sex master?"

Jess snorted. "Honey, that's definitely not what you call him. Is he a Dom or a Master?"

"I don't know." I waved her question away. "He trained with a master for four years, and he said people came to him because he could strip everything away… because of his control." I whispered the last part.

"Lucky girl." Jess grinned.

The waiter brought our champagne. I watched as he and Jessica went through the wine rituals—I knew nothing about those—then he poured each of us a glass before leaving the bottle chilling on ice.

"So yeah, we fit together crazy good and that's so bad for me, which is why I'm here, trying to find perspective on Rebel, but now I don't need it."

"Why not?"

"Because we'll get divorced, go our separate ways.

This was all for show." I gulped down my champagne, needing its numbing effects.

"I understand divorcing since you didn't want to be married, but why give him up?" She frowned at me.

Our bruschetta arrived.

"Tell me about your biker guy?" I urged then stuffed my face so I couldn't talk.

"Zero…the man has untold talents. He's amazing in bed and he doesn't want anything else. The perfect man for me." She grinned at me. "We said one night, but it's turned into four, so far. The man could break a lesser woman."

"Does he know what you do?" I hated to probe, but Jess didn't have a real good track record with the truth.

"Nope and he doesn't need to. We're not in a relationship, not even a fuck buddy one, pure casual sex." She arched a brow at me. "The best kind."

"For you." We'd argued this point a hundred times and I didn't need to make it a hundred and one.

"Tell me about Doris and why your dad's being human again?" She changed the subject on purpose, but that suited me fine.

I told her about Doris's visit and the smug way she'd assumed my life was right on track—the way Daddy wanted it to be. It was hard to admit how I'd been brutally honest about the one-way direction of my feelings for Rebel, but maybe if I said it enough times, it'd kill the last little pearl of hope I held on to.

"So that's why it's got to be over." I sighed, hating the thought of never touching him again. "I love him and he doesn't love me."

"That could change, you guys haven't been together

long." Jess pointed a sexy pink nail at me. "You're scared and running. You always run."

"I don't want to be part of the club, I don't understand it any more than the master stuff, but the women in the club are property. I'm no man's property."

"Why not? It's sexy as hell to be claimed so absolutely." She furrowed her brow in that way that meant trouble. She glared at me with her stubborn look. "You'd be great old lady material."

I cringed at the word.

"Nope, not me."

"Coward. You can't hide from the good things in life." She gave me her I-know-best look, and that just pissed me off.

"There is no us, not where Rebel and I are concerned. He made that clear from the beginning—"

"Change his mind." She hissed the words. "Fight for once."

Rage shot through me and I opened my mouth to lash out, then shut it tight before I closed my eyes and counted to ten. She didn't understand, couldn't understand, what I owed Rebel.

"If this was about only what I wanted, then yeah, I'd fight for him." Those words were true. Surprising since Jess was right, I rarely fought for anything. "But when everyone but you had left me, and I had no one who could help get the one thing I've always needed, Rebel was there."

He'd given me everything even when it had cost him, inconvenienced him, and caused him trouble.

"I won't repay that kind of loyalty by trying to shift the rules, change our relationship, that'd be underhanded, especially when he spelled it all out up front.

I'm not that kind of person." I stared Jess down, daring her to challenge me again.

"Fine." She threw her hands in the air. "There's no way to change your mind if your sense of honor is on the line. You Jacksons would die choking on that honor."

"Damn straight." I grinned at her.

Jess dropped me home a little before three. And in less than thirty minutes I was ready to go bat-shit crazy. I had nothing else to do, but I'd told Rebel I wouldn't be back until tomorrow. Knowing my time with him was short, I didn't want to waste any time away from him, I only had seven days left before I'd be in Dallas full-time, taking the company in new directions.

On my way upstairs to pack, I froze mid-step. What if he didn't want me to stay? What if he wanted me gone right away? Maybe I should just call and tell him about the contract. No. I wasn't going to be a coward. While our relationship would end soon, I refused to hide. He deserved better, and so did I.

I packed a bag and then stopped in my home office to grab an envelope. I stared down at the envelope, not wanting to touch it, or even to acknowledge its existence because taking it meant admitting that my marriage was over. Sucking in a deep breath, I lifted the document out of the envelope and flipped to the last page. I scrawled today's date on the date line on the first page, then flipped to page two and signed my name before shoving it back into the envelope. My half was done, my word still my bond.

My lawyer had been perplexed to say the least when I'd requested the divorce decree the same day I'd given him a certified copy of our marriage license. But being a good man, he didn't question me, instead he'd sent word when they were finished so I could pick them up. I'd dropped them in my desk and tried to forget about them, and had done a damn fine job of it until today.

I dropped the envelope into the duffel and zipped it closed, just like I'd close down the sadness that kept trying to sneak in and immerse me in its gloom. I refused to be its plaything. I'd done what needed doing to save my company, I wouldn't give Rebel even a small reason to regret helping me. By the time I reached his house, I'd be the old me, the happy me. And when I left him, well, I'd have the company to run, to expand, and there'd be no time or room for regret in my life.

Chapter Twenty-Two

Rebel

"Let's get the week planned and get out of here." I sat at the head of the conference room table with JoJo, Delta, and Trisha. She'd picked up the routine quick enough, and I was glad to be done explaining shit to her. Training sucked, even when the person was smart.

Trisha fiddled with her laptop and the first contract came up on the projection screen. "Tim Collins, last seen in Oklahoma City, $25,000 reward for his capture. He's wanted for armed robbery and has ties to Brunk's crew."

"I got him." JoJo wrote down a couple of notes. "Send the file to my email."

Trish gave him a quick smile before the next face appeared on screen. "James Boutilier, known to hang out in Dallas, but no one has seen him in two weeks. We have a contract on him, along with two other companies—the reward is $60,000."

"You want him?" Delta nodded to me.

"Don't really care, you can pick between him and the next one. I'll take whatever you don't want." Normally I chose first and let the guys pick from what was left, but this week none of the contracts really appealed to me. All I thought about was Elle—seeing her again, fucking her, making her laugh. Shit, I was in bad shape.

"Go to the next one." Delta frowned at me but didn't ask any questions, just one of the many things I liked about him.

"Rudolph 'Rudy' Mander, he's a prospect with the Angels of Death and missed his court date two days ago. We have an exclusive contract on him with a payout of $50,000. He was last seen in Dallas at the clubhouse." Trisha looked from me to Delta.

"I'll take Boutilier and you can continue your pissing match with the Angels." Delta nodded to Trish. "Send me the file and do some calling to see if you can get more in the way of usual hangouts. I'll dig through his credit card history and the other crap."

"Will do." Trisha put five other names on the screen. "We also have five more small contracts that I will send to all of you. If you have downtime, you can pick these guys up without breaking a sweat."

"Call if you need backup, I can always send the prospects." I turned to Trish. "Give each of our three prospects one of the small cases, doesn't matter which one, let's see if they can do the easy part of the job."

Trish nodded. "Got it, boss."

"Let's go get busy. Trish, you're in charge here. Call one of us if you get a bond call over $50,000, otherwise let the prospects deal with those too." Delta jetted before I'd finished speaking, no surprise there, he hated being in the office. JoJo grinned over at me. "You and Elle hunting together?"

"Most likely, unless she's got something better to do." I headed toward the front door, ready to get hunting.

"Boss, you can't leave yet," Trisha called from behind me.

With a sigh, I turned away from the door. JoJo laughed when he walked out. Sometimes it sucked being the boss.

Trish sat down behind the sleek black reception desk right in front of the glass doors. "You need to sign all of these." The stack of paper was almost a foot thick, fucking great.

"I can't be this behind on paperwork." I frowned at the stack willing it to vanish.

"You didn't sign all the spots on half of these." Trisha grinned up at me. "You told me to audit the files, and this is what you missed."

"That should have taken you days." I stared down at my young assistant who had three piercings and tats down both of her arms. She fit in with us perfectly.

"This is what I found in the first half I went through. I still have more to go."

"Dammit." I opened the first file and signed in the three places Trisha had marked.

"Are you doing that all here?"

"Yeah," I growled. I didn't want to lug this shit to my office, besides if I actually sat down there, I'd be here for hours. Every time I was in the office it happened.

"Catch the phone then, I'm going to go talk to the other guys." She didn't wait for a response but moseyed away.

I hurried through the stack, willing the phone to stay silent until I got my bitch work done. Thankfully, it did. Once I signed the last post it marked space, I headed to the back to find my secretary.

She sat on Lyle's desk laughing with the three of

them. When I stormed in the prospects lost a shade of color in their faces. I had no idea why they feared me, but all three of them did. I'd never had this trouble with prospects at Bound, but then I'd been around every day.

"Done with your stack, so get your ass back to the desk."

She laughed and slipped off the desk. "Why did you open a bail bonds shop if paperwork makes you grouchy?" She turned and waved to the prospects. "Let me know what you find."

At her desk, I lifted a hand to tell her goodbye. "Why are they scared of me?"

Trisha tilted her head to the side. "You don't know?"

"Not a clue."

She let out a loud peal of laughter. "JoJo." She tried to say more but couldn't stop laughing. Eventually she calmed down. "Told them stories of what a badass you are, put the fear of Rebel into them. I'm pretty sure he did it just to screw with them. They told me, yesterday, as a warning."

JoJo and his damn pranks. "But it didn't scare you?"

"No way, I'd spent the morning with you. You're no demon boss from hell, just a run-of-the-mill pain in the ass." She winked before she picked up the stack of papers. "Besides Elle told me I couldn't be afraid of you guys and do my job, she promised your bark was the worst part."

Of course Elle warned her. "Let's get one thing straight, I'm never run-of-the-mill, I'm the fucking best...got me?" I grinned down at her.

"Oh yes, demon boss." She bowed to me from behind her desk. "Get out of here and make some money."

I headed to Barden to catch up on some Brotherhood

business before I began digging up dirt on Rudy Mander. I wished Elle was coming home tonight, it was ridiculous how much I missed her. I shouldn't miss her, but I had at least three more months to work her out of my system. If this condition, yeah it was definitely a disease, hasn't passed by August, then I'd worry. Until then, I planned to enjoy my madness.

I stopped in front of Marked Man. Jeremy, one of Rock's new prospects worked the main desk. I gave him a nod. "Zero here?"

"In back, he's got about twenty minutes before his appointment." Jeremy fidgeted in a nervous way.

I didn't get it. I wasn't scary, not at all like Jericho or Dare, let alone Bear. Walking down the short hall to the tattoo room, I considered ways to get JoJo back for his wild stories.

"Hey, man," Rock greeted me then went back to work on some guy.

Big Ang worked on a client and Mark cleaned up. Zero stood and gave me a back-slapping hug. "About damn time. I thought I'd have to chase your ass down." He glanced over to Rock. "Use your office?"

Rock grunted his assent then refocused on the work.

"You caught any really bad guys?"

"Not much, I'm hunting another Angel right now, at least beginning the hunt." The Angels needed an attitude adjustment and if they weren't careful, the Brotherhood would give it to them.

We stepped into Rock's office and Zero shut the door. "How are the three prospects doing?"

"Lyle is damn good—born bounty hunter—because he's got an awesome bullshit detector." I liked him the most even if he was the quietest of the three. "Dan is alright, but he's lazy. I've caught him taking shortcuts twice, once more and he's back to you." Nothing pissed me off more than cutting corners, and I wouldn't tolerate that bullshit, but then none of us did.

"Damn, I hoped he'd improve." Zero scratched notes in a small notebook he'd pulled out of his pocket. "If he screws up again, then he's out."

"West is tight, great with the takedowns, but shit at bonding, for now anyway. He might prove better for Ringer in the long run, but I like the kid."

"Got it. What did you do to them?" Zero grinned up at me. "They've been talking about what a hard-ass you are."

"Fucking JoJo is telling stories, I don't even know if they're true stories." I didn't mind the rep, but I didn't like the way it made them cower around me.

"You could take one with you." Zero gave me his shit-eating grin. "But then you have that hot blonde to partner with."

I flipped him off. "Anything else?"

"Yeah, I want to give you one or two more. I have one who didn't work out with porn, but he's a great recruit, then a newbie."

I sighed. "Send them over. I'll tell JoJo to expect them."

Outside of Marked Man I kick-started my bike. When my phone buzzed, I put the bike into park to check my phone.

Elle had texted me. Headed back now. See you in a couple hours. I sped out of town so I could get home, make dinner for her then we could get down to the serious fun.

At home I decided on pasta and shrimp—easy and

delicious. I heard the rumble of Elle's truck right after I'd added the shrimp to sauté.

Elle walked in and hollered.

"The kitchen," I shouted back, not wanting to leave my shrimp unattended. Thirty seconds was all it took for shrimp to go from perfect to overcooked.

"What smells delicious?" She kissed my cheek.

"Shrimp pasta with basil sauce."

"Ooh, fancy." She leaned against my granite countertop looking good enough to eat.

I tossed the shrimp on top of the pasta and set both dishes in the middle of my retro kitchen table. It had a black laminate top with chrome accents and legs. The chairs matched the table, I'd ordered the whole set online—one of the few things I hadn't picked up at the local furniture store.

"First we eat food, then I eat you." I stalked toward her and wrapped my arms around her waist before I leaned down for a real kiss. She tasted delicious.

Elle's stomach growled and I broke the kiss. I couldn't have my woman hungry, especially given what I planned to do to her this evening.

"You must be hungry." I smiled down at her. Her cheeks were pink.

"I wasn't until I smelled this deliciousness." She waved to the food on the table.

I moved around her to collect two plates and silverware. "You want a beer?"

She nodded, taking the plates from me. "I can barely boil water and you're like a master chef." She filled her plate with pasta and salad. "You won't believe my trip to Dallas." Popping a shrimp in her mouth, she closed her eyes and a look of bliss flitted across her face.

I filled my plate although my appetite had vanished when Elle had come in, but I'd need my strength for what I planned to do to her tonight. Two nights, and I was like a randy teenager. I wished I understood why she affected me so much, but I was putty in her hands, as always.

"You see Jess?"

"I did, and Doris, my dad's assistant, stopped by on Friday."

I hoped the woman hadn't hurt Elle. "Was it bad?"

Her fork stopped midair. "Yeah, it was terrible." She swallowed pasta and stared out the kitchen window. "They had people watching us, and watching my house."

"What the fuck?" Her creepy father was on my last nerve.

"Exactly, I ended up canceling on Jess the first night. Doris just drained me." Her eyes were haunted.

I reached across and squeezed her hand.

"Then this morning when Jess and I were leaving for lunch, a courier delivered papers to me." She gulped and her eyes shone with tears. "Daddy signed the company over to me, no conditions."

The bottom dropped out of my stomach, I was in free fall. "That's great, baby." I managed to say the words and I meant them, but my plans blew away with those words. Her news reset the playing field, there was no reason for her to stay. Could I ask her to stay with me? Did she want that? Did I?

"Yeah, his last day is a week from Monday, then I'll be the owner the next day." She bit her lip. "I've wanted this forever, but now that I have it, I'm scared, really scared."

Appetite demolished. I pushed the plate away. "I understand. I was nervous when I opened Brotherhood Bonds. I knew I could do it, but my reputation, my future, was on the line."

She stood and wiped hands on her jeans. "It also means we don't need to…to live together anymore. Our marriage deal is over." She wouldn't meet my eyes, instead she bent down and pulled an envelope from her bag. "These are for you."

Her hand shook when she gave them to me.

"What are they?"

"Divorce papers, um, I had the lawyer draw them up a while ago."

I dropped the envelope on the table, not wanting to think about divorce papers right now. I rarely thought about being married to her. My finger rubbed the ring I wore.

Liar. I liked being married to her and fuck if I knew why.

"So are you moving back?"

"Do you want me to?" Her eyes were huge and round. "I mean, now. I'll have to move back by June 1 to run the company, but I can leave tonight?"

Silence hung between us as I tried to get my brain working again.

"I'm good with you staying, I even have a new contract for us to work, our last one." I shut down the shit trying to break loose inside me. No way I'd go there. Right now, my only plan was living minute by minute.

She stepped forward and grasped my hands in hers. "That sounds good, real good. Who are we chasing?"

"Rudy Mander, prospect for the Angels of Death." My eyes locked on her plump lips. They drew me down and I lost myself in our kiss, tasting redemption in our frantic exchange.

I pushed up her red tee and stripped it off her before tugging up the sports bra. She took over removing it while I unzipped her jeans and tugged down. The table was full of dishes so I couldn't take her there. I moved her back against the wall. Her greedy fingers tugged up my shirt and I jerked it over my head before slipping out of my boots and removing my pants. She wrapped her fingers around my cock and I moaned, but she wasn't sidetracking me.

I dropped to my knees then traced fingers up the inside of her thighs spreading her stance as I went. I trailed fingers through her wet seam before I lowered my lips to her mound, needing to taste her sweetness. She shuddered and pressed into me, starved for my touch. I lost myself in worshipping her, feeling the build inside her, but never letting her topple over. I needed her frantic, out of control. She was mine, I would prove that to her tonight.

"Please." She rocked her hips into me, searching for what I denied her. "I can't take more."

But she could and I'd show her just how sweet the reward was when she waited. Sliding my finger inside her, she tightened around it. I pressed her for more, needed everything inside her. I had no words for my crazy addiction to her, but this, this way I could share what I felt for her.

Body wound tight, her legs shook; she'd fall if I wasn't holding her up. Sexy noises escaped with every breath, but I'd stolen her words and I'd steal more before we were finished. I craved release but my body didn't exist, only her pleasure. I added a second finger and sucked her swollen nub of flesh between my teeth. Working her up higher and higher until she screamed, climaxing around my fingers. I lapped up her sweet cream, drawing out her release. I owned her as she crumpled into my arms. I'd never witnessed a more beautiful sight.

I gathered her in my arms and carried her upstairs to my room. I needed to be buried deep inside her, so I could tattoo my name on her damn soul. She was mine.

Chapter Twenty-Three

Rebel

I woke early the next morning feeling ten kinds of out of sorts, not even the mind-blowing sex we'd shared the night before made me feel better this morning. Seven days before our world changed and I had no idea how to get right with the idea when I didn't ever want to let her go. I was sure this obsession would pass eventually, it wasn't like I could keep her forever, so it had to go away, just not yet.

After waking Elle up in my favorite way, we headed out for breakfast before hitting the road to Dallas. She drove the new, tricked-out SUV I'd bought with a glass shield between front and back along with the locking back doors. I rode my bike since we'd need it to scope out all of Mander's normal haunts. Saturday was a great day to catch a biker, especially an Angel, since they all loved to party. If the intel I'd dug up on Mander was solid, we might have it locked down tonight, maybe tomorrow.

We made it to Elle's place before four.

"You'll need to be a biker babe if you're going with me." I trailed a finger along her jaw line.

"I love being a biker babe." She clapped her hands then frowned. "I'll need a new T-shirt, the last one got ruined."

I grabbed a black club shirt from my bag and tossed it to her.

"What are you going to do?" She dug through a drawer in her bedroom, coming out with scissors.

"I'm going to dig a bit deeper into Mander's life." I'd had Trisha running credit card information for me, as well as contacting the site we used to track that stuff down. This guy I knew, Sampson, did excellent freelance skip-trace work, as long as you weren't picky about legalities.

I carried my laptop bag downstairs and set up in Elle's office. I had a new report from Sampson and an email from Trish. His credit card showed a history of five bars—I knew them all. There was also some rumors of an Angels party tonight, but if so, I had no way to get an invite nor would I be welcome if I did show up. We'd have to hit the bars and hope for the best.

Elle walked into the doorway of her office and gave me a sexy pout. "Am I dressed okay?"

Fuck. She was on fire. The shirt showed off her ample cleavage and the shorts were painted on, but they stopped too soon showing off lots of her curvy legs. "Damn, baby, you look good enough to eat."

Her pout widened to a grin. "Let's go find our man."

I wanted to undress her then fuck her until she couldn't remember her name, but we'd done that the night before. Besides we had work, and I liked working with Elle almost as much as I liked sharing my bed with her. I couldn't explain why I liked working with her, especially when I didn't even like working with my brothers. We clicked though.

"I have five bars on the list, but we may not find him. There's a rumor of an Angels party."

"And we can't go there?"

I shook my head. "Our clubs aren't getting along real well right now." That was more than I should've said, technically, but it wasn't like Elle would spout my business around town.

"Okay, so where to first?"

"A place called the Orange Iguana, a dive bar outside of town." We left her place on my bike and rode the thirty minutes to the Iguana. I'd been there one other time, but it was too grimy for me. I parked my bike but stopped Elle when she started to walk toward the entrance. "Same rules as before." I tipped her chin up until our eyes met. "No fighting, stick to my side, oh and don't use the bathrooms—they're beyond nasty."

One side of her lips ticked up. "You sound like a girl."

"Do not." I crossed my arms over my chest.

Her chuckle relaxed nerves coiled tight, nerves I didn't even realize I had. No doubt about it, her announcement had rattled me deep. I pushed that thought aside like I had every other one that had tried to creep into my brain. I had no idea how to deal with it, so I'd ignore it.

Inside, I saw a couple guys I'd met before at the bar. We sat next to Patch and I ordered us both a bottle of Corona, wanting to avoid any open containers. This place was really that nasty, the Unwashed Iguana might be a better name.

Patch and I talked about the weather and club politics, who was on the outs with who, as we drank two bottles of beer.

"I hear you and the Angels of Death are tense." He glanced my way.

He wasn't talking about me personally, but my club.

"They made a play on our turf, we sent them packing." We wanted everyone to know we didn't allow interlopers.

"They're trying to be bigger than they are." He sipped whiskey. "Heard they're partying tonight with some special guests from down South."

That was bad news for the hunt. "Hope the Bandits don't get wind of it." I thought about calling Charlie, but no doubt he already knew.

"True that," Patch said.

I paid for our drinks and Elle and I headed out. She tugged me to her when I went to throw my leg over the bike seat. Her kiss pulled me under immediately.

I leaned back and broke our kiss. "You ready to hit another place?"

"Why? Our guy is at the party."

"I heard that Mander has a woman who bartends at one of the places. Likely she won't be there, but we can get some information."

We headed to Tuck's Tavern and Elle worked her magic on the guy tending bar. Mander's girl, Sheila, would be on duty tomorrow afternoon. While she worked I dropped Charlie a quick text. We stayed good friends because of the free flow of information between us.

The next day we made it to the bar by noon, two hours before Sheila, and hopefully Mander, would make an appearance. I started with Corona and Elle ordered a Bloody Mary. We were two of the seven people in the bar, all bikers, but none of them were Angels. The place wasn't one of my favorite hangouts but it was decent. Clean. And the manager didn't take any shit so the bikers behaved.

"Are you going to be able to drink all day and still catch Mander?" Elle spoke low then kissed my ear.

"Baby, I'll be stone sober. What about you?"

"No need to worry about me, baby." She threw my words back at me. "I'm checking out the bathrooms." She hopped off the stool and every eye watched her walk to the back of the bar because the sway of her ass was hypnotic

My phone rang. "Hey, my friend."

"Where are you? We need to get together." Charlie didn't sound like his laid-back self.

"Tuck's, but I'm working, going to take down a guy later." I didn't have time for a Charlie party today. The first time I'd ended up at Tuck's I had been partying with Charlie.

"See ya there soon." He hung up.

The ten-second conversation set me on edge because it was unlike Charlie in every way. He wasn't serious, insistent, or short. No, this couldn't be good news. I had a feeling I was about to see the Bandit side of Charlie, not something I ever wanted to see.

I jumped when Elle rubbed her hand along my shoulder.

"What's wrong?" She sat down next to me.

"Charlie's stopping by, and I don't think it's a friendly visit." I rubbed a hand through my hair and debated calling Jericho.

"But we got our own business. By the way, the back door is right next to the men's bathroom so it would be the easiest takedown."

"If it's just him, we strong arm him out of here, no need for waiting." I wanted this day to be done.

"I like direct." She squeezed my thigh.

"Yeah, look, I got to make a call, if any of these fuckers bother you, take them down." I slid off the wood stool.

"Now I hope they start something." Elle grinned wide. "You never let me beat up bikers."

I snorted at the glee in her voice, but I walked along the length of the wooden bar to the exit in front. I needed to get with Jericho before I was in a corner.

"What?" Jericho answered.

I told him about the news I'd heard last night about the Angels party and then Charlie's insistence we meet. "This sounds like Bandit business. I've known Charlie for years but we've never talked club business."

"Sounds like the Angels have made a big, bad enemy." Jericho paused. "If Charlie's business affects us, then you make the call, you know him, know our limits."

"What…" I had no words. This was above my pay grade.

"You're on the Council, you know the area best. Decide and we'll back your decision." Jericho hung up.

I stood in the parking lot trying to process what my Prez just said. I'd never carried my club like this, and fear shot through me leaving an ice-cold trail in its wake. My throat clenched tight, no one had ever given me so much responsibility. Jericho trusted me to decide the future of our club. The weight of his trust settled heavy on my shoulders.

When I walked back inside, Elle laughing with the bartender eased me. Her laugh righted something inside me, shifting my burden to a much more bearable load.

"Baby, where's the pile of bikers I expected to find?" I kissed her cheek.

She turned into my lips for a deeper kiss. She leaned back with a smile. "Chuck will tell you, I tried to lure someone over, but no one came."

"She even winked at Johnny, over there, but he just left the bar for a table." Chuck shook his head. "She settled with arm wrestling me."

"Who won?"

"Chuck," my woman growled. "He's like an ox."

"Thanks for entertaining her." I gave him a nod. "Two fingers of Jack."

He turned away from us to get my drink.

"What happened to staying sober?"

"Charlie's coming to talk serious shit, that's just a bracer. When he comes, we'll go to a table, and I need you to stay here at the bar until I come get you."

She frowned at me. "Okay, but if the opportunity is there, I'm taking Mander down."

"Fine. No doubt you can handle it, take him in if this thing with Charlie takes too long." I didn't have time to worry about bounties, not until I understood what Charlie needed.

"Your business is serious." She touched my cheek. "You okay?"

"The best." I meant it. My fingertips tingled in anticipation. I wanted to make this deal. "I'm sorry it's screwing with our plan."

"I got your back." She squeezed my hand. "Chuck, I need another Bloody Mary."

Chuck sat down my whiskey and turned back to make her drink.

Charlie walked in the door, he had the same easygoing smile and relaxed strut I was used to. In fact I saw none of the intensity from our earlier conversation. His smile grew brighter when he spotted Elle.

"Hey, *chica*, I like seeing you with my man, Rebel." He stood between us with one arm over each of our shoulders.

"Do I get to beat up bikers while you talk to Charlie?" She spoke so only me and Charlie heard her.

"Yeah, if any are stupid enough to approach, or if our guy is in position." I winked at her. "Charlie, what do you want to drink?"

Chuck stopped in front of us, setting down the Bloody Mary on the dark wood bar.

"Give us a couple Coronas," Charlie told him. Once we got the beer we ambled over to a table in the back corner. "Appreciate you letting me interrupt your business."

"I'd do almost anything for you, compadre." And I meant it. He was a great friend who'd helped me in more ways than I could count.

"What I'm going to ask you for may push that boundary." Charlie's eyes narrowed and intensity radiated from him. "Know I don't ask lightly."

So much for small talk, Charlie went straight to business.

"Man, surely I don't have to butter you up after all we've been through." He smirked at me.

"You psychic?" He'd read my mind.

"Just psychotic." He downed half his beer. "But seriously, here's the deal. The Angels made a deal last night with my club's supplier."

They were dead. The club was living on borrowed time.

"Because I wouldn't make a deal with the supplier to take over your club's territory—not something we wanted to do, and honestly there's not enough profit for the war." His cold analysis sent a chill through me. If that ever changed, the Bandits would rip through us without a second thought.

"The Angels are planning to run meth in and through your territory, want to set up labs in the hills around you since it's close to their base of operations."

"That's not ever happening." Anger ripped through me. We didn't allow drugs in our territory, not because we had a moral cause but because it was our territory. The Brotherhood didn't deal with drugs so no one did in our territory—it was about reputation and pride, the currency of all clubs.

"That's what I wanted to hear. We're coming for the fuckers from the south." A smile colder than Jericho's crossed Charlie's face. "We need you to block them in from the north, not give them a way to escape. We will wipe the club off the map."

"We don't go all the way to Dallas." I spoke without commitment.

"Maybe you'd be willing to patrol, control and put down any strays north of Dallas."

Silence expanded between us. I worked out how to say what I wanted to say.

"We'd be willing to expand our patrols and collect the trash, but you'd have to dispose of it however you see fit. We're not in the disposal business." The Bandits would have claws into our club if we did their dirty work. "We would appreciate if your cleanup and disposal happened outside our borders."

Charlie grinned wide. "You speak for your Prez?"

"Yeah, I called him before our meetup." I held out my hand.

Charlie grasped it tight in a firm handshake.

"You'll deal with me on the Brotherhood end." I didn't want anyone else possibly fucking up the fragile alliance with the Bandits.

"And I'll deal with you. This is my mess to clean up." Charlie leaned back and the intensity left in an instant. He was the Charlie I'd partied with too many times to count.

I glanced over to find Elle, but she wasn't there, and Sheila was behind the bar. Fuck, had she taken Mander?

Chapter Twenty-Four

Elle

After Charlie and Rebel sat at the back corner booth, I moved our SUV to the back alley. Coming in the back door, I took my seat at the bar right as Sheila and Mander walked through the door. Now I just needed the skinny punk to hit the bathroom and I'd be good to go.

Sheila gave him a beer and then went out to take orders at the tables. Mander zeroed in on my tits in less than ten seconds. Maybe this would be easier than I thought. I batted my eyelashes and flashed him a quick smile before looking away. We played this game for about fifteen minutes before I decided to try my luck. I gave him a furtive glance before looking at the dark hallway and back to him. His grin widened, I had him. I'd add cheater to his list of crimes, but then he was the sort of slime who likely had zero morals.

I stood up and sashayed across the bar, making sure I worked my hip sway. Steps echoed on the tile floor behind me but I didn't look back until I reached the back door. Mander leered at me, less than two steps away. Crooking my finger for him to follow, I slipped out the back door at the same time I powered up my Taser.

Mander moved closer. "You're a sweet thing." His fetid breath blew across my face.

"Aw, thanks, sweetie." I stepped forward and jammed the round shocking element right into his chest. He spasmed and hit the concrete. I kicked him over and re-strained him. The little fucker didn't wake up so I had to drag his ass into the back of the SUV which made me work up a sweat. I hadn't even given him the full shock, he was a first-class wuss.

Once I locked him in the back of the SUV, I raised the glass shield between us before I texted Rebel. Got Mander. If you're not out in five minutes, I'm taking him in.

Six minutes passed and still no Rebel, so I sent him another quick text. Processing Mander. Be back to get you in an hour or so.

I had apprehended my second Angel of Death, which made me happy mostly because I now knew how much it pissed off the bikers to be taken down by a woman. Me two, Angels zero.

At the precinct I turned Mander over and waited for the paperwork to be completed.

Satisfied with a job well done, I returned to Tuck's. Surely, I wouldn't have to wait at the bar anymore. I checked my phone again. Nothing from Rebel. Would he be pissed?

I walked into the club and it was déjà vu. Another row of tables were pushed together in the center of the bar with Charlie at the head of it. People surrounded him, but Rebel sat to his right again. He spotted me and gave me a lopsided grin. "Come here, baby."

My biker was already drunk, but he was a cute drunk.

"Here I do all the work and you drink all the booze," I sassed as I sat on his lap.

"Hell yeah, I like it that way." His words slurred and I wondered how he'd gone from sober to drunk in such a short time.

I snuggled into him, loving the leather smell that mixed with the one that was all him. I planned to get him home soon before he was too drunk to play my favorite kind of games.

The shower woke me up the next morning. I glanced at my clock, 6:30 was way too early so I covered my head with my arm and tried to go back to sleep, but I was awake. The shower shut off and Rebel strolled out of my bathroom a few minutes later.

He stopped at the foot of my bed. "Did I wake you up?"

I yawned. "Yeah, why are you up so early?"

"Got a meeting at the clubhouse today."

"Oh yeah, it's Thursday." I stretched and sat up. "I'll follow you up in the SUV."

He prowled to me, dropping his towel. "You'll ride with me. I'll send the prospects down for the SUV."

"Why?" It made no practical sense.

"I like you behind me, feels right." He kissed me, dragging me under before I could reason out what he meant.

Rebel delayed our start with a naughty seduction. His brand of lovemaking defied description, I only hoped I'd be able to survive once he no longer wanted me—a day that was coming very soon.

I rode on the back of his bike even though it was impractical, but I honestly couldn't refuse the man anything. I spent every day soaking up all I could hoping it'd sustain me once we went our separate ways.

Maybe he felt the same way because all week he kept me right next to him, and I ate his attention up, gorging on all things Rebel. The only time we weren't in sync was when I mentioned the divorce papers. They'd disappeared off his kitchen cabinet. I'd asked him if he wanted me to take the signed papers back to Dallas. He snapped that he'd take care of it. I didn't understand why it made him pissy, but I dropped it.

Today was Sunday. The day I was leaving for Dallas—our pretend relationship was over and sadness hovered at the edge of my consciousness, ready to swoop in and drag me under.

Rebel showered getting ready to go to his club's Sunday meeting and I planned on leaving for Dallas. I had my truck loaded and sat on the couch giving Harley some last love when Rebel strolled into the room.

"Why so sad?" He crouched down in front of me.

"I'm not, really. Just thinking about missing Harley." The wily tom purred louder and rubbed his chin against mine.

"Why?"

"What do you mean? Why?" I pushed the words past the lump of emotion I was trying to keep from spewing all over him.

"We won't be living together, but you'll still be up to see me." He sat next to me and the cat hopped to Rebel's lap, as if he approved of his master's suggestion.

"I will?" This shit was beyond confusing. He'd avoided all attempts I'd made to discuss our divorce, so I'd assumed our future was off the table.

"The marriage deal has run its course, but I'm still

down with the sex deal." He waggled his brows in a comical way.

I giggled. And I don't giggle, but all the nervous tension had to find an escape. "The sex deal." I hadn't thought about our no-relationship-just-sex deal. Could I handle that? I was more than a little in love with him, prolonged exposure would only make that love harder to bear.

When I stared into his cinnamon gaze, I couldn't say no but I shouldn't say yes. We were quickly approaching the point where ice cream wouldn't fix my broken heart. Or maybe I'd already passed that point? It was hard to tell since I'd never loved anyone like I did him. Without a point of comparison, I floundered in this sea of feeling with no clue what awaited me once I reached shore.

"Okay, we still have the sex deal." I blew out a breath. "But now I need to get to Dallas and you need to get to a meeting."

"No." He scowled at me. Harley left his lap for mine, giving Rebel the stink-eye. "You're going to the club with me and leaving for work Tuesday morning."

He sounded so damn reasonable, but I'd told him three times I planned to leave today. He'd never said a word so I thought we agreed.

"I'm leaving now." I stood, dumping the cat from my lap. Harley gave me his own scowl before prancing off, outrage in every dainty step.

"Baby, don't push me." He stood and drew me to him. "You need to leave Tuesday, not now." Some emotion swirled in the depth of his gaze, something vulnerable and unrecognizable.

Exactly how did he feel about me? I wished I was brave enough to challenge him or even ask him about it. But, I understood the consequences of his response only too well. One word could send me flying out of control, left with a heart broken so profoundly it'd never be whole again. No, I'd never ask him about his emotions or share my love for him. I was all kinds of stupid for falling for my bad boy, but even I wasn't stupid enough to go there.

"Tuesday?" I tried to read him but like always I was out of my depth. "Anything else I don't know?"

A smile played across his lips before he kissed me, intoxicating me with his touch. Too dazed for thoughts, let alone words, I let him tug me out of the house to his bike.

We saddled up on his Harley and headed to the Brotherhood compound. This was the first Sunday I'd come with Rebel to his club. He said Sundays were for Church—what the bikers called their weekly meeting. He'd been tense since our run-in with Charlie last weekend, but nothing like today. Every muscle in his back and sides was coiled tight. I'd held on to him too many times to count, but this was the first time I ever felt the tension in him. I wished I could take it away, help him, but I had no idea how.

We slowed and turned up the gravel lane to the cinderblock building Rebel called home. When he parked his bike, he didn't head straight for the group of people outside, instead he drew me close. With his jaw tight and eyes empty, I reached up and kissed him, pouring my belief in him into my kiss. I had his back and more, I believed in him. He cupped my ass and drew me closer, devouring me with his mouth as if I were the last oxygen on Earth.

He pulled back and cursed. "Baby, I gotta go. You

stay with Mama and Marr until I come get you. Understand me?"

I nodded. Swallowing to clear the fear that blocked my throat, I met his gaze. "You got this. Whatever you need to do today it's the right thing and your brothers know it."

He stepped back confusion clouded his features. "How—"

I lifted my shoulders in a shrug. "I don't know your business, but I know you." I traced the dent in his chin. "You made the right call."

He bent his forehead to mind and squeezed me. "Thanks, baby."

A moment passed between us and I wish I understood what happened, but all I know is something shifted and in that brief space of time I knew he loved me—maybe only for that second—but right then he loved me.

With a smack to my ass, he pulled away from me until only our hands were linked together.

"Hey, Marr," Rebel called to the six-foot woman dressed all in leather.

She turned and grinned at me. "Hey, Elle, glad to see you today."

"Keep her out of trouble until I come get her." Rebel let go of my hand and left without a word to me.

He confused me more every minute I was with him.

"You still leaving Tuesday?" She frowned at me.

"Still have a company to run." We'd talked about the changes in my life when we'd sparred on Thursday. She hadn't been chatty then, more focused on our workout.

"So Jericho says we got an hour maybe more before they're done." She scowled at the block building. "We

can prepare food and act like all the other hens, or..."
Her grin turned devilish. "We can spar again."

"Let's spar." I started walking toward the side of
the building.

"Keep going to the back. The hens will be in and out
of that door." Marr spoke from behind me.

Marr and I removed our shoes. Hers were thigh-high
boots with a good five inches of heel. My boots were
much easier in comparison.

"You just gonna leave him?" Marr's question hit
hard, worse than a punch.

"Are we clucking or fighting?" I had no room for her
judgments. I was too full of my own.

"Fighting, love." She bowed to me.

I returned the bow and we each fell into our stance.
Thirty minutes later, I dropped to the grass. "Enough."
I panted, trying to get enough oxygen running through
my body. We'd been brutal today and it was exactly
what I'd needed. No doubt I'd have a helluva bruise on
my shoulder and right thigh, but Marr wasn't leaving
unmarked either.

Marr sat on the ground beside me, sucking in deep
breaths. "You are a nasty bitch. I like it."

I chuckled and drew to my feet. I should put on my
boots but I was beat, instead I padded over to the white
porch swing fastened to a rusted swing set frame. I
sagged into the swing, not ready to face the women,
the questions, or my own doubts.

A few minutes later Marr joined me with her boots
back on. We sat in silence, the only sound the creak of
the chain from the moving swing.

"You could have him if you wanted him." Marr didn't
glance my way.

"I don't want him." I didn't even believe myself.

"Better work on that if you're planning to convince anyone."

"No one will ask, so I have nothing to worry about." It was that simple. Rebel wouldn't ask me to stay, to be more than we were now, so I had no one to convince.

"You could ask, that's my point." Marr turned her cat eyes on me.

"And you can mind your own business." I returned her stare.

"Like that is it?" She grinned at me. "All self-denial and martyrdom."

"Sure," I snapped. "They'll saint me when I die."

"So that's not it? Then why?" Marr kept prodding me.

"I made a deal, and I keep my word." I wanted to storm off to give action to the temper rising in me, but she didn't deserve the pleasure of knowing she'd gotten to me.

"Well fuck me, I owe Jericho money."

I whipped around and pinned her with my glare. "You bet on me?"

"Bikers bet on everything. And I'll bet that bastard has inside info he didn't tell me. I bet you'd make a play for more from our Rebel and he bet against me, so did Dare and Rock. Viper sided with me and of course Mama, but she's a romantic."

My life, my torture, my pain—all were just entertainment to them. "What did Rebel bet?"

"Oh love, we don't let the biker or woman in question in on our action." She snorted kind of a half laugh. "The bets on Jericho and I were legendary—we didn't work well together, at first anyway."

I let silence hang between us until I could speak with a calm I didn't feel. "So you just wanted to poke at me? Is this the sadistic part of you?"

"There you are," Rebel called.

I jerked up, surprised. He stood at the corner of the building. Had he heard our conversation? I glanced to Marr, she gave a slight shake of her head, and the overpowering anxiety drained away. He didn't know. I never planned to reveal how much I wanted him to want me.

"You've been fighting again, you're a bad influence, Marr." Rebel walked up to us. "Who won?"

"Neither of us." Marr stood. "We exhausted each other before either of us got the upper hand."

Rebel sat where Marr had been. She was gone, around the building and out of sight. "What's bothering you?"

I glanced over to see the tension lines gone from his face.

"Thinking about Tuesday. I've been gone a month, and the transition…well there isn't one, so I don't know what to expect." It was a good cover, even if I wasn't a tenth as worried about the company as I was about our future.

"You'll kick ass and take names, darling. That's what you always do." He picked me up and settled me onto his lap.

"I always do that?" I teased.

"Kick my ass every damn day, and I always want more." The sensual tone of his voice sent shivers along my bare arms.

We sat together swaying on the swing without talking. With Rebel's arms around me, the heartache that almost choked me earlier ebbed away. "I'm hungry. We need food."

"Let's go then." He lifted me off his lap to the ground. His thumb wiped at the corner of my mouth. "You had a spot of blood there." He grinned down at me.

After I'd slid on my boots we headed around to a whole spread of food. "Do they do this every Sunday?"

He grinned. "Lots of perks to being part of the Brotherhood."

We made our way through the line of food, my plate entirely too full. I followed Rebel to a table. We sat next to JoJo and Delta.

"Hey, boss." JoJo nodded to Rebel. "And Blondie."

"You catch your bad guy yet?" I asked JoJo.

"Yup, last night. Unlike Delta who is sucking last teat." JoJo rabbit punched Delta in the arm.

"Fuck off, my guy was a ghost, but I've found his trail now." Delta's smile turned smug. "And he's worth two of your guy."

From my brief time working with the three, it amazed me how competitive they all were. If my bail enforcement agents were half as competitive we'd close twice the number of contracts.

Bear sat down next to me, his amber eyes zeroed in on me. "Hey, beautiful. What did you ever decide?"

"Bear," Rebel snarled. "Leave off."

"Well, I loved the movies you sent me. Rebel was exquisite." I had no plan of deleting those movies from my laptop. They'd provide inspiration for years of self-love once the real thing was gone.

"You didn't…you watched them?" Rebel sputtered, his glance bouncing between Bear and me.

Bear laughed a deep, ringing laugh that had people

looking our way. His lover, Ollie, picked that moment to sit beside Bear.

I patted Rebel's cheek. "Of course I watched, and you were right—you are fucking awesome." I laughed at the open surprise on his face.

"Isn't it awesome at fucking?" JoJo threw in.

"You've got your share of movies, my man." Bear's announcement made JoJo blush.

"So Elle and I are the only pure ones, then?" Delta razzed his friend.

"Maybe." Bear held up a finger. "Elle was deciding." His intense gaze settled on me.

"Sorry, I'll have to pass," I told Bear with just a tiny bit of disappointment. After watching Rebel, my fantasy of us having sex in front of others only intensified, but business owners weren't porn stars. It was already hard enough for me to earn the respect of the men who dominated my business without any extra baggage.

"But it's not because it doesn't interest you," Bear pushed. "What do you fear?"

"She said no." Rebel shot a death glare at Bear. One that said he was a second from following with fists.

Hands up, Bear tried to look contrite. It didn't work. "I heard her, just curious. You know I like secrets." His suggestive tone had Rebel out of his seat.

I put a hand on Rebel. "Please, it's okay." Rebel glanced from me to Bear before he sat down.

I leaned over to whisper in Rebel's ear. "The idea excites me, but it isn't a good business move."

His lips closed on mine and the heat of his kiss burned deep inside me. I loved the fire and wished I'd be destroyed by his flame.

"What'd you say?" I heard Bear repeat himself when Rebel broke our kiss.

I flashed him a grin. "Only Rebel can tell you that."

"And that's never happening."

Rebel and the others laughed at the hang dog expression Bear wore like a costume. I'd never seen him show a single thought before now.

After another couple of hours, we left the party, gathering, I didn't know what to call it. Today had a family vibe that hadn't been part of the party I'd attended. The more I was around the Brotherhood the less I understood about them, and the more I wished I belonged. Maybe I didn't want to be part of the club, but I longed for the uncompromising acceptance. I had no one who cared for me the way those guys did for each other. My dad had been my only family but we weren't a family anymore and I doubted we ever would be again.

The people at Jackson Bonds might hate me after the way my family drama played out. I feared Tuesday, more fear built in me each hour that passed until I wanted to run the other way. Not that I would ever indulge my fears. Jacksons made our own luck. Jacksons kept our promises. Jacksons embraced our fears. I was a Jackson.

Chapter Twenty-Five

Elle

"Yeah," I murmured in my dream. Lights shone down us, cameras followed our movements. Rebel kissed my mound and I arched up.

"That's it, baby." Then his mouth found my most sensitive spot, again. I blinked open my eyes when an intense burst of pleasure shot through me. I wasn't dreaming.

Rebel's rust-colored head rested between my thighs. I grasped his hair when he sent another spike of feeling through me. "Inside me, please." I needed him atop me, close to me, consuming me one last time before I left.

He flicked his tongue over my nub and the orgasm crashed through me, leaving me breathless and wanting more. I needed all of him, not these tantalizing bits he doled out.

I leaned up and clasped his shoulders, he glanced up and his wild eyes danced with ecstasy. When I tugged, he crept up my body, rubbing against me with a delicious friction I devoured. His lips skimmed my torso, across my breast and locked on my neck.

So close, the heat from his skin created prickles of

sensation up and down my body. We moved against each other consumed with each touch and breath we shared. Tension built between us, inside me, until I couldn't hold another drop, but still he tormented and teased. My body writhed and the pleasure leaked from me in small noises and panting breaths until I had no idea where he ended and I began.

Then he was gone and my body plunged into frigid cold without him heating me inside and out. "I need you." I reached for him.

He slid a condom on before crashing into me. I swear when our bodies connected, when he entered me, our souls collided. Hungry, without limits, we destroyed any boundaries between us to become one—together in every sense. Heart beating as one, pulse pounding in rhythm, we fell over together into a climax so powerful we shattered into a bliss infinite and carnal.

Lying destroyed under Rebel, fear was the first emotion to inch through my elation. Sadness shattered the bubble but it couldn't steal the bone-melting ease of all my nerve endings singing in joy. I held him to me, kissing his cheek. Gratitude erased all my other emotions. Without him, I'd never have known even a brief glimpse of nirvana. I hoped he'd experienced at least some of what I had, selfish though it was to hope it, I'll admit to being selfish where he's concerned.

With a tender kiss he moved away from me to do the necessary stuff in the bathroom. I used those few seconds to bury the feelings his lovemaking had breathed to life. My blossoming love had become a force to be reckoned with, one I'd battle on my own once I was safe at home.

When he walked toward the bed, a softness made his

face younger, his smile lighter, and his eyes...those were dangerous, swirling with a storm of emotion. Emotions I had no experience to read or any key to detect what any of this meant to him, to me, to us.

He lay in bed beside me, rolled onto his side, his fingers finding mischief up and down my sensitive flesh. We cuddled together, neither wanting to break the moment. I had no words I could say.

No one's ever made love to me before.

I love you.

You captured part of my soul.

None of those words were my friends.

That was great.

You're a stud.

You broke me.

Too little, too late. No way could a clever deflection mask the moment.

I took comfort in his silence because maybe that meant words failed him too.

My phone alarm rang, interrupting the soft kisses he scattered across my cheek. I turned into him and kissed him as if he were my everything, giving up all the churning emotion I couldn't release any other way.

Breaking the kiss, I rolled out of bed without a word and headed to the shower. Some might call me a coward, and in some ways I was, in others I was brave enough not to diminish the moment with callous comments.

The hot water beat down on me and with the water, I suppressed my feelings until they were a manageable size, one I could hide and take out later to explore. Body clean, mind balanced, I quickly dried off. When I returned to the bedroom, Harley greeted me. Rebel was downstairs in the kitchen, it sounded like he was making breakfast.

"Hey, lover, you going to miss me?"

Harley purred and brushed my legs. I dressed quickly then picked up the huge tomcat for some ear scratches, his favorite pleasure.

"You be nice to him. And I'll bring you treats next time I come up." I scratched under his chin before setting him back down. He scurried out of the room. I picked up my duffel bag and purse before I headed downstairs. When I hit the stairs, the aroma of bacon and coffee hit me, something Harley had smelled long before me.

In the kitchen, Rebel stood barefoot in jeans at the stove. His Jericho Brotherhood tattoo flexed with his muscles, a truly delicious sight.

"Hey, sexy." I hugged him from behind.

"Grab the plates, baby, I've got breakfast ready."

I set plates on the table then poured a cup of coffee. "You need coffee?" I noticed Harley in the corner with his own bacon strip. Rebel was a pushover for his cat.

"Got some." He brought over a bowl of scrambled eggs and plate of bacon. The eggs were more than just scrambled though, with cheese, peppers and more mixed into them. I'd miss his cooking too.

"You nervous about today?" He scooped up a huge serving of eggs and picked up a few slices of bacon.

"Nope." He'd fucked the nervousness out of me— and then some. "It'll work out or they'll work somewhere else."

"Good girl." He grinned at me.

I tucked into breakfast. "God, these eggs are almost as sinful as you."

He gave me his lopsided grin. "You just want me for my cooking skills."

"Definitely like all your skills." I brushed his hand with mine.

"I'm good, a fucking genius."

I burst out laughing at the cocky expression he delivered with his over-the-top praise.

"How can you say that shit with a straight face?"

"Because it's true." He met my gaze a moment then looked away.

Was that regret I saw? More likely me looking for what I felt.

It was already a quarter to seven, time to go. I finished my last bite of eggs and carried my plate to the sink. When I turned around Rebel had my bag and was moving toward the door. I grabbed my purse and caught up.

He put the bag in back then turned to me. "Be safe, text me or call me tonight, I want to know how today goes."

I opened my mouth to respond but his kiss stole my words. Brutal, breathtaking and beyond description, he stole more than my words with no effort.

"Baby, I'm coming your way as soon as I get a free minute."

Dazed I stared up at him. "I have no words for what you do to me."

"Just the way I like it. See ya soon." He disappeared inside the house before I even turned the truck on. I was halfway out of town before I realized I'd never said goodbye or asked about the divorce papers.

At ten on the dot, I walked into the overflowing conference room of Jackson Bonds ready to face my third hurdle of the morning. My first hurdle had been ordering my dad's furniture stored and his office redecorated. I'd wanted to push that one off, but Alice, my assistant, insisted it'd be better this way. My second hurdle came in the way of Chaz Carter in my office at nine. He'd wanted to make sure there were no hard feelings, and I sent him packing in under ten minutes but he left his slimy presence behind.

I stared at the people who'd worked for us for months to decades, too many emotions were reflected in the faces of my employees. I spotted the three I expected, grateful there weren't more who hated the idea of working for a woman. I seriously doubted any of the three would be working for me by the end of the month. I could win over almost anyone, but hating me because I'm a woman, I couldn't fix that and wouldn't tolerate disrespect.

"It was The Who that said 'Welcome the new boss same as the old boss' in 'Won't Get Fooled Again.'"

A few grins met my opening statement.

"A Jackson has run this company for a hundred and fifty years, a new Jackson owning the business won't change much."

"The others weren't women" I heard from my left.

I'd been looking right so I didn't know who said it, but it didn't matter.

"That's one of two changes you will come to accept working for me." I stared Johnny Leander in the eye because I was 99.9 percent sure he was the one who'd made the crack. "I am a woman. You now work for a woman. If that doesn't agree with you, there's the door." I pointed to the door of the conference room. "You can leave or I can fire you." I waited three beats before I spoke again. "Because you will respect me if you work for me.

"You know me, in fact have known me for years, so you should understand what kind of person I am. The no-bullshit kind."

A few chuckles sounded in the room.

"If you have no problem working for a woman then you and I are off to a solid start." I let my words sink in and readied myself for the second announcement. "Second change, I plan to expand Jackson Bonds as soon as it is financially feasible by acquiring other bail bonds agencies. It's the way to grow today."

Shuffling and grumbles met my words. It wasn't a favorite concept among long-time bail enforcement agents. They were territorial and didn't like working with people they'd considered competition.

"Short and sweet. Now I'll take your questions."

"Where's your husband?" Mel, another of the misogynists, spouted off.

"My husband has no interest, legal or otherwise, in this business." I wouldn't have a husband by the end of the week, if my marriage lasted that long. "You work for me."

"Why did your daddy up and leave so fast?" Loretta, one of our best skip-tracers, asked.

"You'd have to ask him. You all know he and I hadn't seen eye-to-eye in a while. When he sent me the note telling me of his early retirement, he didn't give me a reason or invite me to come before today." He hadn't said not to come either, but I couldn't see any way a few hours together could mend what was broken between us.

"You selling out to Chaz Carter?" I didn't catch who let the question fly, but I was glad he had.

"Jackson Bonds will never be for sale. We may merge, change our business model, but our name is our bond. I'd rather eat my boots than sell out to anyone."

After the meeting, the rest of the day sped past as I reviewed paperwork, requested financial reports, and debated how to structure the company. There'd always been a pecking order, and I needed to decide soon how I should change it. Right now Mel Tyler was third in command and he hated my ownership with every fiber of his being. I needed to restructure to decrease his influence on the business or I had to fire him.

I made it home to my townhouse by seven, after stopping for Mexican carryout on the way home. I flipped on lights, dropped the food off in the kitchen and my duffel bag in the laundry room. The place didn't feel lived in, like it had changed while I was gone. Ridiculous. If anyone had changed, it was me. I no longer wanted to come home alone to my empty place, eat takeout and work until I was too tired to keep my eyes open.

He'd changed me. Reset my expectations.

"Time to reset again," I said aloud in my too quiet kitchen. Maybe I should get a cat, like Harley.

Dammit, my mind was going nowhere good. I flipped on the radio in my living room before I carried the takeout to my home office. The room smelled like Rebel, then I remembered he'd worked in here last week. Fine. My nose would quit smelling the sexy scent soon enough.

I ate tacos while I flipped through Mel's employee file. He was my first big decision and I wanted to make the right decision.

My phone buzzed. How was the first day, boss?

A sappy grin spread across my face at Rebel's text. Good enough. Now I have to decide if I'm going to fire one of my employees. I hit send.

My phone rang. Rebel's sexy face appeared on my call screen.

"Hey, sexy, what are you doing?"

"Lousy paperwork before I head out on club business," he grumbled. "What's with the guy you're firing?"

"It's nothing." I didn't need to bore him with more of my problems.

"It's something. Tell me."

"Mel Tyler, third in charge at the company now, and he believes women are best seen not heard and best not working with him. He won't accept me as boss." I laid it out there. Daddy and I used to talk through problems like this.

"He done anything yet?"

"Not yet." I wished he had. "If he had, then it'd be a simple decision, but it's more insidious. Do I let him undermine me, he's done it before but he backed off when Daddy threatened to fire him, or do I prevent the damage."

"Is he good at his job?" Rebel's voice stayed neutral, no hint of what he was thinking in his voice.

"Not so much, especially in the last two years, he's let a lot slide. And he's a good fifteen years away from retiring." I flipped through his file. His evaluations were mediocre and his bonding was haphazard. "I feel like I'm trying to read tea leaves."

"Then don't." He spoke with a sharp edge to his words. "I cut a prospect from the club today. Sloppy work."

"Dan?"

Rebel chuckled. "Yup, see you spotted it too. I gave him three tries and he fucked up the contract I sent him out for, last strike. And I don't feel bad, not a bit. I have to have people I trust at my back."

"I need to know if I can trust him." I talked to myself more than Rebel. Then it hit me. I didn't need to spend hours analyzing his file. I needed him alone with me in my office. "An hour together should tell me that."

"Exactly. You're a damn smart boss." I liked that he didn't say woman. I don't know why, but it made a difference to me.

The next morning I had Alice catch Mel right after he'd arrived. I wanted to check him off my to-do list and I didn't want him to have time to get comfortable.

He showed up at my door an hour after he arrived, not immediately. The first strike, but I'd keep an open mind.

"I'm busy, let's reschedule this for next week." He stood at the entrance to my door, but hadn't entered my office, yet.

"No, we'll do this now. Come in, close the door." I didn't stand or offer any other comfort. He needed to understand who was boss.

"Power already going to your head."

"Excuse me?"

"You heard me, force out Jack, then come riding down on the rest of us." His face contorted into a nasty sneer. He stood at my desk leering down at me a long moment before he sat down.

"See, Mel, that's why you're here today. You and I

have had problems in the past because you didn't like working for a woman."

"You were never my boss, Jack was." Flecks of spittle flew from his mouth.

"I am your boss now." I spoke clearly and without any of the anger Mel exhibited. "Say it."

He stared at me. "You own the company."

"You report to me." I leaned forward with a smile, not a friendly smile, but a let-me-show-you-my-teeth predator smile.

"I quit." He stood up, hands balled into fists. "I'm not working for a fucking cunt."

I stood. "I'm glad we understand each other. Clear your desk, security will meet you there and escort you from the building."

His face turned almost purple it was so red and he opened and closed his mouth.

"You want to do something stupid, Mel?" I moved to the side of my desk, ready if he attacked.

He battled with himself another second before he stomped out of my office.

I buzzed Alice. "Security—"

"Out here and escorting him as we speak." She sounded damn happy to see Mel gone.

"Right. Good then. Have payroll pay him a month's severance," I told her. Mel had worked for us for fifteen years so he deserved that much respect, but no more.

I sat down and let the adrenaline from the confrontation ease away. Satisfaction replaced the hyped-up awareness. I was a damn good boss.

Chapter Twenty-Six

Rebel

I was pussy whipped and had no idea how to cure it. Seven days and a handful of hours without seeing Elle and I was close to breaking. Between the bail bonds crap and now the Angels operation, I had barely slept and had no time to spend in bed with Elle.

"Boss." Trisha barged into my office. "Got a call for bonding in Dallas, who do I send?"

"Fuck me, am I the only one who can fucking make a decision?" I yelled at my assistant.

Color drained from her face. "JoJo said you made the call about Dallas, for now." She glanced at her feet.

The fucking Angels of Death, I wished this shit was over and done with instead of just beginning. "Dammit, I'm sorry I yelled, Trish, JoJo is right, I make that call." I slumped back in my seat. "Who's here?"

"Lyle and the new kid, Heath." She bit her lip.

"Give me five minutes, then send Lyle to me. I'll have him go down but I have some special instructions." I met her gaze. "We good?"

"Yeah, we're good." She gave me a ghost of a grin.

I called Ringer. "What do you need?"

"Some muscle to go with my prospect to bond a guy out in Dallas." I wished I could do it and see Elle while I was at it. But we had an operations meeting in two hours then it was my night to ride lead on the Angels hunt.

"Got it, I'll send Blast over to meet him at your shop. Be best if they didn't ride bikes down." He had brought in almost half of his guys for this operation. Some for patrol, but more for protection.

"Thanks, I'll let Lyle know. See you in a bit." I hung up right as Lyle walked into my office.

"Close the door," I told him. "You up-to-date on the Angels situation?"

"Zero told all of us." He swallowed hard.

"Good. A brother, Blast, I don't know him, is heading over here and he'll ride shotgun with you to do the bond in Dallas. Don't take bikes."

"Can I use him to pick up a contract while we're down there?" Lyle asked.

"Sure, just be home before dark, if you can."

"Got it." The kid stood up. "How's Elle doing?"

"Kicking ass and taking names, I just wish one of those names was mine."

He laughed and headed out of the office.

I finished paperwork and stopped by to have Heath move to the second desk out front. It was unlikely an Angel would make it this far into our territory, but I wanted to be sure Trisha was protected. So far we hadn't found any of the trash north of Dallas, but Charlie told me to expect that to change today.

I grabbed my sidearm from my saddle bag and stuck it in my waist band. I wasn't paranoid, but I was cautious. The ride to the clubhouse did nothing to ease my mind, which was unusual. Twenty minutes on my bike normally cleared my head, but nothing worked lately. I wished it was the situation with the Angels that had me jacked up, but it wasn't.

Elle had worked down deep in me and I should just be done with her, done with the temptation, done with pretending I could keep her. Maybe by the time we'd finished with the Angels, I'd be ready to fix my Elle issue. A swift pain swept through my middle, I'd had knife wounds that hurt less. Every time I thought of letting her go, the pain hit hard, stealing my breath and my resolve.

Fuck me, I was so screwed. Wound tight about a woman I couldn't keep, yet all I could think about was sinking into her, loving her the way we'd made love the last time. It was the last morning with her that had changed me. We'd been in deep waters before, but the way she surrendered to me that morning had thrown me into a whirlpool, one I couldn't break free from, worse, I didn't even want to try.

I parked my bike next to Jericho's in the clubhouse lot and just sat there a minute, clearing my mind of all the bullshit I didn't have the time or ability to fix now, or ever. I strode through the wooden front door into the heart of my brotherhood. This was home, now and forever.

Jericho and Dare sat on the stage, I headed over to join them. A few of the guys already sat at the mismatched tables, even though we had a half hour before the meeting started.

"You good?" Jericho asked when I sat next to him.

"Yeah, I have the map broken out into zones. Zero is bringing the copies and the assignments. He had some of his prospects do the grunt work." I considered grabbing a bottle of beer, or maybe whiskey, but I needed all my wits tonight.

"How's your woman?" Dare glanced over at me.

"Haven't seen her in days, says she's good." I shrugged.

The two eyed me. "You have eyes on her?"

Cold dread ran down my spine. Fuck me, I hadn't even considered Elle might be in danger. "I'll take care of it."

I sent a text to Ringer. Need protection on Elle, send someone her way.

He responded a few seconds later. Send me the deets, I'll send someone tonight.

After I sent him her work and home address, I sent Elle a text. She'd spot the guy and I didn't want her giving him grief.

We have some tension with another club, sending a guy to shadow you, in case. I reviewed the text and knew I was in for a bunch of questions I wouldn't be able to answer.

My phone pinged. Be safe. What club?

You can figure that out. We don't talk about club business. I'm always safe.

So that's why my vibrator is getting a workout. Well that and those videos. Her response sent all my blood straight to my hard-on, the last thing I needed now.

Damn, woman, that's just mean. Miss you too. Gotta go to a meeting. My thumbs hovered over the keyboard. I hit send even if I should have deleted most of that message. I dropped my phone in the pocket of my cut and tried to forget about Elle and her messages.

The tables by the stage filled up. Zero strutted in

with the papers under his arm. I gave him the nod and he started handing out zone maps and getting the guys organized together. Once most of the shuffling was done, I stood up. "Alright, now let's go over our plan." The guys quieted. "I've made more specific assignments, and highlighted a few of the spots you may want to stop and check out tonight. We have guys in a lot of those spots now, and have had the day shift watching the major routes out of Dallas." Most of the guys who volunteered were members but a few prospects were sprinkled in every night.

"We have intel that says tonight we should start seeing the rats flee, if you catch a rat, call for cleanup. We have prospects ready to drive out and pick up. They'll take them to the drop-off site. And our job is done. We ride from seven to seven, when the next shift takes over. You got questions?"

"What if there's a group of them?" Delta asked.

"Call it in, we'll bring a crew, you and your partner just watch and wait." I glanced from him around the room. "I don't want any of us hurt, so play it safe."

The rumbling from the guys at the tables said they weren't a fan of safe. "Not like my granny safe, but no stupid moves, these guys are on the run and scared, that makes sensible a thing of the past. They are dead men riding."

Quiet filled the room. "They want what's ours, so we're going to round them up. They took what the Bandits owned, so they'll deal with them."

Nods met my words. This wasn't pretend, and I didn't want anyone on this ride who didn't understand the consequences. "I won't be on a bike tonight, I'll be in one of the pickup vehicles, call me if you need anything, and stay with your partner, always."

Jericho stood up. "Let's get this settled and move on. Got me?"

Again nods, no one had a doubt this was club business. We'd gone twenty years without a club war—our first and only had been with a club up north who thought the fledging Brotherhood would be easy prey. We'd proved them wrong; tonight, we'd be sure the Angels of Death were taught the same lesson.

West drove and I monitored my phone, getting updates from each pair on the hour. Delta and Zero reported the first spotting at nine. Two Angels sped up I-35 by Gainesville. I called in two other trucks and we merged on to I-35 about five minutes ahead of the bikers. Forcing the Angels off the road was more dangerous than finding them stopped but we'd make it work.

"West, we're the side car, got the drill?"

West nodded, I climbed over the seat to get in the back where I could point my shotgun right at the guys. The bikers came up on us, the lead truck slowed and Thorn settled in beside them. Wise to our move, the bikers drove off road, slowing their bikes enough to hop off the back and they started running cross country, firing behind them.

"Off road," I told the others while West headed the SUV toward them, we caught up in seconds, but stayed far enough back their wild shots wouldn't hit. Thorn took his 4x4 around and cut off their path.

"Drop the guns," I shouted out.

Eyes wide with fright they turned to fire again but both guns were empty. The one gun had been clicking for the last four rounds, but now they were both out.

Easier that way, I hadn't wanted to shoot them, even if it was only to wound them.

I hopped out and ran forward, punching the first guy, knocking him down, the second guy turned to run and Thorn knocked him out before he made it three steps. I restrained both their hands and feet with disposable cuffs before Thorn and I carried each of them to the SUV.

"North of here about half a mile is a dirt road, looks like the best exit plan." West pointed it out on the GPS.

"I'll return to the original location." Thorn gave me a two-finger salute and returned to his Jeep.

"Let's go to the dumping ground." I climbed in the passenger seat. West had already raised the window between the front and back.

"You good?" I asked him.

"Good." He glanced over at me. "Why wouldn't I be?"

"No reason." We rode in silence a few minutes. "You believe that shit JoJo told you?" I still had no clue what he had said.

West grinned wide. "Not after the first few days. Lyle believed longer, until a couple weeks ago, I think."

"Good then." I wasn't admitting to the fact I didn't know what JoJo spouted off.

"I mean you don't even have a dungeon at Bound, I checked." His grin spread wider. "So surely you don't get off on whipping prospects who disobey you."

Fuck me. He'd told them a half-truth.

"Get it straight." I glanced over at the kid, trying to look tough at the ripe age of 21. I remembered those days. "I don't enjoy it, but I have done it and would again if I had to."

The kid gulped. "No shit?"

"I ran Bound and I'm a Master. Fuck yeah I whipped the Bound prospects who screwed up." He hated remembering those sessions, not because of the discipline but because of the Old Man. "It was Jericho's father, the guy who doesn't run the club anymore, who enjoyed watching."

"Fuck me." He whispered the words. We rode in silence a bit longer. "You didn't do that to Dan."

"Dan wasn't meant to wear the cut, so I wouldn't waste my time on him. Besides, you fuck up now, Zero takes it out of your hide first. Or both of us." Prospects didn't need to think we were easy.

"Got it, don't fuck up." West nodded as he spoke.

"You're a good biker, decent bounty hunter, shitty bonder. You have nothing to worry about." I clasped his shoulder and he jumped.

"So work on the bonding, then." He glanced at me.

"You've been with me about four months now, you like the work? Or would you rather be working with the operations guys."

"I'm not military, and I like working with you." He glanced over at me.

"Then quit believing all the sob stories," I told him.

"I caught all my skips." He jutted out his chin.

"Which is why you haven't met my fist." I grinned and sat back in the seat.

On the way to the drop spot, two more Angels were picked up at a dive bar east of Gainesville, so far we were keeping them out of our territory. I liked that.

We arrived at the abandoned church south of Gainesville on a country road. "I'll take them in."

"I got one." He climbed out of the truck.

We dragged the babbling guys into the church and set them down on the rotting wood floor.

"You can't do this, they're going to kill us," the skinny one pleaded.

"And you made a deal to make meth in my backyard." I stared down at him.

His brother spit toward me but I just walked away. I texted Charlie. Two for pickup. Two more in forty minutes. Will text to confirm that delivery.

Headlights flashed further down the road. West turned the other direction and we drove away. Once we were on the highway again, my nerves settled down. I didn't like being on the same road with the Bandit death crew.

"Does it bother you?" I asked West. This was the hardest part of being a brother. He'd volunteered for the work, but it didn't mean it set well with him.

"Not even a little." His hands were relaxed on the wheel, and he showed no sign he was tight about it. "You fuck with us, you pay the price. Way I see it, this is the simpler solution."

He was right. Our two clubs were similar in size and a straight up war with the Angels over territory would be nasty—some brothers dead and others in jail. We wouldn't be able to stay on the right side of the law and deal with them. Charlie was a great friend and a better businessman.

When our shift ended at seven, we had captured nine Angels. A few fist fights but no gunshot wounds on either side. I wasn't sure we'd make it to the end of the fight with a clean record, but I hoped so.

I had West drop me at the clubhouse before he headed back to Ardmore to his place. I needed to update Jericho and crew then I planned to crash here. I was too fucking tired to drive anywhere.

My phone buzzed. By our count 12 are out there.

I sucked in a breath and ignored the icy fingers of panic. The Angels had 66 members and another 17 prospects. We'd captured nine, the Bandits had eliminated more than 60 Angels without any help from us. I texted him back. Got it. Still patrolling.

The Prez and an enforcer are still out there.

Passing it along. I texted as I headed into the Council chamber for the debriefing.

I sat down and yawned wide. I hadn't slept ten hours combined in the last three days, and now it was catching up with me.

Jericho, Ringer, Dare, Thorn and Zero sat in the Council chambers. Zero looked damn uneasy sitting in his chair, but he'd get comfortable because he had leader tattooed on his fucking forehead.

"What do you know?" Jericho growled.

"71 Angels of Death went down last night, intel says there are 12 remaining, including their Prez and a top enforcer. Now they know we're part of this, so we need to be on our toes."

"Fuck me," Zero said what we all thought.

"We will stay alert on protection details and keep up the zones. Worked great last night." Ringer nodded to me.

"Watch our women, and all roads into Ardmore and Barden?" Dare confirmed.

"Yup, unless we find a bigger threat. Whoever we don't catch today likely won't be moving for a few days, but we need to keep up the pressure." Thorn's deep voice boomed in the quiet room.

"If it were me, I'd bring together as many guys as I could and hole up in Dallas a few days, make a plan," Ringer said.

"If it were me, I'd never piss off the Bandits." Jericho grinned. "Anything else?"

We broke up the meeting and I started for a room. "Rebel," Jericho called after me. He walked over to me. "You good?"

"Yeah, got this." I met his gaze.

"You're doing better than got this." He slapped my back. "Now go get some sleep."

I picked the first open room and crashed on the bed. I toed off my boots and climbed under the covers. Elle's bright blue eyes were my last thought.

Chapter Twenty-Seven

Elle

Five days with my shadow and twelve days since I'd touched Rebel. Our relationship was over. He hadn't signed the divorce papers yet, but that was a technicality. Twelve days of over, but I'd only realized it last night lying alone in my bed. If he'd wanted me, he would've found a way to see me. I'd volunteered to come to him last weekend, but he'd been too busy. Everyone slept and I came with my own shadow for protection, so he was making excuses. Time to let him go, like I'd promised.

A tear slipped out, I wiped it away. I had shed enough tears into my pillow in the wee hours of last night. Today I needed to be on my game, figure out my expansion plan, and move on with my damn life.

Once I was in my office, I texted Gator, who thought up biker names anyway, that I was in my office until lunch time. When I'd brought him a big mug of coffee the first morning, he'd given me a toothy grin. We'd exchanged phone numbers and now we were texting buddies—he knew my schedule better than me. Of course that might be because I'd given him access to my calendar after the first time I'd left without him, forgetting about him actually. I'd say we were friends except he refused all my offers to share takeout or to come inside while he watched over me in the evening. He just said no, no negotiation.

Putting bikers and their stupid rules out of my mind, I went over the numbers from Finance again, even though I'd already admitted defeat, for now. Daddy had been right, we didn't have the cash flow to acquire any of our competitors, at least not the caliber I wanted. Unlike Daddy, I'd sent Chet, my numbers guru, back to his office with the task of figuring out how much revenue we needed to generate to be able to fund my expansion plan.

Alice buzzed the intercom. "There's a biker at front reception, wanting to work out a bond for someone. He asked for you."

Was Rebel or one of his guys in trouble? I hurried out the door and past Alice. "Wait. Should I call security?" She gave me a worried frown.

I slowed and the Angels flitted through my mind, but my shadow wouldn't let them in the building. "Have them on standby."

I moved down the back steps and came out the side door beside reception. The biker's back was to me, he wore an Angels of Death vest, or cut as Rebel called it. Shit. I hadn't brought my gun. I stepped forward, my boots clicking on the tile floor. He turned to me, pulling something from under his vest.

Time slowed.

I spotted the gun handle when he moved his hand. No one brought a gun to my company, threatened my employees.

I spun on my heel and kicked up, hitting him in the

wrist with the side of my boot. The gun clattered on the floor.

He lunged forward—Spike, Enforcer—I read the words on the leather vest.

I dodged to the side but his glancing blow sent me staggering back, he'd have broken my jaw, or my whole face, if he'd connected better. Kicking out I struck his knee, spun and kicked up hitting him under the chin, sending his teeth together in a jarring snap. He wavered leaning forward before he fell back, his body thumping against the floor.

"Don't move," my security guards shouted, guns pointing at him.

He was out cold, either from the kick or the hit to his head when he fell back, probably both.

The receptionist held the phone in her hand, frozen.

"Put down the phone," I told her. "We don't need the police."

She frowned but did what I told her.

"Restrain him. You have cuffs?" I asked Jed, the senior security guard.

He nodded and bent to cuff the bastard. I grabbed my phone and punched Gator's number.

"Yeah, darling?" He had a Southern drawl that wasn't Texan.

"I have an Angel here," I told him.

"Fuck, fuck, I'm there." He ran in the front doors seconds later, phone still held in his hand.

He glanced from me to the guy out cold on the floor. "You do that?" Then he narrowed his eyes and moved in closer. "The motherfucker clocked you?" Anger heated his face.

"Glancing blow, he'd have smashed my face to bits if he'd clocked me."

"We need to call the police." Larry, the younger security guard, glanced nervously at Gator.

Gator gave a single shake of his head.

"No, we don't. You two." I pointed to Larry and Janet, our receptionist. "Go upstairs and take a break. I'm locking our front door, for now. No police, hear me?"

Both nodded.

"Jed could you give me a minute."

He nodded and walked into the back hall.

"What do you need?" I suspected he needed to take the guy.

"Don't know the details." He ran a hand over his shaven head. "No police and we need him out of here. Can we take him to your truck?"

"Can you carry him?" I glanced at Gator. "Here are my keys, I'll follow in a minute."

He stared at me as if he wanted to ask questions, but he just nodded. He lifted the still unconscious Spike in a fireman's carry and I led him to the back door.

Jeb stepped up beside me, worry creasing his lined face.

"Please take care of the cameras then get someone else to cover up front for a while." I clasped his arm.

He'd worked for us over twenty years and Daddy had dealt with more than a couple hot heads off the books. "You got it, Ellie, just like your daddy." He left for the security offices.

I walked up to the truck and heard Gator talking on his phone.

"She was tucked inside, I went for a piss break."

Then silence.

"She knocked him out, and he had a gun."

Then silence again.

"Got it. Sorry, brother, I had no idea he'd walk into the fucking business." Head hanging low he hung up. "I will take you home, and if it's okay, I'll borrow your truck for a bit."

"That's the plan, then." My face pounded with pain and my headache was building fast.

Gator got behind the wheel and I let him. Alternate endings played through my brain. I didn't want to think of other scenarios where I didn't kick the gun out of his hand. I'd acted on instinct and training, now that it was over, my body had the jittery let down of an adrenaline overload.

"How'd you take him out?" Gator glanced at me.

"Karate, I'm a black belt, let's just say I'm badass." I tried to make him feel better.

"Good thing, because I fucked up." He wore his guilt plain for me to see.

"You're one guy, you did your job and things went sideways. Can't be the first time?" I grinned over at him. "Last time things went sideways for me, Rebel came running, shooting his gun at the guy choking me out."

"Yeah?" A hint of a smile showed on his face.

"Yeah, and he didn't even know me then. It's how we met." I chuckled, and tried not to replay the conversation in the diner that day. I had wanted him, even then.

Gator pulled into my driveway and I pressed the button for my garage door. "Leave the keys in the mailbox, I may be asleep. See ya later, Ali-Gator."

He flipped me the bird.

Inside, I went straight to the freezer for a pack of ice-cold peas then I hit the cabinet for some pain relievers. With the peas pressed to my face I checked the front door to be sure I'd locked it before I headed upstairs.

I changed into one of Rebel's T-shirts before I slipped under the covers and fell asleep.

I woke with a start, the low light said I'd slept away most of the day. Then I heard footsteps on the stairs. I eased open my nightstand and drew out my bedroom gun, small caliber but it'd put a hole in someone.

When footsteps continued toward me, I moved to the side of the door where whoever came through wouldn't see me.

Gun aimed, I held my breath. Rust-colored hair registered first. Exhaling, I lowered my gun. "Goddammit, Rebel, I could have shot you."

His wild eyes met mine, he took me in and smiled wide. "I see you're feeling better." He took the gun from my hand and set it on the dresser. "You worried me." He stalked back to me.

I opened my mouth to yell some more when his lips crashed into mine. Hot, furious and full of need. He clasped my wrists above me as he ravaged my mouth. I wanted to touch him, to rub my hands all over him, but the bastard wouldn't let me go. I pushed my body into his, sucked his lip into my mouth and bit down. He groaned before he picked me up and carried me to my bed.

Dropping me onto my bed, he stripped, but his eyes never left me. I started to take my shirt off.

"That's mine. I'll do it," he barked.

I'd never seen him like this and I didn't know what

had created the beast before me. But I knew he was more animal than man right now.

Naked, he prowled forward until he straddled me in bed. Intensity radiating off him, he jerked off my shirt before sliding my panties off me.

Then he just stared down at me. Chiseled perfection all the way down to his rock-hard cock, there wasn't an ounce of softness in him right now. He excited me, I wanted him to take me, to own me.

"You're mine. Understand me."

I nodded.

"Say it."

"I'm yours."

Satisfaction, raw and unchecked, settled into his expression. He kneaded my breasts with strong hands that promised pleasure and a little pain. I arched into his touch.

"He bruised you. Hurt you."

"I kicked his ass."

His nostrils flared but he didn't speak. He reached over and grabbed a condom from the nightstand drawer. "Put it on."

I caressed his cock as I rolled the condom over him. His eyes fluttered closed when I cupped his sac. Then he moved down me, a single finger slid through my seam before he plunged deep until I held all of him inside me.

Holding himself up with his arms, he thrust into me, hard and deep every time. "Mine."

I reached up to his shoulders, digging my fingers into him, needing to feel him with every part of me.

He shuddered and drew closer to me, moving faster and faster inside me. "Come now," he commanded me.

My body, already amped up from his possession, lit up at his words. I was on the edge, so close, but I wasn't giving up that easily. He'd have to force my orgasm from me.

Chapter Twenty-Eight

Rebel

I stared into her blue eyes and lost myself completely. She'd been hurt because of me but she was the only thing that could stop the panic digging out my insides.

Seeing her, knowing she was safe. Feeling her, knowing she was mine.

Twelve days since I'd tasted her and I never wanted to stop, but my body had other ideas. Each stroke tightened my body, priming me for the release I tried to hold at bay.

"I said come."

"Make me." Challenge sparked in her mesmerizing eyes. She pulled me under, I had no choice but to surrender. I dipped to her sweet mouth, lips swollen from my kisses, and claimed her. I showed her my need in that kiss, the desperate need that had churned in me for days, then turned into this primal force driving me now.

She quivered and moaned into our kiss and she squeezed me tight when she climaxed. I drove hard, needing her to know I owned her body and soul. I could have lost her today, but I hadn't. She was alive and quaking under me. Her mouth slid past my lips and she bit my neck. I lost the last thread of control, coming hard with her name on my lips. Her body under me but she owned me, body and soul.

"I missed you, Rebel," she sighed before her eyes fluttered close. Asleep again.

She'd almost died because of me. I moved away long enough to dispose of the condom before I crawled back in bed with her. I drew her into my arms and held her. While the danger wasn't eliminated yet, it was almost over. Tonight I'd protect her while she slept, but tomorrow I'd have to finish business.

Elle woke me, trying to slide out from under my arm. I opened one eye and watched her ease her way out from me. When she'd almost made it, I pulled her back to me. "Where do you think you're going?"

In the bright morning sun, her left cheek had turned blue mottled with purple. White-hot rage burned through me again.

"I need to get ready for work." She turned to face me.

"No you don't. I told your assistant yesterday that you were home safe and would be taking off today."

"You did what?"

"You heard me." Damn, I'd slept better last night than I had in days.

A slow, sexy grin spread across her face. "Are you spending the day in bed with me?"

Fuck. I couldn't do that. I had to end this shit so she'd be safe. I sighed.

"Don't bother." She threw my arm off her. "You don't need to make up excuses."

She stormed across the room to her dresser and pulled on shorts and a T-shirt. "Go. The sex was great.

See ya next time." She didn't even look at me as she threw daggers into me.

"What the fuck?" I sat up in bed, not sure when I'd lost the thread of our conversation.

"Nothing." She left the room before I'd made it out of bed. I threw on my clothes and hurried downstairs after her.

"What's up with you?" I stopped midway across her kitchen.

Pain and sadness riddled her face.

Like a punch to the gut, pain radiated in me. Had I caused that pain?

She turned away from me. "Nothing, you have stuff to do and I apparently don't."

I crossed to her. "Elle, what's this about?"

"Look, no harm no foul. It's just a sex thing." Dead eyes stared up at me.

"You're mine. This is more than a sex thing." No way she was evading me.

"When...when did we make that deal?" Anger turned her eyes icy. "We made the marriage deal, but you didn't divorce me."

"The Angels, it isn't safe for me—"

"We made the sex deal, but that's off now." Her words were clipped and short, dagger thrusts. "I think what we got is a guilt thing."

I stepped back. How had she come up with that?

"We were done, I get that."

I was far from done with her.

"Then, I get hurt, you feel guilty. But really, I don't need you to save me anymore." Her eyes bore into me. "You can be done with me and that's fine."

"That's not fine. I'm not done with you." I threw my

own daggers. She'd tied me in knots for days and now she dismissed me. Not hardly.

"Why? Do you love me? Do you want to spend forever with me?"

I did. I couldn't. Fuck. I turned away from her.

"Say something."

What was there to say? Nothing. It had to end, better now than later. "I care for you." Hollow words, not the ones she deserved.

"Ha." She marched up to me, getting right in my face. "I've known Gator a handful of days and I care for him." Her face overflowed with emotion—passion, spirit, anger—transforming her. "But I loved you. Now that deal is done. All our deals are done."

I opened my mouth to say the words. I loved her, I'd never love anyone but her.

But she didn't want my world, wouldn't be bound by it, so I gave her the only thing I could. "All deals done then." I walked out of her house, leaving my fucking heart on her kitchen floor.

I don't remember the drive home, I found myself at the clubhouse sitting at the bar staring at liquor I couldn't drink because the shit with the Angels wasn't over. Likely the guy Elle had taken down would tell the Bandits where his friends were, but until I got the word from Charlie I had more important shit to do than drink myself stupid.

Sometime later my phone rang. "Yeah?"

"Hey, compadre, it's over, everyone is accounted for." Charlie's happy voice sounded so foreign. "You still in Dallas, I'm partying tonight."

"Nah, I'm back home."

"Tell that girl of yours thank you from me." He said the words that broke my last reserve.

"She's not my girl." I hung up and retrieved the whiskey. I planned to drink until I passed out, then wake up and repeat until this shit no longer hurt so fucking bad.

Chapter Twenty-Nine

Elle

The door banging shut signaled the end. I bit my hand and willed myself to be strong, but the first sob worked up over the lump of regret in my throat and burst from me, bringing a storm of tears. I sank to the floor in front of my sink and sobbed, huge ugly heaving sobs.

Gone. Gone. Gone. Nothing would ever feel right again. My love for him—the stupidest mistake of my life—had broken me. I sucked in a breath and tried to let the pain drain away—the pain of my cheek, my pounding head, my raw throat were nothing compared to the pieces of my shattered heart cutting into me with every breath.

His face played on repeat in my mind, not only had I sent him away, I'd devastated him too. He'd refused to say the words, but I'd seen the love shine in his eyes, the same love I saw when we'd made love, then he shoved it away from him. Rejected it. Rejected me and walked out of my life.

But I'd achieved the most important goal, I'd given him back his life. I'd sworn to let him go, well it had turned more into a shove out the door, but I'd kept my word. My principles did nothing to ease the emptiness he'd left in me.

My tears dried up, but I remained on the floor. Standing required energy, walking to my bed was more than I could contemplate. I curled onto the floor, the cold tile against my uninjured cheek comforted me. I closed my swollen eyes and the sting was another reminder I was here, miserable and alone.

The doorbell rang, I ignored it. Two more quick buzzes. Whoever it was, they weren't going away. Was it Rebel? A small kernel of warmth glowed inside me.

Someone leaned on the doorbell and pounded on the door at the same time. Time to answer that door. I gathered all my energy and step by step, I climbed up from the floor. Staggering like a drunk, I made it down my hall to the front door.

Gator stared back at me through my peephole. Unlocking the door, I threw it open.

"What happened to you?" Gator barked and strode into the house past me.

"What do you need?" Forming each word became a monumental effort. I'd known deep inside it wasn't him. He'd never be at my door again. The ache became a primal pain, growing stronger with each breath.

"Rebel."

His name sliced me.

"The trouble with the Angels is over. I'm heading back to Barden."

Of course, he'd want me to know I was safe. There was the guilt again. I nodded when Gator kept staring at me.

"What happened? Did you and Rebel fight?" Gator frowned down at me.

"That's over too." Three words, each a nail in the coffin of my dead heart. I moved past him toward the steps. I could make it to my bed. I would. I wasn't falling apart again, especially not in front of Gator. "Show yourself out."

One step, another, each one consumed my focus.

"Elle."

I didn't have the ability to turn back, so I focused on the next step and the next until my bed loomed in front of me—my safe haven. I sank down into my bed, cocooned in my blankets. Tears leaked from my closed eyes. I hoped oblivion came soon.

Chapter Thirty

Rebel

The pain still ripped through me with every breath I took. I grabbed another bottle of whiskey and drank, sooner or later the pain would go away.

The door opened behind me but I didn't bother to look. I still hadn't drowned the pain. Right now I wished I was a masochist because then I'd be in heaven.

"What's up?" Jericho sat to my left and Dare sat on my right.

"Drinking." My words slurred. Then why the fuck didn't my pain go away.

"Why?" Dare looked at me then grimaced. "How did you fuck it up?"

"She had to go, she wanted to go, I let her go." I drank down the whiskey and the second bottle was empty but the pain blazed bright.

"I'll get you another." Dare moved behind the bar and handed me a new bottle.

I drank and drank until I didn't even remember my own name. I woke, reached for a bottle and drank myself unconscious again.

I was on a binge and I didn't see an end in sight. I

stumbled into the shower, threw on some clothes and headed back to the bar in the main room. People were here today. Fuck, was it Sunday? Probably. I got a few bottles of whiskey before slinking back to my room. I wanted to see no one, talk to no one, be no one. I finally understood why Dare had spent all those months drunk on his ass when he and Mama had split up, it was the only way to survive without your heart.

"I can't have her," I shouted to the room.

"Can't have who?" Viper walked in the door.

Fuck Viper, anyway. He didn't know shit about living without his heart. "Fuck off."

"Can't. I got babysitting duty today. You are, I quote, 'not supposed to get piss-ass drunk before Dare shows up.'"

He picked up the three bottles of whiskey from the floor and carried them out of the room. I still had the one bottle so I didn't worry, besides there were more out front.

By the time Viper came back, I'd drunk half the bottle. He snatched it out of my hands.

"Give that back," I hollered but stood and headed for the door.

"Do you know what day it is?" Viper blocked the door.

"Sunday?"

"Thursday you drunk fuck." He shook his head at me. "Get your shit together."

"Don't wanna." I ambled back to bed. "Life's over anyway."

"Why the fuck didn't you keep her, you want her, she wants you. Why the fucking drama?" Viper threw his hands up.

"The club property clause. She owns a business, and

she's not giving us a share for any reason," I mumbled, head in my hands.

"You asked her that?"

"I'd never fucking ask her to do that, would you give up that shit for love?" No one would, and more, I wouldn't take what was hers. "I signed a sheet, I promised her I wasn't after her company."

"Shit, you always have to be complicated, different, go a goddam different path than the rest of us." He sat beside me. "Couldn't fucking believe you married her. Did you divorce her?"

I shook my head. I'd have to but I didn't want to do it. I liked Elle being my wife, if only she could be my wife and my old lady. But that wasn't happening. Fuck I needed a drink.

I stood and he pulled me back down. "No booze."

"Fuck off." I went to stand again.

His arms shot out and knocked me off balance.

"I must still be drunk."

"Yeah, totally pickled." He looked at me with disgust. "I told one of the guys with a woman they should do this, but the fuckers were pussies. Rock flat out said he'd give you all the booze you wanted. Dare wasn't even there. Sad when it was down to me or Thorn."

I shuddered. "Thorn would just have knocked me unconscious."

"Don't think I'm not considering it," Viper growled.

A knock on the door had him up and moving to it, he turned back to me with a pot of coffee and a cup. "Drink it all." He set the pot on the stand next to the bed.

I poured a cup although I didn't want it. Already the dull ache had transformed into pulsing pain flashing through me with each breath. But I knew Viper too well, the bastard would tie me up and pour it down my throat if I didn't comply. The coffee chased away the last bit of whiskey fog. I headed to the bathroom and caught a glimpse of myself in the mirror. Fuck, I looked like shit. Where did I get the black eye? I'd blacked out long hours, but surely I'd remember a fight.

Pathetic. I wasn't pathetic. No, not me, not anymore. I stripped and showered again, then shaved the start of the beard from my face. Dressed again, I walked out into the room.

Viper nodded. "That's better."

I shrugged on my cut. Time to bury Elle in a deep hole and move on because pitiful drunk wasn't in my vocabulary. I'd played that fool once before and sworn to never do it again. No, I had control and experience with living with rejection. Unlike with my parents, this was my fault. I'd walked away from her love, sure it'd been for the best reason, but I'd left her, destroyed her faith in me.

"Who gave me a black eye?" I touched the black bruise under my eye.

"You don't remember?" Viper arched an eyebrow. "Of course not. Gator gave it to you, punched you out that first night."

Fuck. He'd been the one to let Elle know she was safe. What had he witnessed? I didn't want to know. Already teetering on the edge, knowing exactly what pissed him so much would send me back to the bottle. I needed out of here, out of this room, away from the clubhouse.

I hadn't made it three steps toward the back door before Viper blocked my path. "Dare needs to talk to you. You stay here."

"Get out of my way," I growled.

"Rebel, get your ass over here," Jericho called from the other end of the hall.

I stared down Viper another minute before I turned and stomped toward my Prez. I sat next to him in the back corner.

"You look better." Jericho grinned at me. "You're a talkative drunk."

I held my hand up. "Don't tell me."

Dare strode toward us, an envelope in his hand, and a murderous look on his face. He threw the manila envelope at me. "I fucking hate lawyers."

I'd only opened up the envelope when he returned with a bottle of whiskey and sat across from us.

I glanced through the papers, a merger agreement between Jackson Bonds and Brotherhood Bonds. I dropped the papers to the table. "I don't want her company."

"Stupid fuck," Dare mumbled.

"This merger lets you claim her as your old lady." Jericho tapped fingers on the table.

"How do you figure?"

"Fucking stubborn ass," Jericho growled. "Fine, I'll lay it out for you. We get 10 percent of her company and she gets 10 percent of ours. Then we provide a line of credit, our cash, for the two companies to do the expansion you both want. The holding company buys them, each partner owning 50 percent of all new businesses. The name of the new companies, your company, hers, all of that is up to you guys to decide. She has the experience, we have the money. The merger trumps the property clause."

My mind reeled from information overload. "Okay,

ut she doesn't need us." She already planned to do
what Jericho suggested.

"She needs you," Dare grunted.

"And, the attorneys seem to think Jackson Bonds
doesn't have the cash it'll take to expand. Of course, if
the deal goes through, our books and hers will be ex-
amined by lawyers, everything up and up."

"What's in it for us?" I didn't understand why he'd
even consider this.

"More revenue. Our family made whole." Jericho's
fierce scowl made me want to back away. He looked
like he was a question away from decking me. "Dare's
been working on this since you married her, but we
had to speed them up when you fucked everything up."

I stared between them. "That long?"

"You love her. You want her. This makes it all work
out and gives us a stronger business."

Dare stood up. "Read that shit forward and backward, then go get your woman."

A flicker of hope sparked to life. Maybe she wasn't
gone. I could fix this. It'd take groveling, but I'd beg her
to forgive me. I wouldn't give up until she was mine.

Chapter Thirty-One

Elle

My new life was simple—work and bed with frequen
ice cream binges in between. All the ice cream in th
world wouldn't fix me, but it was the only food grou
that appealed.

After today, the weekend loomed large. I needed t
make a plan that didn't involve hours in bed watchin
sappy Hallmark movies

The intercom buzzed. "Chet's here."

Time to work out the long-range plan for expansion
another dream dashed, well more like put on hold.

"Elle." Chet sat down across from me at the smal
conference table in my office. "You look terrible. You
okay?"

A dry laugh escaped. *Well, Chet, no I'm not okay
I'm a fucking wreck, but let's pretend I'm fine.* Why did
people do that? Tell me how bad I looked then hope
wouldn't unburden my problems on them. "It's been a
shittastic week, but today's the last day, so there's that."

Chet stared at me, caught in the no-man-zone o
women's emotions.

"Give me your projections." I cut the poor guy a break.

"Yes, well, here it is, unfortunately, it'll be a bit before we can expand."

I scanned the projection, seven years was too damn long. I studied it closely. "How much of our revenue did you put to this goal?"

"All the profit, which is roughly 40 percent of what we bring in. I anticipated a modest 10 percent growth each year, but we've been growing revenue at 13 percent." He talked numbers more but I tuned out, focusing on the yearly projections.

"If we grew at 20 percent, how long would it take to be ready to expand?" I tapped my pen on the table, thinking about how I might refocus our team on earning more.

He typed on his laptop keyboard. "Three years, but realistically we can't—"

"Redo this projection, assuming 15 percent this year and 20 percent each year after. We should be able to begin acquiring in the last quarter of year four or maybe early in year five." I handed him back the spreadsheet. "Email it to me this afternoon. I will work on the plan to achieve the revenue goals over the weekend."

Chet opened and closed his mouth. "Have you considered a loan, we have collateral and could get a $350,000 line of credit, added to our bottom line, that would be ample funds—"

"I want at least $450,000, on top of our safety margin. Debt isn't the best approach, no we'll wait until we have the money." I closed my acquisitions folder. Disappointment settled on top of my general unhappiness, beating me down until drawing in breath took conscious effort. "Thanks, Chet. I'll expect the report after lunch."

He closed his laptop. "Got it. Sorry we can't move faster."

"We'll focus on improving at home before we move to acquisitions." I didn't have a clue how to motivate my employees, to be honest, I'd lost my own way, how the hell could I lead others.

Chet left and I moved back to my desk to sign off on last night's bonds then approved payroll before moving onto the report on each of my commissioned employees. Both bonding agents and bail enforcement agents earned commission based on their work, it made up more than half their pay.

My door banged open. I jerked up my head from the latest report to find Jessica standing in my door, arms crossed and serious attitude tattooed across her face.

"Why the hell am I hearing about your breakup from Zero and not you?" She stormed in, leaving the door open. Great, now half the office would get an update on my personal business.

"Hey, Jess." I had nothing, no energy for her, for anyone.

"Oh, sweetie." She sat in the leather chair in front of my desk. "Men are bastards. Please quit looking so sad."

Is that how I looked?

"Come on, get your skinny ass up out of that chair, we're going to lunch and you'll tell me everything." She stood and when I didn't move she tapped her high heel on my carpeted floor, the muffled tap, tap, tap the only noise in the office.

She wouldn't leave, and she would turn obnoxious. But if I left, I wasn't coming back, telling Jess would ruin me for work, for life, so I packed my laptop before heaving myself up. I'd swear it'd gone from thirty pounds to eighty pounds overnight.

I stopped at Alice's desk. "I'm heading to lunch and home. Call me if you need anything. I'll be on my laptop later this afternoon."

"Got it." She gave me a quick wave before turning back to her keyboard. Alice had been the only one to not ask me a thousand questions this week, and for that I should send her flowers or chocolates, maybe both.

"We're going to the diner." My favorite lunch spot in the world, and it was only two blocks away.

We seated ourselves in a back corner booth and Mamie, one of two waitresses who worked the greasy spoon, showed up in seconds. "The usual?" she asked.

"Yup." They had the best Reuben sandwich in town.

"I'll have the cheeseburger and fries, sweet tea." Jess stuck her menu back behind the napkin container.

Mamie hurried away to another table.

"So many fine dining choices and you pick this *place*." Jess scratched at something dried on the table with her sleek pink nail. "Now tell me, what did he do?"

"Nothing, he didn't do a thing. I told him I loved him and he didn't do anything." I bit back the tears that wanted to flow free. No more tears, not here, not anywhere. I unloaded the story, starting with the twelve-day absence and ending with Gator stopping by.

"What about the divorce papers?"

I shrugged. "I told the lawyer to call when they he received them, I haven't heard from him."

"Isn't that weird?" Jess tapped her nails on the laminate tabletop. "Zero said he's fucked up about it."

Emotion lit up inside me, surely I wasn't petty

enough to be satisfied he hurt too. Yep, I was exactly that petty. I didn't want it to be easy for him even if he didn't love me.

"So he's had a rough week, doesn't matter, he walked out. We're done. It's over." I killed the hope trying to take root inside.

"So it's over, and you went and fell in love." Jess stared at me, reading between the lines, in the way only a best friend can. "That's a first for you."

"I can't say I'm eager to repeat the experience."

Mamie delivered our food. The scent of corned beef and sauerkraut lifted my mood. I gave Mamie a half smile before I bit into the deliciousness. Closing my eyes I savored the flavors. At least I still had this little piece of heaven.

We ate in silence a few minutes and the Reuben fortified me.

Jess patted her mouth with one of the cheap table napkins, the gesture looked ridiculous in here. "You make up with your daddy yet?"

She sucker punched me. He was a whole other kind of nightmare I didn't want to deal with. "Not going to." I bit into my sandwich to prevent her from grilling me, not that it'd work. She was crafty and patient.

"He signed over the company, you told me he tried to make amends when you introduced him to Rebel, really, you can't shove away everyone who loves you."

"I didn't shove Rebel away." I spoke with my mouth full. How dare she insinuate I had?

"Maybe you pushed him, pushed it more than he was ready for." She shrugged her shoulders. "But if he didn't man up and admit his feelings, then you're better without him." She pointed her finger at me. "Your

Jaddy is another matter. You have to make up with him. He's family."

I missed Daddy, our talks, Sunday brunch at his house, everything. He was my only family. The outrage from six weeks ago had faded but the sharp pain of missing him remained.

Narrowing her eyes at me, Jess opened her mouth to lay into me again.

"Okay, you're right. I need to call him, but next week. I can't do emotion yet."

Jess gave me a huge smile then ate a fry drowned in ketchup. "Good. You need to make it right with him, soon."

"Got it, quit nagging."

"I do not nag." The indignant arch of her brows was too much.

I laughed, scratchy at first, but it turned into a full belly laugh when she laughed with me.

"Maybe a little," she admitted.

I hadn't laughed since Rebel left, and it felt good, freeing, like maybe a little bit of my old self remained. I'd find myself again, find happiness again, one day.

Jess and I spent another hour talking about nothing, stories about her work, me firing Mel, and somewhere in the mix, a little bit of perspective returned. My world wasn't over, the heartache still stole my breath at times, but each day would be better. Jacksons didn't quit. And I was a Jackson.

At home, I refused to hide in my PJs in bed. Instead, I cleaned the house from top to bottom then went to work on my plan for work. My eyes started burning and I yawned. I glanced at the clock, surprised it was already after eleven. Tonight I was tired from working, not ready to sleep because I needed to hide from reality. That was over. I saved the rough beginning of my plan and shut down my computer.

Upstairs, I changed into pajamas and climbed into bed. I spent a few seconds wondering if Rebel missed me like I missed him, but then I shoved the thought away. He was my past. I needed to focus on my future.

I woke feeling better than I had since…no, I wasn't going there. I hit the shower and spent extra time pampering myself with a masque and my in-depth skin routine. Jess did this stuff religiously, but I only remembered a couple times a month, still my skin tingled and my mood lifted. I threw on my lazy day clothes, comfy gym shorts and tank top, then went to feed my grumbling stomach.

Downstairs I ate a couple toaster waffles before I settled into a new book. My doorbell rang right when the cowboy was ready to get under the skirt of his new love. I ignored the doorbell, surely the salesman would go away. The doorbell rang again, an irritated trio of rings. Leaving my tablet on the end table, and my hero a page away from what we'd both been waiting for, I hurried to the door.

"Settle yourself." The person had moved to pounding on my door.

I glanced through the peephole—my body froze, pain barreled into me fresh and new—I stared into Rebel's face.

What was he doing here? I couldn't deal with him, no way. He could pound away, I wasn't talking to him. I let out a breath I hadn't realized I held, then my door knob turned.

The fucking key. He still had the key to my place. Anger flared to life, almost making me forget the panic and pain. I threw open the door. Rebel glanced up and down me before the sexy grin I couldn't forget spread across his face.

"What?" I barked out over the anxiety holding my throat hostage.

"Baby, we need to talk."

Shocked by the sensual tone of voice, he slipped right past me into my house. I stood there unable to process what was happening. Why? Who? My brain clogged with unanswered questions and my heart wept with overflowing emotion. Those simple words had shattered my defenses, letting a flood of feeling sweep me away.

Rebel stepped to me, inches from me. The scent of leather and man wafted by me, then the door shut with a bang, bringing me out of my stupor.

"I'm so fucking sorry." Then he kissed me.

Pushed back against my wall, he devoured me with his kiss, lit me up and for the first time since we'd fought, I was back. Passion exploded inside me and I couldn't stop it, didn't even want to try. I pressed against him, my hands lost in his hair, my body alive again.

When he stepped back from me, the air left my lungs. I couldn't breathe. No, he had to stay, come closer, make me forget the nightmare of the past week.

I closed my eyes and tried to find rage and only came up with hurt and loneliness and a desperate fear he'd leave me again.

Was I that pathetic?

"We need to talk." He glanced down at his boots then met my stare.

I had to look away, move away or I'd jump him like

the loser I apparently was. "Didn't we say it all last week?" I booked it to the living room. I needed distance, but his scent lingered on me.

"Not even close."

I sat in my recliner, not trusting myself to be on the same couch with him.

Rebel knelt at my feet then he grasped my hands in his, finally our eyes locked in a silent communion. "I love you, Elle. And I'm an idiot for hurting you."

Elation swept through me before reality crashed down. This was a dream. If I was dreaming then I could excuse my lack of backbone. Besides, I'd only hear those words in one of my dreams. If he loved me, he'd have told me last week. Why put us both through the misery if he loved me?

"I have to be dreaming," I mumbled, hoping saying the words would wake me up.

Rebel pinched the skin on my forearm.

"Ow." I frowned down at him. "That hurt."

He gave me his lopsided grin. "Baby, this isn't a dream. I'm sorry for leaving you, I thought it was the only thing I could do. I promised, and I had to keep my promise."

"What?" I struggled to find words. "Explain yourself in a way that makes sense."

He looked away from me and for the first time I could think. It was impossible to think with his cinnamon eyes staring through me. Rebel was here. He loved me. How could he have hurt me if he loved me?

"I didn't think I could keep you forever, so I let you go, even though I loved you." He squeezed my hands. "To be mine forever I'd want you to be my old lady in the club, to be part of all my life."

"And you thought I'd say no? I love… I mean loved you." I shut my eyes trying to keep the tears from falling, but a tear slid down my cheek anyway.

"I promised you I wouldn't take your company." He met my gaze. "When you become part of the club, you become my property."

The term still made me uncomfortable. "Mama and Marr explained that."

He scowled deeper. "Did they explain, I own your company then, the Brotherhood can take part of your profits, then?"

"What the hell?" I pulled back from him. Outrage lit me up. "You bunch of pigs."

"It's the same for me, all of us in the club." He stood and paced away from me. "You give up part of who you are to belong, that includes business. Normally it's not a big thing, but for us, it's a big fucking deal." He ran fingers through his hair. "When you and I agreed to this marriage, I had no intention of falling for you like this, of loving you, so I thought your business would be safe."

"And you would be safe," I shot back, seeing exactly how it worked. He couldn't get too close to me because I wouldn't give up the business I was fighting for.

Chapter Thirty-Two

Rebel

"Yeah, that's what I planned." No use in denying it. She saw right through me. "But that didn't work out for me because I love you." Saying those words sill created a spike of fear in me. Everyone I'd ever loved had rejected me.

"So why are you here then?" She threw the words at me.

"Because my brothers had my back before I even knew I needed help." I wasn't making sense but everything inside me was jumbled into a huge mess. No matter what string I tugged, it turned into a giant tangle of emotion. Fuck, I hadn't thought straight since I'd left her place last week. "Jericho and Dare had some lawyers working out a merger between our two businesses."

"A what?" She stood up, hands on hips.

"A merger—basically if you agree—our two companies merge, each of us keeping our own identity or taking on your company name if you prefer. The Brotherhood provides the capital for our expansion and you and Jackson Bonds provides the experience to run such a complex operation."

She opened her mouth and shut it. "So business was why you left me?" Hurt shadowed her words.

"I promised you I didn't want your company, and I don't, I want you. However, I come with strings, lots more strings than your daddy had for you." I hated saying it, hated handing her the reason to send me packing.

"You didn't think I'd give up my company—"

"It'd have only been a small percent, but goddammit, I keep my word." I shouted the words, losing all my fucking cool. This woman meant more to me than my next breath but I wouldn't ever take from her, let alone break my commitment.

"So you devastated me, killed my heart, to keep a fucking promise?"

Shit when she said it like that, I guess I'd fucked up, and I knew I was screwing up even as I walked out the door. I had no reason to expect understanding, let alone forgiveness.

"We're a pair." A sad laugh followed her words. "I pushed you out, pushed you to commit because I'd promised you…to let you go…once I had the company. If you didn't love me too, then I refused to hold on to you, even though I knew I could."

Son of a bitch. We were so much alike, maybe we weren't meant to be together. Fuck that, she was mine, and I wasn't leaving here until she agreed.

"We're too much alike, maybe we'll fight more because of it, but I can't do life without you. Now that I know what it feels like to be with you, in you, to love you, I won't settle for less." Those honest words ripped me open and left me totally exposed, she could end me with a word.

She closed the distance to me, taking my hand in

hers. "I guess we better figure out the details because I won't settle for less, either. I love you." She kissed me and I surrendered to her, unable to resist her for another second.

I lifted her tank to touch the soft skin I'd missed so much, moving up until I touched her tits. She moaned into my mouth and I needed to touch her, to claim her, to own her. We broke the kiss when I tugged off her top. She wiggled out of her shorts then her hands were on my fly. We stayed tangled together while I undressed, unable to stop touching, feeling the other one.

I picked her up and carried her to the couch, needing inside her right now. I ran a finger through her seam. "So ready for me, baby."

"I love you." She tugged my arms until I moved closer to her.

I kissed her. "I love you. You're mine," I spoke into her lips.

I leaned back, ready to thrust home when it hit me, no condom. "Baby, I need to get a condom."

She held on to me when I tried to move. "I'm on the pill, don't bother."

I drove into her, needing to feel her around me. She was my home, my heart, my life. Each stroke brought me closer to her. Her sexy noises increased and she rocked up into me faster and faster. Elle was finally mine. I'd never let her go again.

Chapter Thirty-Three

Elle

Rebel loved me, wanted me, even more he needed me. I was never letting go. I wrapped my legs around him and abandoned all attempts of control, letting him possess me in every way. We connected, fused together perfectly.

I tensed and the familiar quake pushed me closer, took me higher, until I had no choice but to fall. The sweet release of my body was nothing compared to the way my soul soared. "I love you," I chanted, his gaze locked with mine.

"Mine." He grunted and drove into me hard and fast until he shuddered and came undone. Panting in my ear, he whispered, "I love you, baby, now and forever."

My world was right again. I held tight to him not wanting to ever let him go, needing to feel this closeness between us again. Our relationship scared me, the future and his club frightened me more, but nothing would ever keep me from his side because not being with him wasn't an option. I'd straighten out all my worries so our relationship was rock solid, one strong enough to last a lifetime.

I kissed his cheek and held him tighter. Was his touch sweeter because I knew how miserable I was without it? Maybe. Or maybe that was bullshit.

We spent the rest of the weekend at my place, and the only time we left my bed was for food. I'd read through the merger agreement twice and it looked solid. Monday, Rebel and I would start the process to bring our businesses together. The deal was more than fair and allowed both of us to grow faster together.

I rode to work Monday morning on the back of Rebel's bike. It was a perfect way to start my morning. Alice didn't even blink when Rebel accompanied me into my office.

"Alice, make five copies of this document, for your eyes only. Get Chet in here as soon as possible and schedule a meeting with our attorney today." I gave her the merger document. Her eyes widened when she read the first paragraph, but she hustled away.

Less than fifteen minutes later, Alice buzzed again. "Chet's here."

"Send him in." I glanced at Rebel and the nervousness in my stomach evaporated.

"We got this." He smiled wide.

Chet walked in. "Who are you?" He frowned at Rebel. Disapproval clear on his face.

"Rebel, this is Chet, I want you to read this here, then we'll all talk." I handed him the merger paperwork and turned back to my computer. I was typing up a summary of the key points of the merger for when we were ready to share it with other members of the staff.

"You can't be serious?" Chet looked over at me less than five minutes after he started reading. "We can't do business with bikers."

"Why not?" Rebel shot back.

"Elle, we need to talk in private." Chet glanced from me to Rebel and back again.

"No, we don't. Say what you think." I had no idea what he was so worked up about.

"They're bikers, a gang." He emphasized the words. "Besides we'd be foolish to announce our strategy to the other side."

"What other side?" I joined him and Rebel at my table. "This isn't hostile, we aren't negotiating. Of course, we'll have our attorneys make sure that all the numbers are supported by their books, and complete all the other due diligence, but we aren't bargaining."

"Why not?" Chet gritted his teeth.

"If you read it, you'd see it's very fair, and it accomplishes both our business goals." I worked to keep the irritation out of my voice. Chet had barely made it through the first page and had an attitude.

"Just say it, Chet." Rebel drew out each word.

"Do you know what his problem is?" I turned to Rebel.

Anger darkened his face.

"We're not doing this." Chet slid the agreement to me. "We aren't taking dirty money because you want to grow too damn fast."

"What did you say?" I turned to Chet. "Think carefully."

"His vest says 1 percent, the definition of illegal. It's obvious they're using us to launder their dirty money. Surely you're not so gullible." Chet's face turned red.

"Actually it denotes a lifestyle where the club is first, among other things." Rebel gave Chet a cold smile.

"Chet, the lawyers will confirm the money is legit-

imate but I already know it is." I was disappointed in
my CFO's prejudice, unfortunately I wasn't surprised.

"Really? How is that?" Chet sneered.

"This is my husband. And he gave me his word the
club is legal."

Chet's eyes bulged. "You married *him*?"

This was going from bad to worse. I didn't want to
go through a merger with a new CFO but that was looking more and more likely.

Disapproval lined Rebel's face but he didn't say anything. This was my situation to handle.

"I did and we're merging our bail bonds businesses.
Is that a problem for you?" I clasped my hands in front
of me.

"I don't know." Chet deflated. "This is unexpected.
You'll be using our law firm?"

"Of course, both our firm and the Brotherhood's firm
will be executing the merger. Rebel and I will be im-
plementing it. The question is whether you'll be part
of that team." I gave him my full attention, hoping he
saw how serious I was.

"I will, uh, whatever the law firm says is good by
me." Chet gulped. "I'm sorry to both of you for jumping to conclusions." He met both my and Rebel's gaze
when he apologized.

"Glad to hear it." I nodded to him. "I'll send you a
note with the time of our meeting with the attorneys."

Chet stood up.

"You, Alice, Rebel and I know about this. Make sure
it stays that way." I dismissed him.

Once the door closed, Rebel appraised me, his eyebrow arching up. "Damn you're hot."

"You like a bossy woman?"

"I love you." He kissed me. "But I don't like that guy."

"He didn't like you either, we'll see if he improves."

Rebel glared at the closed door. "He doesn't get a second shot. No one bad mouths my club."

"I know and I agree, he is a word away from being fired."

The meeting with the lawyers went much better than the one with Chet, or at least they had poker faces worthy of their large hourly rates. We would get a schedule for the merger next week, with a rough estimate of six weeks before we'd be ready to execute. Of course that was after Rebel negotiated from 16 weeks to six weeks, agreeing to pay the extra fees to expedite the process.

The next couple weeks passed quickly between merger tasks and splitting my time between Dallas and Ardmore. We stayed close to each other, not going more than a night apart before we figured out a way to be together again.

I'd called my dad and made plans to go to his place for dinner tomorrow night, the nervous tension grew inside me until I couldn't stay still. I'd tried reading, watching TV and working, but nothing distracted me.

"You going to tell me the problem?" Rebel leaned against the doorway into the kitchen.

I had out all my plastic storage containers, reorganizing them. "Nothing big. I'm seeing my daddy tomorrow and it has me messed up inside."

"That's big." Rebel strolled over to the counter, watching me match lids and restack my leftover containers.

I shrugged. "It's time. Past time, actually."

"You need to clear the air, see what's left then." He had that distant stare I sometimes saw.

I wondered if he was thinking about his own parents. They were fools to turn away from him, and I know it still bothered him.

I put the last of my bowls back and stood up with the few lost lids I'd found. Tossing them in the trash, I moved to Rebel and wrapped him in a tight hug.

"You want me to go with you?" He spoke low in my ear.

I'd scheduled it for Thursday night because he usually wasn't here. I hadn't wanted to pressure him to go, but now that he'd asked me, I wanted nothing more than for him to be by my side.

"You have business tomorrow in Barden." I bit my lip.

"I can cancel that, baby. Do you want me to go?"

"Yeah, would you?"

He chuckled and squeezed me tight. "Anything for you, baby."

We pulled into Daddy's ranch house on the edge of Dallas, the same house where I'd grown up. My ulcers sent mini-volcanos of acid shooting pain through my stomach. Rebel parked his bike beside my dad's truck. I slid off the bike and wiped my sweaty palms on my denim shorts.

He clasped my hand in his. "We got this."

"Yeah." While only three months had passed since Daddy issued the challenge, the distance between us was huge, or maybe just one hug away. I'd ridden the emotional roller coaster from hell all day, but right now it felt like I was on the biggest precipice of all. We walked up the short walk to the front door. Daddy threw open the door before I reached his front step.

"Sugar dumpling, it's about damn time." He threw his arms wide and I walked into them. He crushed me in his embrace and I was home. My father was a huge man, over six foot and built like a linebacker, well an old linebacker, but I loved hugging his big frame. He made me feel safe, loved.

I stepped back. "Daddy, I'm sorry."

"Me too, honey, so damn sorry I caused you so much grief." His blue eyes were sad. "Now no more apologies, introduce me to your man." He nodded to Rebel.

"Daddy, this is my husband, Rebel, he's part of the Jericho Brotherhood."

"Nice to meet you, sir. Gus has told me stories about you." Rebel held a hand out but Daddy just folded him into a back-slapping hug.

"Don't believe a damn word that old coot says." Daddy grinned wide at the two of us. "Come on out back. I've got the grill started and Doris is here."

"What about Megan?"

"We divorced in April." Daddy grunted. "It wasn't meant to be."

That's all he'd ever said about any of the women who had left his life. In fact, I'd never heard him speak ill of any woman and very few men. He was more of an action kind of guy, a lot like my own man.

"So tell me, how'd you work it all out?" Daddy opened the screen door to his back deck. Doris sat with her feet up with a beer in her hand.

"Doris, I'm glad to see you." We hugged. I hated how we'd left things after our last conversation.

"That was my fault, sir." Rebel cleared his throat.

"Stop callin' me sir, it's Jack or Dad, pick your poison." Daddy grasped Doris's hand and brought it to his lips for a quick kiss.

"When? Are you two…?"

Doris cackled. "Since he isn't my boss anymore, I asked the idiot out. He's hopeless when it comes to women."

I grinned wide.

"But not with you." He winked at Doris.

"Spit it out, you were telling us why you're here with Elle." Doris crossed arms over her chest. "Last we spoke, Elle was pretty sure you weren't the staying type." She shot me her stink eye.

"About that, it's complicated, but we're working it out." I folded my own arms across my chest. "The important thing is we love each other."

"Now that's the damn truth." Daddy laughed. "Welcome to the family." He handed Rebel a beer.

"We're merging our companies," I told Daddy.

"Don't give two damns about that business. Should've retired years ago." He gave Doris a knowing look and I honestly hoped he wouldn't say more. There were lots of things a daughter shouldn't know.

Doris and Daddy were too cute through dinner, and for once, I thought Daddy might have a woman who'd stick.

"When are you two tying the knot?" I dug into Doris's chocolate cake.

"We're not." Doris frowned over at Daddy. "The fool man has asked me three times already."

"Don't be that way, Dee." Daddy winked. "I'm working on her."

"I told you if I want to be married, I'll do the asking." Doris snorted. "You are cursed."

"That's telling him." I squeezed Rebel's knee. "Not everyone can get married first and hope it works out."

Rebel grinned at me. "I did."

"Rebel, come play a game of horseshoes with me. Leave these women to clean up."

Doris harrumphed. "Get out of here."

The two guys barely made it down the deck steps before Doris turned her stare to me.

"Fine. I'll tell you everything while we wash dishes. But I didn't lie, he broke my heart, he just put it back together again."

Chapter Thirty-Four

Rebel

I walked away from Elle, sure this was when Jack told me how much he didn't approve of me marrying Elle. He'd been all smiles around his daughter, but I expected the truth now that we were alone. He'd have to get used to me because I wasn't letting her get away no matter what her father thought about it.

"Son, you are a miracle worker." He clasped my shoulder. "I haven't ever seen my girl so happy. Thank you."

I whipped my head to him but he was serious. "You don't care that I'm a biker?"

"Known lots of good men and more than my share of bad ones—being a biker doesn't make you one or the other. But loving my daughter, putting that smile on her face, that makes you the best kind of man." He slapped my back. "Besides, Gus vouches for you."

I stopped. No one had ever accepted me so easily, sure he'd had time to check me out, dig into the Brotherhood, but his approval eased something inside me that I didn't even know was there. "I love your daughter, and I'm happy you two worked things out."

"We're too much alike, hell I raised her to be a carbon copy of me, so no doubt she got my stubborn streak." He shook his head. "Thank god she did because I'd have made a mess of her life if she'd let me. Hell, I didn't do a great job on my own."

There was a no-bullshit honesty about him I liked. Elle had it too, but hers was tempered with diplomacy. Jack had given up diplomacy.

"Tell me about the last couple months, and why this merger is so damn important." He picked up four horseshoes. "It's more exercise if we walk end to end, and Doris bitches that I need that exercise."

"Fine by me, but really Elle should tell you the story." I didn't want to piss him off now that he liked me.

"Just the basics." He threw the first horseshoe.

"Well, I guess it all started because you pissed me off." I was a no-bullshit kind of guy too. I told him about our business deal, then the marriage deal. "In my club, a woman you want to be with forever joins the club with you as property."

I threw a horseshoe, waiting for the explosion.

"Know about that shit." His face didn't give away any clues as to what he thought about it.

I threw another horseshoe, this one rang on the pole. "Anyway, part of that would involve her business, but I didn't want her business, just her, so I thought it better to walk away. My brothers had a different idea. The merger gives us an equal stake in each other's companies and we provide the cash to expand the bail bonds businesses and Elle has the experience to run the whole thing, plus it gets around the business worries I had."

Jack nodded. "You'll let her lead the whole thing?"

"She's the one who was raised in the business, I've

been doing it a few years, way behind on that curve."
Besides, no one let Elle do anything. "Elle earned that
place."

Jack grinned wide. "Knew I liked you first time we
met."

"I didn't like you, but you're growing on me." I
tipped my beer to him.

We continued playing the game and talking. He was
a tricky bastard and beat me soundly.

"So what's my girl's last name?" We walked back
toward the deck

I stopped. "It's Jackson, she isn't changing it."

He frowned at me. "Why?"

"Bikers don't really do marriage, hell I hardly use
my name. No reason for her to take it." I had no desire
for her to wear my father's name. I sure as hell wasn't
proud of that heritage.

"Hunh." He started walking again, whistling "The
Yellow Rose of Texas."

I collected Elle from the kitchen and we said our
goodbyes with a promise to come to dinner next week.
We'd have to work out the day since Sunday brunch was
out unless they wanted to come to Barden.

"You okay?" I asked as we walked to my bike.

She turned to me, happiness lifted up her face.
Damn, I loved seeing her happy.

"I'm real good, making up with Daddy and Doris
healed something inside me." She laid her fisted hand on
her chest. "I was so worried about it and it was so easy."

"He loves you, baby."

"Yeah, he does. He likes you too." She leaned up on
tiptoes to give me a quick kiss.

And maybe the dinner healed something inside me.

Not many people accepted me, let alone trusted me with a treasure like Elle, but her father did. I had no doubt about it.

I paced in the living room of Elle's townhouse. She was upstairs doing whatever women did to drive men crazy. "Get your ass down here," I yelled up the steps. "Dresden will be gone before we get there."

A moment later, Elle appeared in the red dress. The dress she'd worn the first night I'd seen her and she looked even hotter tonight than she had then. "Fuck, baby, you can't wear that."

"Why not?" Her face puckered into a pout.

"I'll be fucking hard all night, and where's your gun?" I tried to sound anything but desperate.

She slid up the slinky red material to show me her thigh holster. "Right there, honey." She gave me a sexy smile and I was lost.

"Good thing we're taking your truck," I grumbled.

We made it out of the house and to the club without me losing my mind and fucking her right where she sat, but I really wanted to.

"Let me help you down," I warned her before I hurried to her side of the truck. I lifted her down, letting her body slide down mine. It was sweet torture.

I placed my arm around her and we walked into the Red Light Club. The dance music irritated me when we walked in the door but Dresden was the designer drug dealer to the dance crowd. Tonight he was supposed to be here, so I'd suffer the music. Elle's body moved with the beat as she made her way through the crowd. My intel said Dresden liked the corner stool at the bar.

We walked toward an open pocket at the bar. When I

got closer, I noticed a cut. Fucking Charlie sat at the bar, the crowd stayed away from his Bandit cut. This was the last place I expected to see him. "Amigo, you swim in strange waters." I grasped his arm in a handshake.

"I was about to give up on you." He whistled. "Damn, Elle, glad I stayed for the show."

She leaned up and kissed his cheek. "Good to see you, Charlie."

I convinced the two guys next to Charlie to move on, helping Elle up onto her bar stool before I sat next to Charlie. "What can I do for you?"

"Just wanted to say thank you and share a drink." The bartender set a bottle of whiskey between us.

I leaned over to Elle. "Maybe you can take care of Dresden while I catch up—"

"Oh no." She grinned at me, knowing I was giving her grief. "Last time I came back to collect you, you passed out on the way home." She ran her fingers down the deep cut of the dress. "You will be fucking me tonight."

"Oh, baby, you can count on that." I grinned at her. Charlie handed me a glass of whiskey which I passed to Elle.

He held up his glass. "To friends." We clinked glasses before I downed my whiskey. Elle sipped hers while watching our target.

"You made it work between you." Charlie spoke into my ear because the damn music was loud and entirely too fast.

"Yeah, we made it work." I remembered telling him she wasn't my girl. "I'll be patching her into our club soon."

"She'll be hotter with your patch." Charlie poured another round of whiskey.

"If that's possible. You good? Everything settle the way it needed to."

"Better than I expected. Life's good, and I'm here in Dallas now, overseeing our business here." He smiled wide. "Lots of time for us to get drunk."

"Sounds like a plan, but tonight, I'm a working man." I waggled my brows.

"Working to get that dress off, maybe." He glanced over at my mark. "Elle could take him. Can't believe she took Spike down on her own."

I laughed. He was right, she could do it on her own but she didn't have to, she had me. I'd always be there for her. "She's tough, but I like keeping an eye on what's mine."

Chapter Thirty-Five

Elle

Since I couldn't hear myself think, there was no way to hear what Rebel and Charlie said to each other. Instead, I nursed my whiskey and kept an eye on Dresden. If our intel was right, he should head out the back soon. When he left, I'd follow to take him down, and Rebel would bring the truck to the back.

Dresden moved off his bar stool. I tapped Rebel, who gave me a nod before saying something to Charlie. When Dresden began moving through the crowd, I followed behind him. Since he had on a teal shirt, he was easy to spot in the crowd I pushed through. He was headed to the back hall, just like he was supposed to do. I followed, drawing my Taser from between my breasts. While my gun chafed my thighs, I hoped I didn't have to pull it. This place was too crowded for a gun, too much could go wrong.

Why had I worn this dress? I slipped between two guys, one brushed my tits and the other groped my ass. I considered shocking the shit out of them, but then I'd have to knock Dresden out with my fists, and that wasn't the plan. Rebel got grouchy when I improvised.

Only Dresden and I were in the hall now, we'd passed the bathrooms and turned the corner to the exit. It was too early in the night for the walls to be lined with couples doing the nasty.

Dresden started to turn but I stuck the round end of my Taser into his back. "Keep walking if you don't want me to ruin that shirt."

"Okay, honey." He oozed sleaze. "We can come to an arrangement. I'm sure I have what you need."

He stepped through the exit door into the Dallas night. Garbage and the smoggy smell of the city met me. Headlights blinked, that was Rebel.

"Walk to the truck," I told him, pushing the barrel into his back.

"Gotcha." He didn't even resist, sure he could talk his way out of whatever trouble he was in, more likely buy his way out of it with drugs or cash.

Rebel stood beside the truck. "Wait." He slowed when he saw Rebel. "What is this?"

I sent the electric current through him. He fell to the ground, stunned.

"Couldn't resist?" Rebel secured his hands before checking him for a weapon. Nada. Then he hauled him into the truck.

"He was so slimy and gross. He needed a shock." I liked my Taser, maybe a little too much.

I hiked my dress up and climbed into the truck.

"No panties, you are naughty." Rebel grinned over at me.

"You like me naughty, now let's turn this garbage over to the cops and go home." I unstrapped the annoying thigh holster and tugged down the skirt of my dress.

"Baby, I love you." His serious tone made me look his way. Love shone bright in his eyes.

"I love you too." I reached out and squeezed his hand. "Now drive. I want you to take me home and strip me bare."

"Damn, baby, you might break me."

"Nah, you can handle me, you're the only one who can." I loved my tough biker who owned me heart and soul. And he understood me better than anyone, but better, he loved me just the way I was. I never thought I'd find that.

"That's right, only me."

* * * * *

Acknowledgments

Thanks so much to the great editors at Carina Press, especially Lauren. And it's been wonderful working with my agent, Jessica, on this series. There are so many friends I want to acknowledge in helping me get here. My critique partners—you know who you are—have helped me improve my writing and supported me as I learned about publishing. I also can't say how much I have appreciated my writing groups and the open community of romance writers in general.

About the Author

I live in Kansas City with my children and animals in less than organized chaos. From an early age, bad boys piqued my interest as much as the strong women who could meet them challenge for challenge.

A romance addict, I turned to writing when my own stories refused to stay in my head. A true-believer in happily ever after, romance has always held the number one place on my bookshelf, and now my tablet. I enjoy escaping to new worlds and meeting all kinds of people who live in the imagination of others. Now that I have brought my imaginary world to life, I find I cannot write fast enough to bring those ideas to you.

My floor may not always be vacuumed, but laughter and craziness surrounds our family of four, spurred on by our cat, dog, and school of fish.

If you would like to know more about my upcoming book releases or anything else Jade-related, visit me on my website www.jadechandler.com. Or enjoy my social media ramblings at any of these sites:

Facebook: Facebook.com/groups/1745864482348641
Twitter: Twitter.com/JadeChandlerRom
Pintrest: Pinterest.com/14jadechandler
Goodreads: Goodreads.com/user/show/37229091-jade-chandler

Get 2 Free Books,
Plus 2 Free Gifts -

just for trying the *Reader Service!*

YES! Please send me 2 FREE novels from the Essential Romance or Essential Suspense Collection and my 2 FREE gifts (gifts are worth about $10 retail). After receiving them, if I don't wish to receive any more books, I can return the shipping statement marked "cancel." If I don't cancel, I will receive 4 brand-new novels every month and be billed just $6.74 each in the U.S. or $7.24 each in Canada. That's a savings of at least 16% off the cover price. It's quite a bargain! Shipping and handling is just 50¢ per book in the U.S. and 75¢ per book in Canada*. I understand that accepting the 2 free books and gifts places me under no obligation to buy anything. I can always return a shipment and cancel at any time. The free books and gifts are mine to keep no matter what I decide.

Please check one: ☐ Essential Romance ☐ Essential Suspense
194/394 MDN GMWR 191/391 MDN GMWR

Name _____
(PLEASE PRINT)

Address _____ Apt. #

City _____ State/Prov. _____ Zip/Postal Code

Signature (if under 18, a parent or guardian must sign)

Mail to the **Reader Service:**
IN U.S.A.: P.O. Box 1341, Buffalo, NY 14240-8531
IN CANADA: P.O. Box 603, Fort Erie, Ontario L2A 5X3

Want to try two free books from another line?
Call 1-800-873-8635 or visit www.ReaderService.com.

*Terms and prices subject to change without notice. Prices do not include applicable taxes. Sales tax applicable in NY. Canadian residents will be charged applicable taxes. Offer not valid in Quebec. This offer is limited to one order per household. Books received may not be as shown. Not valid for current subscribers to the Essential Romance or Essential Suspense Collection. All orders subject to approval. Credit or debit balances in a customer's account(s) may be offset by any other outstanding balance owed by or to the customer. Please allow 4 to 6 weeks for delivery. Offer available while quantities last.

Your Privacy—The Reader Service is committed to protecting your privacy. Our Privacy Policy is available online at www.ReaderService.com or upon request from the Reader Service.

We make a portion of our mailing list available to reputable third parties that offer products we believe may interest you. If you prefer that we not exchange your name with third parties, or if you wish to clarify or modify your communication preferences, please visit us at www.ReaderService.com/consumerschoice or write to us at Reader Service Preference Service, P.O. Box 9062, Buffalo, NY 14240-9062. Include your complete name and address.

STRS17F

Get 2 Free Books,
Plus 2 Free Gifts—
just for trying the Reader Service!

HARLEQUIN
ROMANTIC suspense

Get 2 Free Books,
Plus 2 Free Gifts—
just for trying the Reader Service!

◆ HARLEQUIN™

INTRIGUE

YES! Please send me 2 FREE Harlequin® Intrigue novels and my 2 FREE gifts (gifts are worth about $10 retail). After receiving them, if I don't wish to receive any more books, I can return the shipping statement marked "cancel." If I don't cancel, I will receive 6 brand-new novels every month and be billed just $4.99 each for the regular-print edition or $5.74 each for the larger-print edition in the U.S., or $5.74 each for the regular-print edition or $6.49 each for the larger-print edition in Canada. That's a savings of at least 12% off the cover price! It's quite a bargain! Shipping and handling is just 50¢ per book in the U.S. and 75¢ per book in Canada*. I understand that accepting the 2 free books and gifts places me under no obligation to buy anything. I can always return a shipment and cancel at any time. The free books and gifts are mine to keep no matter what I decide.

Please check one: ☐ Harlequin® Intrigue Regular-Print   ☐ Harlequin® Intrigue Larger-Print
                          (182/382 HDN GMWJ)   (199/399 HDN GMWJ)

Name	(PLEASE PRINT)
Address	Apt. #
City	State/Prov. Zip/Postal Code

Signature (if under 18, a parent or guardian must sign)

Mail to the **Reader Service:**
IN U.S.A.: P.O. Box 1341, Buffalo, NY 14240-8531
IN CANADA: P.O. Box 603, Fort Erie, Ontario L2A 5X3

Want to try two free books from another line?
Call 1-800-873-8635 or visit www.ReaderService.com.

*Terms and prices subject to change without notice. Prices do not include applicable taxes. Sales tax applicable in N.Y. Canadian residents will be charged applicable taxes. Offer not valid in Quebec. This offer is limited to one order per household. Books received may not be as shown. Not valid for current subscribers to Harlequin Intrigue books. All orders subject to approval. Credit or debit balances in a customer's account(s) may be offset by any other outstanding balance owed by or to the customer. Please allow 4 to 6 weeks for delivery. Offer available while quantities last.

Your Privacy—The Reader Service is committed to protecting your privacy. Our Privacy Policy is available online at www.ReaderService.com or upon request from the Reader Service.

We make a portion of our mailing list available to reputable third parties that offer products we believe may interest you. If you prefer that we not exchange your name with third parties, or if you wish to clarify or modify your communication preferences, please visit us at www.ReaderService.com/consumerchoice or write to us at Reader Service Preference Service, P.O. Box 9062, Buffalo, NY 14240-9062. Include your complete name and address.

HI17F

Get 2 Free Books,
Plus 2 Free Gifts—
just for trying the Reader Service!